Peony House

Anne S Paisley

To My Family
With Big Love

1

What happened to Addie Morgan that winter and spring she later described as a lot of little accidents that, in hindsight, she could see were unseen hands pushing her toward a new life. In a way she knew it was a lazy description and that the truth underlying how any of us meet strangers and change our minds, our hearts, and our lives as a consequence, was more intricately beautiful and frightening. She likened it to swimming in a lake where you can't see the bottom.

Addie was awake but her eyes remained closed. Her three year old toy poodle, Buck, was under the covers somewhere near her feet. He wasn't touching her but she could feel an aura of warmth coming from his direction. She found his soft apricot fur with her foot and stroked him good morning. He licked her big toe once and let out a sigh. She kept her eyes closed. She didn't want to get up. No, it wasn't that she didn't want to get up; it was that she didn't want to go to work. She thought of the depressing bumper sticker a neighbor had on his trashed Escort: *Same shit, different day.* Thinking she might share a sentiment with the lank-haired, beer gutted guy who drove the beater filled with an ever- shifting array of sad junk was just the spur she needed. She opened her eyes in a first step toward dispelling the unfortunate association. Buck wriggled out first, popping his head out from under the blanket and giving her cheek several go-team-go licks.

"Ok, I'm coming. Keep your curly shirt on."

Standing outside on the small grassy patch behind the apartment building, Addie pulled her heavy terrycloth robe tight and shivered in the freezing February air. Buck picked his way around the edge of the grass, sniffing for just the right spot to dribble some pee. He'd already taken care of the urgent business and now he was in secure-the-perimeter mode.

"Buck! C'mon, let's go!" Buck, acting as if he was hearing impaired, ignored her and stopped to carefully sniff and then lift his leg against a limp rhododendron.

"Buck! Come!" He caught the sincerity of this second command and dutifully trotted across the grass and through the door Addie was holding open for him.

"Good boy." Buck went ahead of her as if to show the way. She followed the trail of dirty little paw prints he left on the tired linoleum floor.

2

It was that afternoon, after she'd finished seeing clients, that she first saw the caretaker ad for Pen House. As was her usual practice, she'd come home, changed into jeans and hooked Buck up to his leash so they could go out for a walk. Sometimes they ambled around for over an hour and sometimes it was just a fifteen or twenty minute walk around a couple of blocks.

The sun had come out and shifting patches of blue sky could be seen. Spring was still a month away but the daffodils were blooming in nearly every garden, their yellow petals and orange trumpets like flags coaxing weary winter travelers on toward the finish line. Even though Seattleites very rarely had to crawl out from under long snowy winters or temperatures below the mid-twenties, these exuberant reminders of spring's near-arrival meant a great deal in the Northwest. Each flower was a well-earned prize after a difficult stretch of short gray days and long nights. As for the famous Seattle rain, it was only occasionally heavy and the yearly totals were surprisingly humdrum. But it seemed to get doled out a little every day so that sometimes, by the time

January finally came to an end, it was hard to remember when the last sunny day had been. It could feel like never.

Regardless of weather, Addie made it out most every day to walk Buck. Because of this commitment she'd made to him, she'd discovered with a certain amount of surprise that winter in the city had a genuine beauty. Yes, the trees were bare and the sky was clouded more often than not. But those trees were like great and gifted actors, able to reveal something essential using only their stripped down form and the scrim of a late February sky. And the sky wasn't simply gray; it was many tones and moods of gray. True, it sometimes hovered in an abysmal monochrome stillness. But often she watched it move and even roil in a fickle wind as if coming to a cold boil, changing from light to dark and back again in just a couple of charged minutes.

She noticed for the first time how many bushes and trees had over-winter berries. She'd had an idea about winter: that it was colorless and lacking in definition, as if God had hit the pause button. But she'd been completely wrong. Everywhere she looked she saw snowy whites, crimsons, lavenders and fiery oranges. Even the way plants shriveled and died back had an affecting poignancy. They hinted at shapes sometimes realistic, sometimes abstract and always, she thought, sculptural. Some were drooping and rounded like a tight-curled nude, some seemed to mimic an industrial landscape in the way they jutted upwards like rebar out of broken concrete, intruding on the softer forms that surrounded them.

She loved to look at a tree's reflection cast in a puddle of rain, even one dirtied by a rainbow slick of petroleum leaching out of the indented asphalt. The distorted image reminded her of a dreamscape and, like the dream world, it reminded her to refresh the way she looked at things. She'd discovered that seeing and feeling the loveliness of winter was only a matter of looking more deeply and dressing to stay warm and dry. And she knew that if you succumbed to Seattle's winter, sat inside and waited for spring, waited for God to press play, it led to thinking in circles. It led to loneliness.

Fortunately, Buck was always an enthusiastic walker. His sturdy cheerfulness and expectant tail wags shamed her into many an outing she would have otherwise found a hundred excuses to avoid. He would signal his desire to go by standing next to the basket by the front door that was filled with a handsome array of his sweaters, fleeces, raincoats, all of which, with resigned dignity, and for the price of a decent amble, he let Addie put on him.

At the end of the walk Addie stopped to pick something up for dinner at the little grocery store that was a couple of blocks from her apartment. The ad was on a community bulletin board just to the left of the metal café table, the leg of which Addie was preparing to tie Buck's leash around. She caught sight of the words "Peony House" in large hand-printed letters at the top of an index card. Her eyes just incidentally brushed the surface of the two words and yet there was a fleeting sensation that rippled across her solar plexus. She felt momentarily giddy and unsettled and then it passed as quickly as a hiccup. Addie shivered. The wind had started up again, tossing her hair into a crazy shape and stinging her neck and face. She looked down at Buck who was shivering under his plaid fleece coat. He had recently been groomed and his naked poodle paws looked bony, pink and vulnerable. She reassured him she'd just be a minute, patted his head and hustled in to the store. Standing in line she briefly remembered the words *Peony House* with a pinch of curiosity and the intention of having a look at what the ad was about. She forgot about it by the time the checker was bagging her groceries. Outside again the wind had retreated and the now setting sun cast yellowy-orange reflections on the windows of the houses across the street. Buck was sitting attentively, never able to relax until he caught sight of her. He greeted her as if the parting had been hours long instead of minutes. She untied his leash from the table leg, hefted her grocery bag and headed for home.

Home was a small third floor one-bedroom apartment on a wide, noisy street. Her block was lined with mature cherry trees, gnarled with age. Addie had to watch her step where tree roots had buckled the sidewalk.

She didn't mind. She liked the irregularity it created and the way the roots pushed against something so heavy, so apparently permanent, and prevailed.

She had lived in the same brick building for years. First she had lived there with Sean. They'd found it together. Now she lived there with Buck. As she unlocked the front door to the building, she recalled the day she and Sean found the apartment. She remembered them sitting in the cafe, eating breakfast and looking at apartment ads in the paper, marking possibilities with a red pen. She remembered he had on an old and holey navy blue sweater where she could glimpse here and there the white tee shirt he wore underneath. She remembered they talked about how this apartment was in a good neighborhood; close enough for her to walk to her new office and on a busy street with a bus that went downtown for him. She remembered them climbing the carpeted stairs to the third floor apartment. It was small, smaller than either of them had admitted to thinking. But the afternoon light coming in through the kitchen and living room windows made a rich golden spill on the recently swept wood floors. The price was okay, just squeaking in under the high end of their budget. They wrote the landlord a deposit check right there and then.

This memory was what played through her mind nearly every time she came through the apartment building's front door. It was a review that took no longer than picking out the key on her key ring and turning it in the lock. It was a way she had of lightly checking in with the woman she thought she was, reassuring herself of where her edge was and where the rest of the world started. She considered herself level headed, analytical even, but she didn't subject this small ritual of remembrance to scrutiny. She only knew, vaguely, that neglecting to do so would feel like walking under a ladder.

She unfastened Buck's leash and let him run upstairs ahead of her to the apartment. He stood with his paws up on the door waiting for her to catch up, wagging his tail. She marveled for the thousandth time that Sean had never known Buck. That someone she'd loved as much as

9

she'd loved Sean had never even set eyes on the force of nature that was Buck, seemed like it defied some law of physics. Surely the paths of two as connected to her as they both were, should have crossed at some point. But Addie and Sean hadn't shared Buck. Sean's going had crushed the air out of Addie's life. In Buck she imagined the possibility of hope. Buck was fine and happy and he had never known Sean. She looked at Sean's picture on the table by the front door. There he was, frozen in a moment. One tiny moment.

That night Addie dreamed she was moving. She pushed a laden cart up a steep ramp and just as she was near the top her strength seemed to abandon her. She started to lose her grip on the cart. Someone, a man she didn't know, came from behind to help her push the cart that last little way.

"I'm not as strong as I used to be," she said to no one.

Now she found herself on a narrow asphalt path raised just a little bit above water. The water was on both sides of the path. To her right it stretched away to the horizon and to the left she could see a shore comprised of city buildings, warehouses. The water was deep and clear, a gorgeous aquamarine. The path was only slightly wider than the wheels of the cart. A panicky fear that she would tip the cart and herself into the water rose up and wrapped around her in a claustrophobic fog. The water was calm, perhaps even tropically warm. She could swim. Still, it was unimaginable that she could survive a fall into waters so deep. She pushed her cart with great care along the serpentine ridge of asphalt, eventually making it to the other side.

Addie woke up to Buck's growling from under the covers, something he did when she shifted in the bed and disturbed him. She stroked his back with her foot and tried to determine the time by the amount of light she could see around the edge of the curtains. The window was open a little and she could feel the air moving in the room. It was cold and she pulled the covers up around her chin. The sun hadn't hit the apartment building yet but she thought she could tell from the quality of the light that it was going to be sunny.

Addie reviewed the dream. There was a stirring of unease when she considered what it might mean that in the dream she had been moving. Was the dream an omen that something new was going to be asked of her? So much had already been demanded. She dismissed the fear even as she noticed herself refusing to look. This noticing self quietly suggested she might have dwelled a little longer on the dream and been more kindhearted about her uneasy feelings. It was a source of continual painful irony that she almost never followed the advice people paid her to give them. Nevertheless, she made herself get out of bed immediately to derail what she concluded was, overall, an unhealthy line of thought. Buck wiggled out from under the covers and jumped down. He stretched, first the front legs, then the back. Every morning his routine was the same and Addie felt pulled into his ritual with tremendous gratitude.

Addie looked at the clock, just a little after seven. Good. She still had two hours until her first client. She had scaled back to five clients a week. Wednesdays were the hell day of three appointments. Monday and Tuesday each had just one. The dread had lessened a little each time she was able to wean a client away from her. Where that was ultimately leading in terms of her career, she had no idea.

What a fraud she was! She had gotten in to this to help people for God's sake. Now she could barely remember what had inspired all the schooling, all the ideas of the difference she could make. Most days it seemed like all she could authentically lay claim to was her ability to listen. And she did listen. When she was asked directly for advice, she often felt as if she were reading from a Therapy for Dummies textbook. Strangely, her clients didn't seem to notice. She even got thanks from them with some regularity. It wasn't that she didn't feel for them. She did. In fact, their pain felt dangerously close. *Like the dream cart starting to slip backwards*, she thought, as she poured boiling water into the little black cone holding the coffee. Addie mulled over the words spoken to the unseen man: *I'm not as strong as I used to be.* Aloud she said, "I'm not anything I used to be." Buck wagged his tail in acknowledgment that she must be talking to him since no one else was there. She scratched behind his ear and congratulated him on his superior logic.

After breakfast Addie bundled herself and Buck up and went out for a walk, one hand holding the leash and one holding the travel mug of coffee. Buck seemed to know that she wasn't the person to yank along on the leash. Not because she was stern with him, far from it. No, it was as if Buck understood that she needed him like a blind person needs their guide dog. Even as a puppy he had seemed to study her. And he had taken her measure well.

The air was sharp and the sun, while bright, lacked punch, a pretend sun standing in for the real thing. The wind was awake and bullying some big white clouds across the sky. Like a curtain being opened and closed and opened again, the light shifted rapidly from light to dark to light.

Buck was frisky and pranced along the sidewalk stopping frequently to sniff and lift his leg. Her steps too felt energized by the swirling and unpredictable movement of the air. Her body was responding as it always had to blustery weather, with a physical sense of hope.

But checking in with her head, she felt the familiar disconnect between her body and her thoughts. There, in her thoughts, energy and hope seemed purely academic. She wasn't aware of feeling sad. She felt removed. Her buoyant feet and tingling cheeks seemed to belong to a different Addie, a younger self that still uncovered joy in everyday places. *I feel like I'm waiting for a train*, she mused, *and I have no timetable, and no itinerary.* Buck stopped to relieve himself against a fire hydrant. She smiled at him, at the corny pose of his leg cocked against the hydrant. *And waiting for a train? With no timetable? C'mon*

3

Her one client of the day was a woman who was a good twenty years older than Addie. She had children that were grown. Her husband was an alcoholic and Addie spent a lot of their time together simply working with her to keep her separate from her husband's drinking. As Virginia recapped her week, the usual dread snuck up on Addie again. What did she know of later middle age? What did she know about raising kids? What gave her the right to presume she could help anyone? *I've never even lived a life*, she thought and quickly upbraided herself for veering off into thinking about herself. This woman was paying a small fortune for what, a daydreamer? *Focus, damn it!*

"...Peonies," her client said, which jerked Addie back into her chair.

"Excuse me, Virginia, would you repeat that?"

"I dreamed Dan brought me a bouquet of peonies," she dutifully repeated.

"I came home from work and they were in a vase and I knew they were from him. I smelled them and was surprised there was no fragrance. I don't know what it means." She trailed off and looked at Addie as if she might have the key.

"What do peonies mean to you, Virginia?" Addie inquired.

"I have a beautiful tree peony in my garden. Sometimes the blooms are so heavy, the stalks can't support them and they bend way over. Their fragrance is powerful. My mother loved peonies."

Virginia paused, lost in thought. Addie was moved by Virginia's earnest inquiry. Sometimes it seemed all she was doing was spending the hour watching and listening to her clients form deeper connections to themselves. She felt that the great secret she held was that their wisdom surpassed hers by a long shot.

What do peonies mean to you, Addie?

They mean nothing. No, that wasn't exactly right. *It's a flower name I saw on an ad outside the grocery store. Do I know what peonies look like? Would I recognize one? Are they like roses?* She remembered that Sean had wanted a garden, wanted a place that had space for him to garden. Addie tightened her throat, choking off what felt like a tsunami rolling toward her head from her guts. This was the feeling that had caused her to start dropping clients; the sense that she might lose control, even though she wasn't clear what precisely that meant. This was the dread.

"My mother said that peonies smelled so uniquely that she would be able to call them up in her memory even after she was dead. It never really made sense but I knew what she meant." Virginia's eyes were cast downward, half closed, and her mouth was a little crooked so that Addie couldn't read whether this memory was pleasant or not. Perhaps it was just concentration as Virginia continued to search for new associations.

Addie forced herself to become completely absorbed in the woman sitting across from her. She looked at the short thick gray hair, simply but expensively cut. The thumb and forefinger of her right hand turned the gold band on the other hand round and round. She had manicured nails, buffed but unpainted. She wore a wool skirt of brown plaid with a white blouse and fawn sweater. She had her legs crossed at the ankles and wore pumps that matched one of the lighter browns in her skirt. A whiff of her perfume or soap, something like grapefruit, hung in the air between them. Slowly, Addie calmed her sense of panic.

Their hour together came to a close. Virginia seemed to leave the appointment with a sense of peace about what the dream had meant to her. Something about expectation. Something about meeting love where it was instead of where you thought it should be. Something about her mother.

Addie pondered how unnecessary she was. She was swept by a wave of longing to get home to her dog, to the little creature that loved her. His need for her was real and, by showering her with companionship that was both steady and infinitely patient, he soothed an ache in her. *I need time.* How much longer would she need time?

4

As she put the key in the lock to her front door she heard the sound of Buck's nails on the bare wood floor. She knew if she were to feel the seat of the old leather armchair it would be warm from where he had been curled up both sleeping and waiting for her return.

"Hey buddy," she greeted him as she walked in.

He put his two front paws up on her legs managing to both greet her and stretch at the same time. His poodle pom wagged and she bent over to scratch him behind his ears and tell him how handsome he was. She promised him a walk as soon as she had something to eat.

The day had continued to bluster. She sat at her kitchen table eating left over Thai food. Looking out her second story window she could see the wind bullying the cherry trees' branches. Cherry blossoms now carpeted the street and sidewalk, the delicate pink and white petals mostly now a mushy brown. The new leaves would be much more tenacious. They wouldn't let go until next October.

Will I hold on that long? The thought snuck in and she felt both guilty and ashamed. Of course she would. What would Buck do without her? She abhorred the thought of, what? Suicide? Was that what she had been thinking about when she'd compared herself to the sturdy new green leaves? She had always felt angry that people killed themselves. As a therapist she should know better. She had witnessed people in pain so acute that the sufferer's identity became consumed by it. But privately Addie felt repelled by the act. She thought of her parents. They didn't live close by. She didn't talk to them often. But Addie withered under the thought of the anguish she knew they would endure were they to lose her. So, what did she mean when she wondered would she be able to hold on until October? Was she in danger of a breakdown? *No. Of course I'm not.* She tried to reject the thought as a non sequitur, but it only partially quelled her unease.

When she and Buck were both in their coats and Buck had his leash on, they headed out for one of her favorite walks. It was a loop walk that took them along the edge of the lake for about a mile and then back up the hill and home. She let Buck sniff and relieve himself and then they walked in earnest. The sun was encircled in a large halo of blue. The wind snapped and nipped and she pulled her stocking cap down so every bit of her ears were under cover. Buck was frisky and seemed to be prancing rather than walking. She felt his vibrant life energy come up the leather leash and into her own hand. She imagined it spreading like slowly immersing her body in a hot bath.

They passed the lakeside houses that she had seen so many times before. Originally these mostly tiny parcels had been the ground for extremely modest post war homes and vacation cabins. Where she now walked had once been a railway line. Sixty feet from the bone rattle of passing trains could hardly have been desirable property. You still saw those first homes now and again, some of them not much more than shacks, wedged between houses four or five times their size and infinitely more ostentatious. This was now prime lakefront property. The BMWs and Mercedes' were parked in front and the pleasure boats were tied up at the piers that extended from many of the tiny backyards.

She imagined the people who'd first lived in those little dwellings no doubt thinking they had found a pretty and affordable spot to build far from downtown's noise and bustle. A place to quietly grow old. But the world had changed quickly around them. Since Sean had gone she had become acutely aware of how people sought permanence and how flimsy and bound to fail their efforts were. She too longed for an anchor, something to hold her still, something to finally satisfy, once and for all, the starving maw that everything got chomped up in sooner or later.

She stole looks into the windows of the houses she and Buck strode by. She saw a woman standing at the sink in her kitchen. A television flickered on the counter behind her. The woman looked up as if knowing Addie's eyes were on her. Addie turned away quickly before eye contact could be made and looked beyond the houses to the lake. A cormorant sat on a pylon, wings outstretched. She could hear the lake lapping at the shore.

They approached one of her favorite houses. It had been one of those modest little homes and instead of pulling it down and building a three-story monolith, the owners had chosen to work with what was already there. The house, which had been not much more than a simple rectangle of concrete blocks, now had a new roof with deeply overhanging eaves. There was an awning of corrugated steel that extended out over the front door, creating a sheltered entry. The old front door, which Addie recalled as battered and nondescript, had been replaced. The opening had been doubled in size and there were now two doors, the right hand side bearing a beautiful big round brass handle. The doors themselves were painted canary yellow. The concrete blocks had been painted white. The window casings were a bright red and the windows' grilles were the same yellow as the front door. There was a knocker on the door, a lion's head with the ring for knocking in the lion's mouth. None of these houses had much of a yard and this house was no exception. It was crowded with potted trees and plants that sat on granite paving stones.

She felt the drag on the leash as Buck stopped to sniff one of the pots. There were little shoots the color of rhubarb just rising up out of the soil. There was also the stubble of last year's growth.

"May I say hi to your dog?" Addie, startled, looked up from the pot. A man who looked to be in his mid to late sixties was walking toward her from the side of the house, his confident stride that of someone who inhabits his body with great comfort.

"Yes, of course. He's a little shy at first but very friendly."

The man reached down and put a hand out toward Buck. Buck leaned forward and sniffed the man carefully. The man didn't rush him but waited quietly, hand palm up under Buck's twitching nose. Finally Buck gave his hand a little kiss of acceptance. The ice thus broken, the man squatted down and scratched Buck's chest.

"I've had many poodles. Miniatures, toys, standards. My wife and I always had them…"

His wife is dead, Addie thought.

"They are fine dogs, aren't they?"

"Yes, Buck is really just about my best friend in the world," Addie admitted.

"Buck, huh? That's a pretty sturdy name. You're a real gentleman, Buck. It's good of you to see this lady gets safe passage in her travels." Buck wagged his tail as if to say *you nailed it mister.*

Addie smiled down at the man. This kind of goofy anthropomorphizing was something she related to. She often created conversations for Buck, ascribed feelings to him, had him tell her his impressions. When it came to dogs, this man was obviously a kindred spirit.

"I'm afraid Buck's been peeing on your pot." She pointed to the pot she'd been looking at. The man straightened up.

"Ah, peeing on the peony." Gently, he ran a finger along one of the tender folded-up leaves.

"When it blooms the flowers will be deep pink, and so huge I always think they'll snap the stalk. But they don't. Some years are more glorious than others. Wonder what this year will bring?" Buck put his paws up on him, something he rarely did to strangers.

"Sorry Buck, didn't mean to ignore you." Buck stayed with his two front paws up on the man's leg, making it easier for him to resume scratching his chest.

"Buck likes you." *and so do I,* thought Addie.

"Do you live here?" The answer seemed obvious since he had walked out from around the side of the house.

"I'm sort of on a permanent visit. It's my son and daughter-in-law's house."

"I love this house. I always look at it on our walks. I love how they made something out of what was here rather than tear it down."

When was the last time Addie had felt such an immediate level of comfort around a stranger? She found herself envious of this son and daughter-in-law, having such a great father. Her most annoying therapist voice reminded her that family members usually had a wildly different experience of their relatives than did outsiders. *Go away voice, let me just indulge in nice thoughts for a minute.*

"I think it was a combination of money considerations and artistic challenge that made them choose to work with the existing house. With heavy emphasis on the money. Both Sarah and James are architects, not too long out of school. Sarah has found a position with a firm downtown. James is working in construction and hoping to find work soon."

He gestured toward the house, "this is their first home and they did it on a shoestring. Two architects under one roof is pretty heady, let me tell you."

He smiled revealing straight strong teeth. He was handsome. It was his warmth that made him so. With a ripple of alarm, Addie imagined this nice man wrapping his arms around her. In her mind's eye he was gently pushing the hair out of her face where little strands had been stuck by tears. *Where the hell did that come from?*

"My name is Leo," he said, extending his hand and looking into her face.

"I'm Addie and you already know Buck." She smiled up at him and realized for the first time how tall he was. She was 5'9" and he had her by another half foot.

"Where did the name Addie come from? That was an old fashioned name when I was a boy."

"It's short for Adeline. I was named after my great grandmother. She died a million years before I was born. What about the name Leo, any relation to that doorknocker?"

Addie couldn't believe she had made such an inane joke. *God, I hope I haven't offended him.*

He looked at the haughty lion face as if noticing it for the first time and then chuckled.

"Maybe. I've got a fair amount of brass in me. My real name is Leonard, which I've always thought was an awful name. The "Nard" in Leonard always jumped out at me in an unpleasant way. I mean, what kind of sound is that?" Addie laughed and it sounded strange and a little surprising to her ears.

"Adeline, would you like a cup of coffee and a cookie? I just made macaroons. Buck is welcome too, of course."

Addie went through a quick checklist in her mind. How did she feel about this stranger? She had to admit she felt fine and Buck, who was pulling on his leash toward the house, seemed even more comfortable with the invitation.

"Maybe I can come in for a few minutes." This said as if she had a busy life, a place to be, someone to come home to.

5

"Let's go in through the side door. That's where the kitchen is. I think it's the best room in the house. But I'll let you decide about that."

She followed him along the path between a crowd of potted plants. He pointed out another peony by the door, this one's shoots more delicate and green.

"Peonies seem to be following me for the last couple of days." Addie meant it to come out lightly but Leo seemed to hear something else.

"Let me get the coffee going and you can tell me about that intriguing statement."

He was looking at her with something she couldn't quite name. Sympathy perhaps. She heard the therapist voice urging her to act professional. Then she told herself to hush, Leo wasn't a client. Nevertheless, she mentally rearranged herself into a more protected posture.

The kitchen was lovely. The first thing she noticed was the coconut aroma of the freshly baked cookies. The sun was streaming in at a slant and making a golden patch on the brick-patterned linoleum floor.

Sarah and James, the strangers whose house she had found herself in, had brought the kitchen to life as if the house were brand new. The cabinets were pale green with Wedgwood blue Bakelite pulls. The walls were a buttery yellow. The blue ceiling matched the cabinet pulls perfectly. The yellow and green of the walls and cabinets reappeared in the ceramic tile counter and backsplash. Even though the butter cream-colored appliances gleamed with newness, they were designed to look mid-twentieth century. The overall effect was like being in her grandmother's kitchen. *That is*, thought Addie, *if Grandma had been ridiculously hip.*

Buck wagged his tail at nothing and Addie felt the same. Courteously, Leo filled up a bowl with water and put it down for Buck by the door they'd come in. He then put a kettle on to boil. He waved his hand toward the vintage dinette set sitting in the patch of sun coming through a window that looked out onto the choppy waters of Lake Washington.

"Have a seat, Miss Adeline."

No one had ever called her Adeline. Even when she was scolded as a child, she was always simply Addie. Was he seeing her as an Adeline? Was she an Adeline after all or maybe becoming one? She wore it like a new coat. Not sure if it fit. Not sure if it suited her.

She certainly didn't see him as a Leonard, however, and agreed completely that the name didn't fit him at all. On the other hand, he wore the name Leo like a driving glove. He had a physical confidence; a graceful way of moving that age hadn't diminished. His white hair, receding at the temples and a little thin on top, still had heft and body. He wore loose jeans and battered desert boots and a red cardigan partly buttoned up over a soft blue cotton shirt.

She sat at the table and Buck hopped up on her lap, turned a couple of circles and curled up. While Leo ground the beans and took the cups down off their hooks, Addie stared out the window and let a comfortable silence settle between them. She felt as if she was catching up with an old friend, a friend she had forgotten was so dear to her heart. The feeling floated in the air, warm and delicious like the smell of the macaroons.

Her gaze settled on the little back garden. A mossy square of grass gently sloped down to the lake's edge. There were plenty of whitecaps and the columnar shaped, bare-limbed poplar that stood between Leo's yard and the house next door was leaning this way and that, as if working a kink out of its trunk. The sun was making the water's surface sparkle, almost too bright to look at directly. Everything was in movement. Officially it was still winter, but spring was going to win, like it did every year.

Leo put a mug of coffee in front of her and then brought over his own cup, a little pitcher of cream and the plate of cookies.

"Do you put sugar in your coffee?" Addie shook her head and inadvertently made a face expressing distaste. He laughed at her.

"Tell me what you think of the cookies," he said, pushing the plate a little closer to her. She bit into one. They were amazing, light, soft, rich, perfect.

"These are fabulous. When did you take up cookie baking?"

"I feel a little dishonest having you try my cookies like it's a new recipe I just clipped from an AARP magazine. I was a pastry chef by profession. I retired just a few years ago from C'est Magnifique. Have you been there?" Addie nodded. In a town with a lot of good bakeries, it was well known and loved.

"I've been there for lunch. It was fantastic."

"I could make these in my sleep." He hung his head in mock shame, as if he had fooled her terribly and then switched gears quickly.

"Tell me about the peonies."

Addie sipped her coffee, strong without bitterness, as

24

wonderfully right as the cookies. This man had it going on in the kitchen without a doubt. What about peonies? Suddenly the whole thing seemed flimsy, silly.

"It's nothing really. Yesterday I was at the grocery store, the one at the top of the hill. I glanced at the bulletin board out in front, do you know it?" Leo nodded. Addie continued.

"I saw an ad out of the corner of my eye. Well, I assume it's an ad, I haven't actually read it yet. I just saw what I think said Peony House. I meant to take a minute to read it when I came back out, but I forgot."

"And Buck forgot to remind you?" he asked in a seemingly serious voice. Buck opened his eyes and looked up at Leo.

"It's ok, friend, we all forget things sometimes." Leo reached out and stroked the crown of Buck's curly apricot head.

Addie thought the proper thing to do was to laugh. It was a joke, right? But the kitchen was quiet and there was that comfortable silence again.

"Well, among all your talents, Leo, I guess you are also psychic because Buck was with me and he did "forget" to remind me to read the ad." Something caught her eye, seemed to run across the back yard. She turned her head but not in time to see whatever it was.

"Actually, I have no idea why I was even struck by the words Peony House. Anyway, this morning a client told me she dreamed her husband gave her a bouquet of peonies. This seemed odd and I admit somehow synchronistic. And then I found out from you that this house that I've looked at a million times has a potted peony in front. And now you are right up to the minute in this mystery."

"Who are these clients?" Leo's hands were cupped around his coffee mug as if to warm them. Addie noticed his knuckles were a little enlarged with arthritis.

"I'm a therapist. I don't have many clients, I've scaled way back on my practice." She caught herself from running on any further.

"So your client had a dream with a peony reference. That is interesting, I agree."

She felt a rush of gratitude toward him. *Thank you for taking my profession in stride, for not making a fuss or the usual uncomfortable jokes.* A large weighty cloud had pushed its way in front of the sun and ate up the light that the table had been basking in. Almost immediately fat raindrops started falling. The lake's surface was peppered with them and the wind turned and blew them against the window.

"We should go." The rain seemed to be sending a message that she had stayed longer than she should. Buck immediately hopped down, ready for the next thing.

"You should go read that notice on the board." Leo's conversational tone was unchanged by her sudden conviction she needed to bolt. Buck looked back and forth at each of their faces trying to determine the drift of the conversation. Finally, he put his paws up on Addie's lap. *I'm with you*, he told her with his eyes. She stood up and carried her cup to the sink and filled it with water.

"Thank you so much for the coffee and fabulous cookies, Leo." She held out her hand to shake his. He took her hand with both of his.

"Make sure and tell me what that notice said. Maybe it's just the thing you're looking for." He patted the back of her hand and she was suddenly afraid she was going to cry.

"It was nice to meet you, Leo. I'll get back to you about the peonies. Thanks for listening." She couldn't help but notice she sounded just like one of her clients. Is this how they felt? Listened to? Elevated somehow by simple interaction?

"I'm just glad to show up somewhere in your synchronous events." He reached down and patted Buck once more.

"Nice to meet you Buck. Take care of Adeline." Buck wagged his tail and gave Leo's hand an acknowledging lick and then one more because his fingers smelled like cookies.

Leo walked her back out to the street. The little squall had stopped but the sun was still obscured by clouds.

Leo said, "are you going up there to look at that notice now, before you go home?"

Addie felt gripped by apprehension. After all this time of moving through her life as if someone else inhabited her body, she was feeling something come in to focus inside her. It was the sense that there was change on the way. And this frightened her because, though she certainly couldn't claim to be happy as she was, she at least knew the lay of the land.

"I guess I could stop by..." The words felt like a lie as they came out of her mouth. A way to wiggle out of an uncomfortable moment. Leo picked it up.

"You'd only be looking. You don't have to do anything." He looked at her and smiled a kind smile. "Not 'til you're good and ready."

Addie and Buck headed back up the hill. Maybe she should go

have a look. Didn't she tell her clients all the time that they had choices and the right to exercise those choices? Looking wasn't anything but looking. All true, but why did she feel like an agoraphobic being shoved out the door? She wished Leo had come with her. He probably would have if she had asked. Her hand still felt the warm presence of his two hands clasping it. Without noticing, she put that hand up to her chest.

6

The ad was hand printed on a fading orange three by five index card. It was so short, so nondescript, Addie was surprised it had ever caught her eye. Most surprising of all was that it didn't say Peony House at all. It very plainly said:

PEN HOUSE

Wanted: Caretaker

Approx. 1 year commitment. House located near

Sutton Bay. Good people skills

How had she misread it? She felt a little deflated. Peony House had sounded so charming. Pen House simply sounded odd. She moved away from the consternation she felt about misreading the name and considered the ad. It was maddeningly uninformative. Good people skills? What did that mean? She had good people skills but couldn't see where that would come in handy with a house. She didn't know where Sutton Bay was but it sounded familiar. *They probably don't want a dog there and that will make this whole thing out of the question.* Almost immediately the next thought came: *Buck will be allowed, welcomed even.* She shuddered involuntarily. There was that damn sense that she wasn't totally in control. Being in control had been critical ever since Sean had left. Another unbidden thought nosed its way in and shook a finger at her: *and way before that as well.*

Looping his leash around the same café table leg, Addie told Buck to stay and ran inside the market to borrow a pen. She copied what was obviously a cell phone number onto her palm. As she scribbled on her hand, she felt light-headed and a little sick to her stomach.

At home she wrote out the number on a piece of paper and it sat by the phone, undialed, for two days. She would catch sight of it on the table and think about throwing it away. *Like I never saw it*, she thought. But somehow she kept leaving it alone until finally she picked it up and dialed the number.

"Hello. This is Mike Parris at Parris Properties. Leave your number and a message and I'll get back to you as soon as possible." Addie waited for the go ahead tone.

"Hi. My name is Addie Morgan and I'm calling about the caretaker position at Pen House." She left her number and hung up. *Now it's a done deal. God only knows what the hell I'm getting myself in to.*

She looked at Sean's photo beside the phone. Sometimes she stared at the picture, sure that she would be able to detect some secret movement, a finger moved just a little, the gaze slightly altered. But it was always as final as an ancient fly caught in a block of amber. She imagined that Sean could look back at her and make the same assessment. She stood there, trancelike, unable to read her reaction to having made the call. It was muddled, confused, obscured so that she couldn't get a clean look at it. Buck snored from where he was curled up on his favorite nap chair and Addie felt infinitely comforted. He would be there with her. *Wherever there was.*

Mike Parris called her back within the hour. Addie reiterated that she had called about the ad and where she had seen the card and then added that she had a dog, aware as she said it that her relief would be enormous should that knowledge torpedo the deal. Then she could simply return to life as it was a few days ago.

"I'm acting as an agent for the owners who don't live there. In fact they aren't even in the country. I'd have to check with them but I don't think the dog would be a problem as long as it's, you know, trained and all. Might even be an asset, you know, for protection."

She assured him a little stiffly that Buck was well trained. Buck wagged his tail from his chair without opening his eyes. *Protection?* She let that comment go.

When he asked what her situation was, she told him she was a therapist planning to take a sabbatical from work, possibly to write a book. She didn't know where the book nonsense came from. It had never crossed her mind until that moment. Was she trying to impress this man? Trying to convince him she was a solid sober citizen, the most responsible for the job?

"The ad mentioned people skills and I was wondering what that referred to?"

"The owners of this property bought it only recently. They haven't ever lived there. There were renters in the house until a couple of years ago. There are problems in the attic and the back of the house. The owners are planning a remodel, including a new roof. They need someone to be a presence in the house while the work is being done. Someone who can be a go-to person on a daily basis and relay information to the owners, through me, as needed. They need someone to make sure things are on schedule and so forth..." he trailed off.

"I don't know anything about construction..." Buck had jumped down off his chair and come over to her, put his paws up on her knees. She gave him a 'just a minute, buddy' wave of her hand.

"Oh, they don't need anything like that," he interjected before she could elaborate, "just a presence. Make sure everything's locked up at night, make sure all the workers are behaving."

"Behaving?" She almost laughed but worried he might be that guy who was sensitive to imagined feminine slights.

"You know, showing up on time, not making off with the family jewels."

"Are there valuables in the house, Mr. Parris?" Once again she noticed her tone, it sounded formal, priggish even.

"Nah, nothing they could easily carry at any rate." There was a brief silence and then he continued, "can you meet me at the property? Then you could see it and we could discuss details."

Addie got down all the pertinent information and a plan was made to meet on the upcoming Saturday at one pm. She hung up the phone, dazed.

"Buck, let's go for a walk." Buck ran to the door, tail wagging, prancing in place.

7

Leo opened the door and the warmth of the kitchen reached out and caressed her cold red cheeks.

"Adeline! Come in, you're just in time." Buck ran in ahead of her, wagging his tail hello.

"I hope it's ok that I'm dropping by. I would have called you but I don't have your number."

"It's more than ok, I'm delighted! Sir Buck, good of you to come as well." Leo squatted down and scratched Buck under the chin and on his chest. He straightened back up and Buck wandered off, perusing the floor for crumbs.

"What am I just in time for?" Addie smiled, genuinely glad to see her new friend.

"Coffee. Some kind of a delicacy. And talk." He took her coat and scarf and hung them on the back of the door.

"Sounds perfect. Can I help?" Addie felt happy, knowing it had been right to follow her instinct to come here.

"Yes. Talk. You look like you might know what Peony House is."

Leo had already turned toward the counter and started to fill a kettle. He opened the breadbox, pulled out a loaf, sliced off four fat hunks of bread and put them in the toaster. Addie watched him and felt tremendously comforted by the confidence he brought to the simple task of making coffee and toast. She noticed he was dressed the same as the last time she'd seen him except now he wore an old pair of leather bedroom slippers and his shirt was pink. For a long time her orbit had felt wobbly, as if she might be flicked out into space at any moment. In Leo she sensed a larger more stable body and she could feel herself coming into alignment with him.

"Well, I know it isn't Peony House. How are you, Leo?"

With a trace of good-humored impatience he said, "I'm good. Dying of curiosity, but other than that, fine."

"Ok, Ok. I feel so lopsided coming here unannounced and launching into my life."

"Let's examine that, shall we?" Leo held up his hand.

"One, as you pointed out, you don't have my number so you couldn't call me. In fact, you couldn't even look me up in the phonebook because you don't know my last name and this isn't my house anyway. Two, and most important, you came here because you need to tell me what's up. Don't you listen to people all the time? What makes you think you don't need to be the talker some of the time?"

He was smiling, three fingers raised in triumph, but his eyes were serious, so serious she felt a momentary sense of displacement, a hint of foreboding.

"And three, what do you mean it's not Peony House?"

Buck barked, one sharp bark that made her jump. She turned toward where he stood at the window, paws up on the sill, looking intently at something.

"What's up, buddy? Is there a cat out there?" She walked over and looked out the window. It was drizzling and there was a great stillness. The lake was a glassy gray expanse. There wasn't a whisper of wind. She felt strung tight and mentally shook herself like she'd seen Buck do multiple times every day of his life.

"I went to read the ad. It's an ad for a caretaker for a house in Sutton Bay. But it isn't called Peony House. It's called Pen House. It is so weird that I made that mistake," she trailed off.

"Come and get it," Leo said, setting a tray down on the table.

"And would you grab the coffee stuff on the counter?" Addie brought the pot and mugs over to the table.

"Did you make the bread?" She felt a sense of safety in the homey smell of toast.

"No. The kneading is hard on my hands nowadays." He spread each piece with a generous knob of butter.

"Help yourself to jam or lemon curd." Addie obliged, dipping her spoon into a jar of marmalade. Leo bit into his toast. Addie could almost see the wheels turning in his head.

He finally said, "seems as if you had an upside down bout of precognition. First, you saw the little ad, which you thought said Peony House. Then your client mentioned a dream about peonies. Then you met me when Buck stopped to relieve himself on my peony." He looked at her for confirmation. She nodded.

"Weird, huh? If I was a proper psychic my client would have dreamed about pens and..." She laughed and Leo finished the sentence, "Buck would have peed on my pen."

She said, "I guess it's just a slightly bizarre coincidence."

Leo nodded slowly. "Maybe it will make sense someday. I have to admit I was pretty attached to the idea of a Peony House." Now Addie nodded. She was suddenly ready to move on.

Leo obliged. "So tell me, what's the story? Why is it called Pen

House?"

"There isn't too much to tell, I called and talked to this guy who does some kind of property management and the owners are having him look for a caretaker to live on site for about a year. I didn't even think to ask him about the name." She continued, recounting the entire conversation as accurately as she could remember it.

"I have so many questions, I'm not sure where to start. So, if you're going to go meet him and see the place next Saturday, that must mean you're thinking about making a pretty serious job change."

"I hadn't been thinking about it at all, at least not really, not in some organized, planned way. Honestly, I'm not that happy with what I do. I don't think I'm really very good at it. I had all this confidence about it all the way through school. Now that certainty just seems ridiculous. Arrogant even."

"What changed?" Leo had a way of cutting to the bone.

Did I feel this way about my work before Sean left? She had asked herself this many times and once again she experienced the feeling that she had led two completely distinct lives. One with Sean and one without. In a way, she liked the with-Sean self less. That Addie seemed like the shallower version. But this impression of herself always threw her. Hadn't she been infinitely happier? Hadn't she felt like life had been progressing as it should, that her actions had purpose?

"What changed?" Leo asked again, his voice a little quieter.

"I lost someone," she said simply.

Please don't let this conversation come off as me feeling sorry for myself. She had never understood people who felt driven to talk constantly about every pain and setback they experienced. To Addie it felt tantamount to being pushed onto a stage, naked. Although she had never shared it with anyone, the irony of her being a therapist and yet conducting herself so guardedly was a source of shame, as if she had cheated on the final exam.

Leo nodded, "thought so. I thought I recognized a fellow traveler." She thought he was going to say *fellow sufferer* but he said something quite different.

"When did your wife die?" Addie felt shy, was the question too personal? Maybe intrusive? It seemed like this kitchen, the three bodies in it, and the extraordinary stillness of the day comprised all of existence.

"It will be a year on the twentieth of next month." A year! Addie had still been out of her mind at the one-year anniversary of Sean's...passing. She still choked on the word death.

"You seem so peaceful." It was with a sort of innocent wonderment that Addie spoke the words.

"Honey, I'm a lot older than you. I just turned seventy-five last month. What are you, thirty-five?"

"Almost forty, but thanks"

"OK, forty. That's still over thirty years I have on you. She was sick for a long time. We had a long time to say all that we needed to say and beyond that we had time to just be." Leo sipped his coffee then continued, "I get the feeling you didn't get the gift of time. Am I right?"

"Sean, my husband, died in a motorcycle accident almost five years ago. It was a perfectly sunny May afternoon. He went out for a drive and was hit broadside by a car that ran the light. Nobody was going all that fast, but the doctor told me later he died immediately. The EMT tried to revive him at the scene but he was gone."

Silence fell between them. This was something Addie didn't talk about. What was the point? Yet she had told this man who was almost a stranger to her. The silence stretched. Buck suddenly made a little snoring sound and both Addie and Leo broke into laughter.

"Buck could do stand up, his timing is impeccable. Don't you love the way dogs bring us back into our bodies?" Addie nodded and added, "I don't know what I would do without Buck. Honest to God, it feels like he is my connection to sanity sometimes."

"If someone had asked you before your husband, before Sean died, how you would have made it without him, you certainly wouldn't have been able to imagine that either. But here you are. Here I am. What are you going to do? Shit happens, as they say, and if you look closely it appears we don't control the outcome."

Addie understood perfectly and even found a measure of comfort in the words Leo spoke. But they also frightened her. Shit happens. Right. And shit could happen again. She couldn't approach the idea. Not yet. She felt a wave of anger and fear at the thought of something happening to Buck. It was an injustice too painful to consider. She could feel herself running away from the truth of Leo's words, running as if it protected her from loss. *I'll be able to think about that later, after I heal, when I'm myself again.*

Leo seemed to know this was as far as she could go for the moment and brought the conversation back to the original topic.

"Did Mr. Parris say what the problems were with the attic and the back of the house? There haven't been renters there for a couple of years, is it habitable?"

Addie hadn't even wondered about the nature of the house's problems. "I guess I figured it must be ok if they need a caretaker. I never even thought to ask." An odd and somewhat defiant voice in her head insisted: *I don't care. I can live in it no matter what. It's going to be a home for us.*

"How does a therapist go about dropping clients?" Leo mopped up a blob of lemon curd with the last corner of his toast and popped it into his mouth.

"I was thinking maybe I could come in to town one day a week and keep most if not all of them. I looked at the map, Sutton Bay doesn't look like more than a couple of hours away unless the traffic is really awful or I have to wait a long time for the ferry."

And Buck could come too. She could set up a little bed for him in the office. She couldn't leave him alone in Pen House. The last thought had come to her with complete certainty. Despite a sense of significance, she pushed it away abruptly.

"That could work. Do you want clients?" There he went again, asking the questions that made her turn inward. But he did it with the great gentleness of authentic curiosity. It didn't feel intrusive.

She laughed, "no. I want to refer them to you. You're ten times the therapist I am. But seriously, it just seems like I shouldn't turn my nose up at the money."

Leo nodded. "Have you sat down and figured out what you do need? You wouldn't have to pay any rent and they must be paying you a little stipend. Maybe you could cut back?"

Addie smiled, "sounds like you're trying to talk me into quitting my job."

Leo's face was calmly serious. "Not at all. I just hear you saying you aren't happy doing what you do. Maybe this is a chance to take time away and see what direction you want to go."

He was right. She wasn't happy with her work and a huge part of the appeal of this entire venture was the thought of escaping the weight of that.

"I feel dread on Wednesdays, when I see the bulk of my clients. I feel guilty. I feel like I'm cheating them."

Leo shook his head, "I don't know about them, but I feel wonderful when we talk." Addie smiled, felt shy.

"But seriously, you're a good person Adeline. If your clients seem to be growing in healthy directions, maybe it's not for you to second-guess what they're getting from the sessions. Maybe all you can do is try to decide what's your next best move." He paused and then clarified, "the best move for you."

Buck, sensing a shift in Addie, jumped down from her lap where he had been curled up. He stretched, first the front, then the back, and then stood watching her, wagging his tail.

Addie danced around her discomfort by blaming her need to drop the conversation on the dog. "Buck says it's time to go. Leo, thank you so much for being here. Honestly."

"You know Teddy, Theodora, that was my wife, she and I talk. Do you talk to Sean?"

He looked at her; his eyes were utterly frank, completely

serious. Addie didn't know how to respond. Was this guy who seemed so grounded and sane, a nutcase? She didn't really know him after all. Did he mean like in therapy? When you had someone face an empty chair and tell their dead father all the things they never said while they were alive? Did he mean he really talked to her and that she talked back?

"No. I don't."

As the words came out of her mouth, she realized she felt envious that he believed he could still talk to his wife. How nice it would be to talk to Sean again. She wouldn't have to be greedy about it. She would be more than happy if they could converse once in a while. *Where are you?* She had asked this question internally a thousand times and always the question seemed to be snatched away to a place she couldn't see or feel.

"You could try it. He might have advice for you."

Leo had reached out and was holding her hand. She needed to change the direction of their conversation or she was going to cry.

"I have to get going. What are you doing Saturday night? Why don't we have dinner when I get back from Sutton Bay and I'll tell you about Pen House. I'm not sure I'd want to hold my cooking talents up next to yours, but we could meet at Andy's, have a burger and some beer?"

Addie was grateful that Leo moved on to this next topic easily. "You're on," he replied.

She hugged him impulsively. "Thanks so much for the toast and coffee. You spoil me with your food and attention."

"It gives me great pleasure and we are definitely on for

40

Saturday."

He held her coat, hat and gloves out to her. She put the coat on and stuffed the hat and gloves into her pocket. The sun wasn't out but the rain had stopped. She put Buck's leash on and was halfway out the door when she turned back to Leo.

"What is your last name by the way?"

"MacLeod. Let me write down my number. And give me yours."

He handed her a pen and a sticky notepad. She wrote the number and under it she wrote "Adeline Morgan...and Buck"

8

For at least the tenth time Addie checked the directions she had written down from Mr. Parris' dictation. The original plan had been to meet him at his office in Sutton Bay and then go with him the rest of the way to the house. He had called in the morning to tell her he was tied up with a client and didn't think he could get back to his office on time and why didn't she just meet him at Pen House. The directions to Sutton Bay were easy. However, the last three miles beyond town were going to demand more of her attention as they involved two left turns, one right and then having to keep her eyes peeled for a rusty blue mailbox, approximately a hundred feet beyond which lay the driveway, on the right, to Pen House.

She drove slowly through Sutton Bay and found it charming. The wide main street had been built in the eighteen eighties and many of the original structures remained. Large edifices of warm golden-brown stone, seemingly all from the same quarry, housed a café, a couple of banks, a thrift store, a women's clothing shop, a Sears store with lots of appliances in the window and a surprisingly fancy looking Italian restaurant. There were also a couple of vacant spaces with for rent signs stuck to their smudged and dusty windows. Still, she saw people on the sidewalks and there was a sense that it was a living, functioning town. This was a relief to her. It would be fun to walk here with Buck. The three miles from Pen House was well within their walking routine and though the area wasn't flat, neither was it dauntingly hilly.

As they left the town behind, Addie began to look for the first turn she needed to make off the highway. Buck came up from the backseat and sat in her lap. Normally this was forbidden but this time she allowed it. His little warm body gave her courage. He looked up at her and licked her cheek.

"Turn around and sit down, buddy." Buck turned so he faced the passenger side and lay down.

"Good boy." She scratched him behind his ears, which were especially soft after his recent trip to the groomer. His tail wagged.

"I'm excited too," Addie said conversationally.

Buck always knew when they were nearing their destination. What was it he picked up on? Did she shift her body? Breathe differently? He was minutely tuned in, of that she was sure. What would it be like to be that awake, that ready? She was always amazed by how he would anticipate a knock on the door, her homecomings, and her moods. Now he lay in her lap but he wasn't relaxed. He was ready for something. His chin rested lightly on his front paws and his eyes were open. His nose was quivering and his ears had the lifted posture that came with intent listening. All his systems were alert.

Addie was grateful when she easily found the road off which Mr. Parris told her she would find the driveway to Pen House. It was called Orchard Boulevard. Whoever had named the street must have envisioned it evolving in a different way. Wasn't a boulevard a city kind of thing? There weren't more than a couple of houses along the mile stretch to the driveway's turnoff. There were orchards, old and wizened apple orchards that clearly had not been tended to for a long time. The trees were big and gnarled and hadn't seen the teeth of a pruning saw for years. Some of them had blackberry brambles climbing up their trunks and festooning the branches. Here and there a shriveled brown apple clung improbably to a branch.

The grassy fields hadn't gotten any spring growth yet and everything looked tired and cold from winter. Still, it was beautiful. The day had become sunny and the pavement, still wet from last night's rain, had a little mist of steam rising up off the asphalt where the sun was hitting it. She rolled down the window and let the clean smell waft in. Buck sat up and stuck his face out the window. His ears blew comically backwards and Addie laughed. He looked back at her with what she imagined to be a wounded expression.

"Sorry buddy, nothing personal. You know I think you're the handsomest boy ever."

Buck resumed his intense sniffing. The air was filled with birdsong and Addie felt an onrush of lightheartedness. It was a quiet surprise, as if she had come across a loved pair of comfy old shoes at the very back of the closet. Lost in the distraction of this feeling, she almost missed her landmark. But there it was, a battered mailbox that must have originally been a cheery sky blue and was now mostly eaten up by rust. The post it precariously clung to listed toward the road and the door of the box was open, giving it a hungry look. A large telltale dent in the side led her to believe that the local kids liked to play mailbox baseball.

She slowed almost to a stop. Somewhat abruptly the road had descended into shadow. Douglas fir and madrone had replaced the grassy meadows and tumble down orchards. She drove on slowly looking for the driveway. She saw the opening and out of habit flipped on her turn indicator. *That's a useless move*, she thought, getting a glimpse in the rear view mirror of the empty road that rolled out behind her. Buck sat up on her lap, waiting, knowing there was just a little way to go.

The driveway was unpaved and rutted. She crept along, not wanting to bottom out. She hoped the trees would thin out soon, hoped the house wasn't in this somewhat oppressive shadow. Addie followed the drive around what she thought would be a grand curve after which the house would be revealed to her. But the drive continued. Finally, thankfully, the big trees receded and gave way to lawn and shrubs. The sun once again glinted off the hood of her car. She knew that once upon a time this forlorn garden had been meticulously landscaped. The grass now had lots of mossy patches and low spots that looked pretty soggy. There were little mounds of rich brown earth where moles had been busy tunneling. Still, she could make out the shapes of the beds and see old rose bushes, some of them climbing messily up trellises, leaves splattered with black spot, tentatively clinging to the thorny stalks. There were also azaleas and rhododendrons and much more she couldn't name. The beds were crowded with weeds, dandelions being the only ones she could confidently identify.

Just as she felt a twinge of anxiety that she might have gone down the wrong driveway after all, she rounded one more large and swooping curve and caught her first sight of the house. It seemed that when she came into the clearing in the trees the house should have been straight ahead of her, but it was to the left. She puzzled over this odd placement only until she saw beyond the house, perhaps another quarter of a mile away, the sparkling blue water of the bay. The house faced south and out all the windows at the back of the house, to the north, must surely be stunning views of the water. She realized how turned around she felt. She wondered if there was a path that led to a beach. Buck had abandoned his manners and not only had his head out the window, but was also whining in anticipation of getting out of the car.

She pulled to a cautious stop about fifty feet from the front of the house. She looked at the dashboard clock. Ten-to-one. There was no sign of another car. She had obviously beat Mr. Parris here. She opened the door and Buck bounded out. He sniffed at an azalea and promptly lifted his leg and had a good long pee. Addie stared at the house, not moving from the side of the car. She realized she had been picturing a cottage, maybe a trellis overflowing with honeysuckle, a charming little path up to...up to what? Little Red Riding Hood's Grandmother's?

Pen House was a two-story edifice made of stone. The stone was the same honey-brown of the buildings in town. It had deep eaves and a steeply pitched slate roof. Some of the slates had slipped and now sat crookedly or were missing altogether. The copper gutters and downspouts were a deep green-blue and were spotted with age and the saltwater laden air. The upstairs windows were adorned with shutters, all in sorry repair. Chalky black paint, largely gone, revealed the wood's natural weathered gray underneath. Many of the slats were missing or askew, mirroring the condition of the roof tiles. The lines of the house were symmetrical, lovely really. What a sad and beautiful house! How did it ever happen that someone put so much into a house and then, over time, it was forgotten? Where did everyone go? It was once a home and now it seemed to simply be braving the elements, waiting... *as hopelessly as a widow waits.* A western gull sunned itself on the lip of the chimney. Addie could see by the white spatters down the chimney's sides and around its base that this was a popular stopping place. The gull cried out, spread its wings, lifted upwards and headed toward the bay.

Addie realized Buck had wandered off.

"Buck, come!" She looked around for him and didn't see him. He came running toward her from behind. He seemed to be smiling, almost leaping as he ran.

"Come on buddy, let's peek in the windows."

Buck ran ahead of her as she walked toward the house. There was a leggy barberry that formed a wall, creating an oddly cramped front garden. The shrub was immediately distasteful to her. It was sharp and unfriendly. On closer inspection she saw that its thorns were wickedly long. She noticed as she passed through the opening gap in the shrub that there was a path leading to the wide stone steps that in turn lead up to the front door. But Little Red Riding Hood was hardly the fairytale that it called to mind. The idea of a wolf dressed up in a nightgown and mop cap had never frightened Addie. It was too silly. This called to mind something sadder, darker and much more impenetrable. She realized she was cold and fastened her wool coat and pulled her gloves out of the pocket.

The path was brick and there were weeds, managing to look both stunted and hardy, growing up through nearly all the spaces between the aging masonry. On the grass to her right was a concrete birdbath with a scalloped edge around the bowl.

Around the pedestal climbed concrete vines. There was rainwater in the slime-covered bowl. She looked down into it and saw the reflection of the clouds scuttling across the blue sky and she saw her face, brown hair hanging forward. Her face looked distorted, both familiar and strange.

She was startled by Buck's barking. She looked up and saw he was barking at the window. She felt a moment of panic. Was someone here? Had they been watching her poking around, seen her foolishly staring at her reflection in a birdbath?

"Buck! Hush!"

He barked again and followed that with a noise somewhere between a bark and a growl. They were both diverted by the sound of a car approaching. She felt a wave of relief. She reached down and picked him up. She had left his leash in the car and didn't want him barking at Mr. Parris.

Mike Parris pulled up nearly to the barberry. Because of the sun winking off the glass, she couldn't see his face clearly through the window of his late model sedan. Addie braced herself for an obnoxious real estate agent type. He climbed out holding a cell phone up to his ear and his other hand, one finger up, indicated he'd be off in just a second. Not exactly her favorite way to meet someone, Addie wondered how much she'd have to interact with this guy. Not much she hoped. And then it occurred to her that she was just assuming this was a done deal. Wait until you see the house and hear the details she told herself. But it felt like that was just pretending to do the reasoned grown up thing. In her heart of hearts it felt inevitable that she would be at Pen House.

"Hi, Mike Parris, sorry I'm late. This has been a crazy day." Mike stuck out his hand and Addie, tucking Buck under her left arm, shook it.

"Nice to meet you. I haven't been here long. This is Buck"

She set Buck back down as she spoke, admonishing him not to bark. Buck sniffed at Mike's pant leg and then turned away, on to something more interesting. At least this guy didn't appear to put Buck on guard. Addie always gave tremendous weight to Buck's judgment.

"Let's go inside, shall we? You can see that this place has seen better days but the new owners have big plans for the house. Maybe turn it in to a bed and breakfast. They'll need to pave that driveway. People won't want to spend a lot of money to stay here only to get their oil pan trashed on the way in." Mike reached up and knocked on the door.

"Is someone here?" Addie asked, remembering Buck's barking.

"No, it's just an old habit from being in the real estate business." He pulled a key out of his pocket and fitted it in the dead bolt above the elegantly curved brass handle. The oak door was large and heavy seeming which Addie was glad of. Mike pushed it open.

"Welcome to Pen House."

9

Addie walked in and was immediately taken with the wide maple staircase that faced the door. The color of the wood reminded her of caramelized sugar. Rising up grandly from the curved swell step was an elegant newel post encircled with carved vines and flowers. The wood of the balusters, as well as the cap on the post that spiraled around and became the handrail, was a dark and polished cherry. The steps went up to a landing, turned to the right, two steps up to another landing, turned again to the right and continued up to the second floor. The entryway walls were covered with flat panel wainscoting that rose up over Addie's head to reach within three feet of the ceiling. The wainscoting's inset panels were birdseye maple and the frames around the panels matched the cherry balustrade. Her gaze was broken by the realization that the house was bitterly cold and that she was shivering under her woolen jacket. She saw that Buck was still standing at the threshold.

"Come on buddy, it's ok." He trotted over to her and put his paws up on her legs in the pick-me-up stance. She reached down and lifted him.

"You're too big for this, but ok, for a minute."

"Is he a poodle?" Mike asked.

No, it's a Great Dane, moron. What more did he need as evidence than a big round pom on the end of Buck's tail and a puff of tight curls on the top of his head? She immediately chided herself for her uncharitable thoughts and answered him.

"Yes, he's a miniature poodle."

"How much does he weigh?" Mike reached out to Buck and got

49

a lick on the hand for his efforts. Buck was ok with this guy.

"About sixteen pounds. Not really all that miniature." She put him back down on the bare oak floor and Buck stayed glued to her leg.

"It's freezing in here," Addie said, and shivered again.

"Yeah, it's a big house to heat and the heat hasn't been turned on at all this season. It does work though. It's an oil fired hot water system. These old radiators make a lot of noise but they work just fine." He indicated a cast iron radiator that stood a few inches out from one of the entryway walls. It was covered with an ornate design of interlocking vines. Addie compared and confirmed it was the same design as that which twined around the newel post.

"What exactly do you do Mr. Parris?"

For the first time Addie really looked at the man next to her. Mike Parris appeared to be in his late forties, maybe early fifties. In his face were the beginnings of the lines that would define his look in old age, but there was also a boyish blush to his cheeks as if he had just done something exuberant like run up a big flight of stairs two at a time. He was average in height and getting wide in girth. His gut pushed against his well-made shirt and threatened to hang over his suit pants. He had a lot of thick disobedient hair that was reddish brown going to gray at the temples. His hands were manicured, strong looking, like a surgeon's as opposed to a laborer. He smelled of aftershave. Too much for Addie's taste. If she had to be around this guy for long she was sure she would develop a splitting headache. She found herself pettishly looking for faults in him, actively trying to override what seemed nice about him; a gentle kind of energy, goofy almost.

"Please call me Mike, Mr. Parris is my dad."

A small smile crossed his face and he continued, "I run a real estate office in Sutton Bay. And I do property management. The new owners bought this property through me about, oh eight, nine months ago. After the sale the house just sat. That's the kind of money these folks have, they can buy something and let it sit until they decide what they want to do. Anyway, they called me last month and asked if I would put an ad in the paper, looking for a caretaker. Said they wanted to start a remodel by late spring and since they couldn't be on site they wanted a responsible party living here."

"But I saw the ad at my local grocery store. Did you put that there?"

Addie realized she was kind of hopping from one foot to the other to generate a little warmth. Mike, seeing her discomfort, said, "come on, we can talk and walk around the house at the same time. Let's go into the living room, there's a little sun coming in those windows."

Just to the left of the entryway were French doors that opened into the living room. Each door had a panel of frosted glass and etched around the edge of the glass was a trail of the same vines and flowers.

"What kind of vines are these?" Addie asked, waving her hand vaguely to indicate the pattern she had seen repeated so often. She realized as she asked that she thought they must be peonies given how many times she had come across them lately.

"I asked one of the gardeners that came in to spiff up the grounds before it was put on the market and she said they aren't any kind of vine at all. They're the leaves and flowers of a tulip poplar.

Addie felt strangely disappointed. "Why is the house called Pen House?"

"I have no idea."

Mike pressed down the brass handle and pulled the right hand door open.

"You can open both doors but this left hand one needs to be unbolted first."

He reached up and pulled down one bolt then bent over and pulled up the floor bolt. He pulled the door but it still didn't want to move. Addie noticed there was an arc of scrape marks on the floor where it had been forced open.

"That's something the contractor will need to see to," he said, walking in to the living room and leaving the left hand door unbolted but closed.

The living room was beautiful and noticeably warmer than the entryway. The room was flooded with light. There were windows facing south, west and north. The afternoon sun left watery images of the somewhat wavy old panes of glass on the oak plank floor. Addie was quietly struck that such warmth and light seemingly hadn't penetrated the entryway by a single degree.

"No peonies," Mike said, "but definitely a tulip poplar." He pointed to the west window.

Looking out she registered the enormous tree, perfectly framed by the windows and surrounded by lawn. Its limbs were still bare but she could see from its elegant shape that it was a grand tree. She could imagine it in leaf, filtering the light and cutting the heat of a long summer afternoon.

Turning to look out the north window, Addie was treated to a stunning view of the shimmering blue bay. She stood still and the quiet of the house seemed to rock her gently. Buck had succumbed to the same sense of peace and stretched out on the sunny floor.

Mike's voice broke into her thoughts.," funny story about that ad you saw. It was the only card I put up. I placed ads in the paper. The response wasn't great. I had a couple come and look at the house. They sounded promising but they finally decided they didn't like the house. They thought it was too big and draughty. I met with a retired couple and we were close to firming up arrangements and then they just backed out. They never said why. Anyway, my daughter, who's a student at the University, lives just about a block from that store where you saw the ad. I was over there visiting her and she asked me what was going on at Pen House. She knows the property, it's kind of well known around here. I told her I was striking out with the newspaper ad and she suggested putting cards up around where she lives. We sat there and wrote out probably ten or fifteen of the cards. She put that one up at the store the next day. But she never got around to putting any of the other ones up. In fact, I talked to her yesterday and she apologized for not doing it. I told her I was meeting you today and let's just wait and see how that goes."

"Have you had many calls?"

"Honestly? None but yours." Mike looked a little abashed, as if he'd been caught trying to pass off shoddy goods. Addie, however, felt enormously relieved to know she had no competition.

Buck continued basking, his head perched on his two

outstretched front paws, his sleepy eyes on Addie and Mike. *I love this room*, thought Addie, *I could live in here. God knows it's big enough.*

"So I'm your only prospect at the moment?" Addie tried to adopt a tone that was business-like but couldn't entirely keep the pleasure out of her voice. Pen House was oddly, quietly thrilling.

"Yep, you're it. Why don't you tell me about yourself."

Mike moved to the other side of the room where there was an arched opening into a back hallway. Addie filled him in as they moved along. When she extracted everything that felt personal, it was a surprisingly short story: professional woman who lives alone in the big city sees ad for caretaker. It just so happens she has been thinking about taking a sabbatical from work and calls on the ad, which looks intriguing.

"So, here I am," she concluded.

"Here you are," he echoed.

He pointed out a bathroom on the left. It had a toilet and a white porcelain pedestal sink. The floor was tiled with little octagonal black and white tiles. There was also a smallish double hung window that had thick frosted glass. It let in light with no hint of the sun's warmth. The cold was if anything deeper here than the entryway. Mike opened a door on the right and switched on a light. Addie looked down a steep narrow staircase. She saw there was also a rounded handrail and thought that was definitely a good thing. She hoped there was nothing in the job that required many trips down there. It was decidedly creepy. She looked down the stairs and could only see a little bit of the gray cement floor at the bottom. Then the light, a bare bulb that hung over the midpoint of the stairs, reached its limit and bumped up against deep black.

"The basement and the furnace room are down there," Mike explained.

"The main electrical panel is also down there. The contractors will be rewiring the entire place. Everything in this house is pretty much original. The new owners want to update it but keep its original look. I know the basement looks pretty…" She knew immediately that Mike's first impulse was to say *scary*. She watched him check the impulse and say, "dark".

"Believe me it gets lit up like a Christmas tree when you hit all the switches down there. The worst part is finding that first switch. We'll put in a little nightlight down there so you don't have to fumble around."

He shut the door to the basement and moved along the hallway.

"If you decide to take the position, I'll show you everything down there, how to replace a fuse if the power goes. You shouldn't have to do anything with the furnace. We have a company in town that does a yearly inspection, changes filters, that kind of thing. I'll show you how to check the oil tank. It should be nearly full so nothing to worry about there."

Now they moved into a mudroom with a door to the left that led out to the back garden. The door, indeed the entire room, was painted white. The door had a glass panel in its upper third and the pane had a diagonal crack running across it. There were shelves lining the beadboard walls. There was also a large porcelain coated cast iron sink with porcelain faucet handles and drain boards on either side. Just to the left of the back door was a built in box seat that served as a storage space as well as a place to sit and take off muddy boots. Addie lifted the lid and looked down. She gasped before she realized what she was looking at. It was a mirror, lying face up and she was looking into her own face, brown hair framing her startled expression. Mike looked over to see what had made her start.

"Oh yeah. Sorry about that. It's the mirror that goes in that little bathroom, the so-called scullery toilet." Mike indicated with his thumb back in the direction they had come from.

"It fell and by some miracle the glass didn't break. I haven't gotten around to re-hanging it. I just put it in there to get it out of the way."

"It's ok," Addie said, laughing, "I just wasn't expecting a face, even if it was my own."

Buck went to the backdoor and whined.

"You need to go out, buddy?"

Addie unlocked the dead bolt and turned the glass handle. She was relieved that the door had a sturdy lock on it. Her next thought, however, that someone could break the already cracked pane and simply reach in and turn the deadbolt, sent a wave of unease over her. She pulled the door open and a breeze off of the water hit her face. The fear proved momentary, displaced by the fresh air and her interest in what the back of the house looked out on. In only a matter of minutes the sun had disappeared behind thick clouds and the water of the bay had turned a turbid green. She could see the flecks of white caps erupting over the surface and smell the saltwater, a scent she'd always found stinky but wonderful. Addie had been expecting only lawn so she was surprised and delighted to see an orchard of perhaps twenty fruit trees. A mass of daffodils, primroses, grape hyacinths and tulips grew singly and in clumps all around and under the trees. The tulips hadn't bloomed and their buds were still green and tightly closed. The other flowers, however, were opening and under the dark sky their petals of purple-blue, yellow, pink and white, glowed against the green of the grass.

"Are those apple trees?" she asked.

"Some are and there are a couple of pears and both Damson and Italian plums. In that very back row are a couple of cherries. You will have more fruit and more birds then you know what to do with in a few months." Mike and Addie stood on the back porch while Buck ran out to one of the trees and gratefully lifted his leg.

"They look well tended."

"One of the first and only things the new owners did was to have a gardener come out and clean all these trees up."

"The same gardener who gave you the tulip tree tutorial?" Addie smiled at her own alliteration, aware of the little spark of friendliness she was stoking.

Mike smiled back, seemingly every bit as willing to be cordial.

"Nope. This was an outfit from Seattle. There was an arborist that came out with the gardener and a crew of four guys. They did prune the poplar and a couple of trees in the front.

They stood quietly for a moment watching Buck, nose to the ground, slowly return to the back porch.

"What do you think so far?" Mike looked at her and Addie could see he really hoped this was going all right.

"The house is unbelievable. It's beautiful. It's a little hard to imagine just me and Buck in this big space."

"You can have friends come stay, boyfriend, whatever." Mike's voice sounded eager, maybe even a little desperate.

"My life is pretty solitary right now, though it might be fun to have a friend come and visit." Addie was thinking how much she wanted Leo to see this place. It would knock his socks off. Would he want to come all this way to see the house? See her? Buck trotted up the back stairs and the tour resumed.

"I think you'll get a kick out of the kitchen. This is the pantry, which is about twice the size of our kitchen at home." Mike's enthusiastic tone sounded to Addie as if he was addressing a prospective buyer rather than a glorified house sitter.

Like a dog hearing a whistle, the word *our* stood out with great clarity. She pictured Mike and his wife, a perky frosted blonde with a ponytail, standing in their kitchen, lace trimmed eyelet curtains tied back with ribbon, wallpaper with...She caught her thoughts and reined them in, thoroughly ashamed of that small-minded Addie who, with no provocation or evidence, disparaged people she didn't even know. She gingerly poked at the possible reasons for her mental meanness, as if feeling for the spot where the worst of the pain originated. What she found, that it made her loneliness more bearable if she imagined someone else's happiness to be shallow, made her cringe.

The pantry walls, like the mudroom, were lined with beadboard. The paint, once livelier, was now faded and mellow, like pale butter. There was an entire wall lined with shallow shelves which Addie imagined had once been full of canned peaches, tomatoes, pickles and jams. Another wall had a tall cupboard flanked by deeper shelves. On the east wall was a half-round window, its top edge just inches from the ceiling, She could see that it opened at the bottom and swung outwards. Just as she was going to ask, Mike showed her a long pole with a brass hook on the end leaning up in the corner.

"This is really easy to use." Mike demonstrated, hooking the window's handle, turning it and pushing the window open. Addie heard the indignant squeak of the hinges. She looked through the windowpane at the scuttling clouds rendered somewhat distorted, in a psychedelic way, through the glacially slumping glass.

She said, "I remember my grade school windows had to be opened like that, with a long pole to reach, I mean." Mike pulled the window closed and leaned the pole back in the corner.

"I think I could put the entire contents of my kitchen on one of these shelves," Addie said.

She hadn't cooked much since Sean's passing. It used to be something fun they did together. She remembered the intense enjoyment of planning and shopping for a meal with him. She remembered how they would congratulate themselves on successfully pulling off a new recipe. This thought drifted to a specific memory that she had revisited several times: It was a cold and gray Saturday afternoon. Rain was in the forecast and Addie and Sean had decided to stay in and cook. They had baked long loaves of French bread, something they had never tried making before. They also made Coq au Vin, looking forward to dipping the fresh baked bread into the stew's red wine sauce. What had actually happened was that, while the stew was still cooking, they ate a test piece of the hot bread. One piece led to another and another, each spread thickly with butter, until one loaf was gone and the other was halfway demolished. They were so full they left the kitchen and sprawled on the living room couch to compare their bulging tummies. They had laughed and horsed around. Then they had kissed and made love on the living room floor. And the Coq au Vin had burned to the bottom of the pot.

She realized she was standing still at the threshold between the pantry and the kitchen, so caught in the memory that she had inadvertently stopped moving. She mentally shook away the feeling of disorientation that her slide from presence had caused and followed Mike in to the kitchen.

Addie's eye was immediately drawn to a large, rather elaborate cast iron range. The butterscotch colored enamel was seemingly in perfect shape. The oven and firebox doors were trimmed with cinnamon brown enamel. It had short squat legs whose feet turned out. It reminded her of an illustration from one of her childhood books; the plump farm wife who, to assuage her loneliness, makes the gingerbread man. She smiled.

"What?" Mike asked. Addie told him her impression. He stared at the stove.

"I guess I can see that, although I think it looks more like the Queen of Hearts."

"No, it's too cheerful for her."

"I think we should wait until that firebox is full and burning before we make a final decision. Her true identity can't possibly be determined when she's cold."

"Ok, at least we agree it has a feminine nature." Addie laughed and held her hands up in truce. She asked him about its provenance.

"The original owner, guy by the name of Davies, had this monster shipped from Boston if you can believe that. I'm sure at the time it was state of the art. I don't know how it is to cook on, I don't know how you'd control the heat of the oven, but I imagine it warms the kitchen up very nicely. In any case, there's an electric range as well." The modern stove looked puny by comparison. She saw there was also a new looking refrigerator.

The kitchen was large without ostentation. It was obvious that the house had been built for a big and well-to-do family. And this kitchen and its adjoining pantry were once the purview of a cook and her helpers. A wave of melancholy lapped at Addie. The big kitchen had done its part, lasting a hundred years. But the family, the cooks and the wait staff, were long gone. *Can't we ever have one lasting thing*, Addie thought? The house seemed to sigh and she shivered yet again. *Damn! It's freezing in here!* Addie consciously put aside the cold and turned toward a more positive observation.

"You know, Mike, the house doesn't seem to be in bad shape at all. I did notice that the outside needs some help but overall the house seems well cared for."

Mike nodded. "The house has always had devoted owners. Even the renters took surprisingly good care of it. It's only had four owners. First was the Davies family, who had the house built in the early eighteen ninety's and owned it until their only child, Laura, went into a nursing home. After that it's only had three other owners. They all started out with the intention to stay, but for one reason or another, they all had to sell. The last owner rented it out. Turns out those renters were part of some religious cult. I think there were about twelve people living here. They really weren't that hard on the place though I can tell you that people around here definitely did not like them, didn't trust them. There were all kinds of rumors that swirled around this place. They seemed pretty harmless to me, a little kooky. Really kooky, actually." Mike stopped, as if his narration had gotten uncomfortably off track.

"Anyway," he resumed, "the upstairs is in worse shape."

"We're almost done with the downstairs tour. Did you notice how the staircase is the center of the house and the rooms circle around it?" Mike pointed this out as they walked into the dining room beyond which was the entryway.

"I hadn't thought of that but of course, we just walked in a circle."

Addie felt charmed by the simplicity of the design. As they had entered each new room she found herself more deeply in love with the idea of living in Pen House. She mentally ran some numbers, seeing if there was a way to do it without dipping too deeply into the money that had come to her after Sean's death. She might keep one client. That would get her into town once a week and give her a little extra cash. It might also help assuage her guilt that she was dumping people who needed her. *I have needs too*, she thought defensively. There was some ferocity to it, as if she was actively arguing her point with someone.

Mike's voice brought her out of her head.

"This is my favorite room. It's the dining room and all that painting up around top of the walls was done by hand."

Addie saw that the walls had the same flat panel wainscoting that lined the entryway. Above the wainscoting, the walls were painted a pale rose. At the top of the wall and running the circumference of the room, were the tulip tree flowers and leaves morphed into a vine motif. The flower petals were gold leaf and the leaves and stems were a deep green. It was delicate and exquisitely beautiful. In the middle of the ceiling was a large ornate circle of the same leaves and flowers, this time rendered in raised plaster. Hanging from the circle's middle was a large and swooping crystal chandelier. Addie could see that a few of the crystal dangles, like loose baby teeth, were hanging by a thread.

"Does it work?" Addie asked.

Mike walked over to the two-button wall switch and pressed the upper one.

"Voila!"

He made a grand sweeping gesture with his hand as if he'd just lit up a fifty foot Christmas tree. In reality, about half of the chandelier's twenty little bulbs were either burned out or screwed in to receptacles that no longer functioned.

On the south wall was a big window, the twin of the living room's front window. It looked out onto the lawn with its surrounding barberry hedge. She was struck again by how wrong the shrub was, both in scale and effect. It was leggy and thorn-covered and truncated what should have been an open, somewhat wild view across the manicured garden and into the thick of the fir and madrone forest.

What a beautiful room this must have been to dine in, Addie thought. She imagined a big bustling family but then remembered Mike saying the Davies' had only one daughter. Her mind's eye view shifted as she imagined a long formal table with only three people sitting down to eat, one of them a little girl whose feet didn't yet reach the floor.

On the east wall were leaded glass windows, below which was the only piece of furniture Addie had seen. It was a large sideboard. The wood was dark, almost black, and Addie found it both ostentatious and grim. The upper stage had a large beveled mirror at its center. The mirror's silver coating was badly eroded and when Addie looked into the mirror her image was interrupted by irregular black voids. There were cupboards flanking each side of the mirror. Twin columns supported the entire upper portion. The main body had three drawers, underneath which was a cupboard that ran the width of the piece. All of the sideboard's drawers and cupboards had handles that hung like big brass tears. The entire piece was ridiculously ornate and the two columns looked like the cabinetmaker had been in the middle of a manic episode while manning the lathe. All that was missing, Addie thought, was a black-framed photograph of Queen Victoria in her older, fatter years, covered in black mourning clothes.

"Wow." It was all Addie could think to say. Mike laughed.

"Has this thing been here all along?"

"As far as I know this baby hasn't budged for over a hundred years."

Mike pulled open one of the drawers as he spoke and the smell of the wood wafted out into the room like a genie out of its jar. It was the smell of wood, but stronger than that Addie could detect the smell of what used to be kept inside; silverware, linen napkins, beeswax candles. Addie opened the drawer next to it and then, together, wordlessly; they opened the third drawer and the two cupboards underneath. The wood had a pleasantly musty smell and they both laughed, a little sheepishly, at the sight of the pulled open drawers and cupboards. Addie stooped down to look in the cupboard.

"What's this?" She reached toward the back and picked something up and then immediately dropped it with a squeal.

"What is it?" Said Mike, peering into the cupboard.

"A bug, I think." Addie tried to put some dignity back in her voice after her girlish reaction.

Mike reached in and brought out a shiny black beetle. Dead as a doornail, it lay on its back in his palm. He turned it over and they looked at it together.

"How'd you get in there, fella?"

Mike placed it, somewhat reverentially, on the top of the sideboard. Together they closed the drawers and cupboards. Mike smiled at her as if to say weird, huh? Addie smiled back but her thoughts were unclear at that moment.

Buck, unconcerned with the sideboard, had his wriggling nose in the air. He stood in the center of the room looking toward the stairs.

The jarring sound of Mike's cell phone echoed through the house. He fumbled in his pocket and brought it out.

"This is Mike."

Addie couldn't make out the voice of the caller, only that it sounded noisy and out of place in the hush of the house.

"I can't hear you, hang on, I'm going to walk outside."

Mike put his hand over the phone and mouthed, "Be right back." Addie nodded.

After the door closed Addie reflexively looked around for Buck. Her sense of isolation was immediate and powerful. After a moment of panic she saw him heading up the stairs, nearly to the first landing.

"Buck! Come!"

Her voice sounded harsh and loud. Buck turned to acknowledge her but then, in a rare display of disobedience, he continued slowly up the stairs, nose to the ground. She followed him, realizing there was no harm in going up without Mike. With just one foot on the first stair she could feel an icy draft coming down toward her. She wished she hadn't left her scarf and gloves in the car.

"Ok Buck, lead on."

She ran her hand along the banister, smooth and well oiled from the touch of human hands. At the first landing she turned back to the front door. She could hear Mike's voice, though not his words, talking on the phone. She felt as though she was eavesdropping on a strange communication from another planet. It sounded muted, garbled, and the cadence of Mike's voice was unfamiliar. With deeper reflection, however, Addie decided it was the house that was the unknown planet and Mike's voice, now so distant it was no longer decipherable, was the transmission from home.

Addie could feel the strength of Pen House all around her. In a way it was like meeting a client for the first time. How would this new relationship build? Would she be called upon to offer up practical help, or did Pen House want more of her? She had the distinct impression that, regardless of how it all shook out, the house needed to be taken seriously and treated with the utmost respect. She felt puzzled about how her intuition would be translated into action. She turned back to her ascent, almost tripping on Buck who was sniffing somewhat compulsively at a stair.

Out loud she said, "I wonder if there are mice in the house?"

She certainly hadn't seen anything resembling a crumb. The house didn't even look particularly dusty.

Now Buck lost interest in the stair and trotted up to the top. The sound of his nails on the wood sounded preternaturally loud. Addie herself was near the top when Buck started growling. It was a fierce growl meaning he was sincerely afraid. Addie had to stifle the urge to run back downstairs. *My god*, she thought, *I feel terrified!* She soothed herself somewhat by distancing from her feelings as if she were a scientist studying herself. Buck continued to growl.

"What's up buddy?"

Her light tone sounded shaky and unreal. She turned to look down the hall to her right. At the hall's end was a closed door and on the outside of the door was a mirror. She experienced a ripple of fear before she realized what she was seeing. Buck was growling ferociously at himself and now her.

"It's ok Buck, it's just us." Buck continued to growl but it was morphing into a whine.

She walked toward the mirror to show him there was nothing to worry about. *What is it with the mirrors in this place?* He followed her warily and didn't really give up his suspicions even after he sniffed his reflection. Addie could feel the draft coming from under the door and she thought surely a window must be open. She jumped when she heard the front door shut and hurried back down the hall as if caught red-handed doing something she shouldn't be.

"We're up here," she called down.

Again her voice sounded false and tinny. *Damn, I am uptight.* This thought made her want to giggle. She took in a deep breath and forced herself to return to the sanity of her body, the beat of her heart, the sound of her breath.

From the hallway she watched Mike appear at the top of the stairs. Buck wagged his tail like they were old friends who'd been parted for much longer than five minutes.

He reached down and patted Buck on the side. "Sorry. I had to take that call." Addie nodded in understanding.

She hugged herself. The first thing she was going to do was get that heater cranked up and get this house warm again.

"Buck was growling at himself in the mirror."

"Go get 'em, buddy." He patted Buck again.

She smiled, feeling both better that Mike was there and fairly irritated by the truth of that.

"Why would someone put a mirror on the outside of the door?" Addie asked as they walked back toward it.

"I have no clue," Mike said, "except to scare the living daylights out of someone."

Addie admitted her fear or at least a tidied up version of it.

"I heard Buck growling and before I realized what he was growling at, I did feel a little spooked." Mike nodded as she spoke.

"An empty house, even one a lot smaller and newer than this one, can seem a little spooky." He stopped and opened a door on the right.

"Here's another bathroom, no shower, only the tub."

Like the downstairs bathroom, all the fixtures were white porcelain and the floor was covered with the same octagonal black and white tiles. There was a large claw foot tub to the left of the door. Addie noted that the feet were eagle talons each of which clutched a glass ball, which rested on the floor. There was a double hung window, much bigger than the one in the bathroom downstairs, and Addie could see a sweep of treetops and the bay once again glimmering in the fickle afternoon sun.

"If you look up here you'll see where we have some problems," Mike said.

A brown stain covered a third of the ceiling and the plaster had fallen away in some spots. In others the paint was curling up, threatening to fall. There was debris in the tub, and on the top of the toilet seat was a large orange bucket. Addie looked into the bucket which, besides having a layer of swept up paint chips and dirt, was dry.

"The roof was leaking. It wasn't a flood of water but it came through in a few places. We did a quick roof patch and I've got big plastic garbage cans in the attic to catch any drips that find their way through. This isn't the worst damage, that's in the master bedroom."

"Is the attic empty?"

"There are a couple of boxes up there and a few odd pieces of furniture, a chair or two. Nothing interesting. I've shoved what little there is into the driest area. The roof is going to be completely redone and then all these water damaged spots need to be re-plastered and painted. They're also putting in all new wiring and adding a shower. They have lots of plans..." Mike trailed off.

"Do they already have someone lined up?" Addie asked.

"Yeah. It's a contractor in Sutton Bay, a family that's been in

69

business there for years. I think you'll like them just fine, if you decide to take the position that is. Anyway, they've agreed to start in early May. The idea is that May is probably the first safe month to open up the roof."

"I'd like to accept the position, Mike. I love the house and it seems like the right thing for me at this point."

Now I've done it.

She felt as if she was free falling, dreamlike, terrifying, just the place in a dream where it came in handy to rescue herself by beginning to fly. Sean came to mind as abruptly as a splinter sliding into the meat of a fingertip. It seemed as if she'd be abandoning him, leaving him behind in the apartment. Now, instead of the designation being *our apartment*, it would soon become simply another place to be accessed only through the ephemera of memory. She quite suddenly recalled the line drawings in her childhood copy of Alice In Wonderland and how oddly placid Alice's facial expression was as she fell and fell and fell.

Sean is dead. She forced herself to mentally repeat the words: *Sean. Is. Dead.* A new fear rose up fully formed: What if this move caused her to miss him less? Who would she be if she weren't grieving the loss of Sean?

She thought her legs might give out, she felt so lightheaded. She put her hand on the wall and closed her eyes. Mike was talking but she couldn't bring herself to focus on him. Behind her eyes she struggled to see Sean's face, to hold the image still. But he lacked substance. Jesus! She was forgetting him already!

She leaned on the wall, eyes still closed, trying to recapture her equilibrium. Just as she was about to declare to herself that the spell had passed, she saw or rather felt a visage so clearly that it seemed to be right in front of her. Was it a child? No, not a child, but child-like. In the wake of her quiet panic, the face was impassive, though not unkind.

"Sean is fine."

She heard the words clearly. She opened her eyes. Mike was just turning around toward her. She knew immediately that she alone had heard the calm, authoritative statement.

"Sorry, I was just yammering on. Are you ok?"

He looked at her questioningly. Kindly. That's why Buck liked him. Where was Buck, anyway?

"It was nothing, a little light headedness. Did you see where Buck went?"

Hearing his name, Buck came walking out of a large closet and also looked at her with inquiry in his eyes.

"Good boy," she said, "stay close." Addie felt abashed in front of them both. She did not like to appear out of control.

"Sorry, Mike, could you repeat what you just said?" She noticed her tone was clipped, business-like. It wasn't at all how she felt and she regretted giving him such a steely impression.

"I was just saying it's great you've decided to take this on. How soon do you think you can wrap up what you need to in town?"

Thankfully, Mike's tone indicated he probably hadn't noticed anything amiss with her. Or perhaps he had and was simply accepting her lapse in presence. Yes, she had the impression that, while he couldn't have known the specifics of what was going on with her, he knew something was up and he wanted her to know he was fine with acting as if nothing had happened.

Whatever the case, face saved, she felt her composure returning.

"I have clients that I need to refer to other therapists and I need to give them at least a month's notice and the same with my apartment. It's already the first of March so I can't do it until the first part of next month. Would April tenth work?"

"I won't lie to you, the owners would like to have someone in here yesterday."

Mike was quick to add that it was fantastic news that she wanted the job and could he call the owners today and confirm that?

Yes, Addie agreed, he could.

There were a total of four bedrooms, two on the west side of the house and two on the east. All of them were ample, the master bedroom being, predictably, the largest by far. It had an en-suite bathroom with a tub, shower, large pedestal sink, toilet and bidet. Here the floor tiles were also octagonal but instead of white and black, they were white and blue. It was the pale blue of a northwest sky, as if clouds had been stirred into a bucket of cobalt glaze. The air was sour, an odor Addie tried but couldn't identify. She conjured up lots of unpleasant smells: dirty socks, body odor, mildew, but none of them quite described it. She was aware, however, of a feeling-tone of sadness and, perhaps, anger. Was she projecting that? She honestly didn't think so.

The views out the windows of the master bath and bedroom soared over the trees and to the water. The late winter sun was shining again, but clouds pressed in on every side. The water was now a frigid blue. A pair of gulls expertly rode the air currents sweeping up over the water. She and Mike stood at the bathroom window for several moments watching the birds' graceful display. Addie had the sense that time had simply stopped for a few moments. Even Buck, who had been engaged in what Addie liked to call a major sniff-fest, stood still at her side.

It was Mike who started the clock again by saying, "I see the gulls all the time and I forget how big and beautiful they are."

"I know what you mean. Sometimes when I'm walking Buck I'll really notice the crows; their big beaks and glossy black feathers, the way they interact with each other, and I'll be amazed by them."

Mike laughed. "Wow. I've never had the experience with crows."

Addie was a little embarrassed. Had she said something too gee whiz? No sooner had the thought manifested, a pair of crows landed on a nearby branch of a bare fruit tree. One seemed to be scolding the other but, upon seeing the human faces peering out from behind the glass, redirected his hectoring cawing toward them.

Mike looked at her as if she had personally trained the crows. She shrugged, a small smile on her face as if to say, *yeah, I'm awesome*.

Addie could plainly see the once elegant master bedroom was no longer habitable. The water damage to the ceiling was extensive. There were brown water stains running down two of the four walls and the oak flooring had a thick dusting of plaster and paint chips. There was a large rug, loosely rolled up, along one wall. No question about this smell, it was moldy wool. She could see the lath showing through the ceiling in several places. *Like a skeleton, the fine, delicate bones of the house.*

Mike pushed a piece of plaster with the toe of his shoe. "I think your best bet is to take that first bedroom I showed you. I'm not sure how it will work once they start in on the roof. You might even need to camp out downstairs." He looked at her with the question in his eyes, will that be ok?

"Maybe I'll just stay downstairs." Addie had an image of waking up to see a roofer peering down at her. "The beetle room, maybe," she said with a little laugh. "Besides, I like morning light." She realized she didn't like the idea of sleeping anywhere upstairs.

"Totally up to you," Mike said equitably. " You can camp out in the pantry or change rooms every night if you want. It's your house for now, you're the boss."

She was glad that Mike was in front of her as they walked down the stairs. She would not have wanted him to see her using her sleeve to hurriedly blot away the tears that had suddenly come to her eyes. The anticipation leading up to seeing Pen House, the near constant stream of thought that had run round and round her mind, sometimes excited, mostly anxious, had finally caught up with her. She was bone tired. She was glad to wrap up the tour; glad Mike had an appointment he now needed to rush off to. She wanted nothing more than to go home and curl up in bed. *And pull the covers over my head.*

10

Despite making the decision to take on Pen House and the ensuing fatigue, Addie's mood seesawed all the way home. She would find herself excitedly thinking ahead to where she would put what, what could be gotten rid of, and what might have to go into storage. Then she would be visited again by that awful disorientation she had felt for a few moments at the house. She was leaving Sean. Leaving him behind. Had his face, little by little and without her realizing it, started to fade? Were her thoughts of Sean, once as visceral as a fist in the guts, now tiptoeing toward becoming only memories of memories? Had she already crossed the borderline into conditioned thought, where direct experience is replaced by storytelling? Was that inevitable? When had that happened?

And then came the question that really haunted her: who was she if she was no longer Sean's grieving widow? And there she stopped, not yet able to approach deeper inquiry. There was a big danger sign nailed over that door and she didn't have the heart or stomach to force entry. She told herself, as she would a client, that it was ok. *My timetable is up to me. There is no rush.* In this way she would calm herself and slowly find herself back to fantasizing about the house. She was going to re-hang the mirror in the little back bathroom, ask Mike if she could get rid of that awful barberry shrub in the front. She imagined a fire in the fireplace and the house being restored to warmth. To love, not knowing just what that might mean.

Buck, in stark contrast to Addie's racing thoughts, stayed curled up, fast asleep on the back seat during the entire journey. Even when she pulled on to the ferry and went upstairs for tea and a newspaper, he only opened one eye in acknowledgment of her leaving. Later, reading the comics and waiting for the scalding tea to cool to drinking temperature, she could hear the reassuring sound of his deep-sleep breathing, sprinkled here and there with a little snoring. *Lucky dog.*

Back in her apartment she felt as if she had returned from time traveling. Something about Pen House felt resistant to the present day. She imagined her laptop sitting on the Victorian sideboard, imagined a phone ringing, the sound of a television's inane droning. She could picture it all but it looked superimposed rather than integrated. This was certainly, in part, Pen House's charm. But it was also disquieting.

For the first time she wondered if there were any neighbors close by. She made a mental note to ask Mike the next time they talked. She thought maybe she should get pen and paper, make a to-do list. Instead she sat, gazing absently into her small living room, unable to conjure up another item.

Her eyes brushed over a wedding photo of her and Sean. She looked away. She was exhausted by the emotions of the day. Just as she was sliding toward the thought of getting to bed early, she remembered she was meeting Leo for dinner. From where she sat on the couch she could see the wall clock in the kitchen. Just enough time to feed Buck and take a quick shower. She hardly recognized this newly energized woman.

11

Leo had already secured a table and waved to her as she came in through the front door. She felt almost giddily happy to see him and hugged him warmly when he stood up and opened his arms. She felt like he was her oldest and dearest friend, this old man she had met just days ago.

"I am so glad to see you Leo!" *Jesus, I'm gushing.*

He smiled broadly, "ditto. I've ordered a beer, you want something to drink?"

She realized she did and a stiff one too. The waiter came around and set Leo's beer down. She ordered a double Maker's over ice. Leo raised one eyebrow theatrically.

"I see I'm going to have to walk you home."

Leo waited to sip his beer until Addie's drink came.

"Cheers," he said, "here's to the truth, the whole truth, and nothing but the truth."

"You know, Leo, I'm a listener usually. I am much more comfortable in that role. For God's sake, I do it for a living..." she paused and he jumped in.

"But you feel like talking tonight, don't you?"

She laughed and clinked his glass with hers, "I really do. The truth, the whole truth and nothing but the truth."

She sipped her bourbon, felt the heat, teetering between pain and pleasure, find its way down her throat and radiate through her body. She launched into the story of the entire day. Whenever she seemed to go lightly over anything, Leo would ask a well-placed question and in this way he teased out a thorough account. Addie talked more than she could remember doing for a long time. She even told him of her panicked moments in the upstairs bedroom, tried to explain the irrational thought that she was abandoning Sean by leaving the apartment.

"It's as if I'm preparing to cheat on him."

Leo nodded encouragingly in a gesture suggesting he both understood and wished her to keep going. She liked that he didn't make a fuss or try to talk her out of her impressions. He didn't try to save her from her mixed up feelings like so many people did. He could handle it and she felt profoundly grateful. On the heels of the gratitude was the fear that maybe she was letting the alcohol fuel a little too much disclosure. She thought she better leave the rest of her drink in the glass and retreat a little.

"Where are you?" Leo asked.

"I don't exactly know," she admitted, "this has been a huge day for me. I basically just agreed to something that's going to change my entire life and I don't know if it's crazy or smart. I feel out of control."

"You don't have to have the experience all down pat, figured out and categorized by bedtime, do you?"

"No, I guess not." She felt like laughing but, as silly as it sounded, that's exactly what she felt compelled to do. She realized her left hand was clutching her napkin. She uncurled her fingers and told herself to relax.

"Relax, honey," Leo said, echoing her thought. "You're fine. As someone famous said, 'everything worth doing scares the crap out of you' or words to that effect. You're making a big change, an exciting one. Maybe you could find it in your heart to congratulate yourself for having some guts. I'll say it...congratulations Adeline."

"Thanks, Leo. You know I can give this advice but the truth is it doesn't come easy in the other direction. It's part of the reason I feel like I'm a less than stellar therapist. Can you imagine if one of my clients heard all this floundering around?"

"Imagine!" Leo intoned with mock horror. She smiled at him and they fell into a brief silence, the first one since sitting down.

"Seriously, Adeline, maybe it will be the best thing for you to take yourself out of the therapist role. Stop being the one with the answers for awhile."

Another silence ensued and then Leo said, "I have three more questions: how did Buck like it, can I come visit, and what do you suppose that voice was you heard after you told Mike you'd take the job?"

"I definitely want you to come visit. For one thing, you've got to try out the kitchen. It's a lonesome place, I know I'll be glad to see you." She paused, took the last bite of her black bean burger, dabbed her mouth with a paper napkin and continued, "Buck was ok. He was really interested in smelling everything. He wasn't running around, he just seemed intensely engaged. He really liked this guy Mike."

There was a long pause. Leo finally prompted her, "And who was the child-like-but-not-child who told you not to worry about Sean?"

Addie tried to remember a face but she had to admit there hadn't really been one. Had she made it up? "I guess it was me, some aspect of me." Strangely, this sounded like what should be the obvious truth but the experience had felt completely different. Trying to understand what it might have been only left her quietly baffled.

Leo put a disappointed look on his face, "I thought maybe it was Laura Davies."

"The owner who's been dead for twenty years? Jesus, Leo. I'm going to be staying there by myself. What are you trying to do to me?"

"If you feel afraid, I can be there in a matter of hours." Leo was smiling but he added, "really, Adeline, there's no need to play the brave soldier." She nodded, not exactly sure why he was giving this advice and feeling a sort of seasick reassurance. She finished her drink.

They parted at Leo's car. Addie was on foot and assured Leo she was fine to walk the couple of blocks back to her apartment.

"Call me," he said.

She nodded yes, gave him a quick hug and turned to go home. The sky was clear and the air cold. She looked up and saw stars despite the ambient city light. She thought she could make out the little cluster of the Pleiades and imagined how much brighter the distinctive grouping would be over Pen House.

12

The task she had been dreading, telling her clients that she was moving and dropping her practice for the foreseeable future, could not be put off. She'd told Mike she would arrive at Pen House on April tenth. All day Sunday she felt a sick gnawing in her stomach. She thought of each of her five clients and how best to tell them. She had put together a list of recommended therapists to refer them to.

The first client she told was Matthew. *Monday Matt*, as she privately and affectionately thought of him, was a college student who originally came to her with insomnia. It didn't take too long, only a couple of visits, before they were talking about his binging, purging and excessive exercise regimen, all of which he initially regarded as necessary to keep himself at the right weight for his wrestling class.

Now she had been seeing him for over a year and she expected he would take her announcement in stride. He was doing well and, because he was also part of a bulimics group that met two evenings a week, Addie felt confident that he already had plenty of support. To her private horror he cried when she broke the news. She kept her face in the kindly neutral expression that was the mask she had come to feel so burdened by. What she felt like doing was holding him in her arms, apologizing for letting him down and reassuring him everything would be all right.

As he cried and talked about his fear of not having their time together anymore, a little ray of sanity pierced her shame-laden thoughts: This was not the same man who had come into her office a year ago. Her guilt had been obscuring the fact that he was now comfortable enough not only to cry, but also to name what was bringing the tears on. Her body relaxed and she looked at Matt with something like wonderment, impressed by the journey he had made since she had first met him. It didn't occur to her to claim any credit. When she told him that, despite his fears and sadness, she was certain he was going to be fine, fabulous in fact, she spoke the truth.

She'd ditched her original thought that she would keep one client. In part it was because the extra money couldn't justify the rent, though small, to keep her little office. But largely it was due to Virginia, her last client on Wednesdays, the last client she broke her news to and the client she had thought she might keep.

Addie was ashamed to admit to herself that she had thought of keeping Virginia because she was *easy*. Virginia wasn't looking for the moon and stars, therapeutically speaking. It seemed to Addie that she merely had to give her a weekly pep talk.

After telling Virginia she was moving to Sutton Bay and adding that she could come into town for their appointment once a week, Virginia pointed out that it seemed like what she was really after was a clean break. Addie looked for self-pity or anger in Virginia's comment but there was none. In fact, Addie felt as if a friend was gently encouraging her.

Then Virginia added, "and maybe this move will help you to finally begin to feel better about your husband's death."

This had floored Addie. Virginia knew Sean had died but Addie didn't talk about it. To do so would have been unprofessional. So what had Virginia seen in her? Addie didn't know what to say. She briefly contemplated an all out lie: *I am fine.* She thought of somehow trying to weave the comment in to Virginia's therapy: *Tell me about the sadness you're feeling, Virginia.* In the end she said nothing.

The last two sessions with Virginia felt awkward. Addie kept wondering how she was appearing. Did she look as muddled and scared as she was feeling? Or was Virginia seeing the part of her that felt empowered by the choice she had made to drop her career and move to Pen House?   Could strangers see her walking down the street and figure her out?   She had always prided herself on her reserve, her ability to not freak out. When they said goodbye Virginia impulsively reached out and hugged her. She wanted to reciprocate, to convey the warmth she felt for Virginia, but discomfort flooded the moment.   Addie, her sense of presence lost, was only aware of two bodies bumping gracelessly up against each other.

After the door closed behind Virginia, Addie cried. It felt strange to reach for the box of tissues she had handed out to others so often. The tears were those of tremendous relief. It was as if she had been on an uphill hike for longer than she could remember and finally she could set down the enormous backpack she'd been carrying.   For a few minutes she sat in the big comfy chair that had been reserved for clients, shoes kicked off, feet up on the matching ottoman. She could hear muffled traffic noise, a phone ringing down the hall. She imagined herself as a slip of paper or a leaf, blown to this spot, resting, temporarily out of the wind.

13

Deconstructing the apartment she had put together with Sean mostly left her with a feeling of disconnection. She watched herself pack a box, roll a rug, sit pondering over a drawer filled with paper and photos. She had a nagging voice in her head that told her it was important to analyze this detachment. She answered the voice: *Fuck off. I am too tired right now and this is too stressful. Later, when I'm settled into Pen House, I'll have time to think, to write, to explore my feelings.* She didn't exactly disbelieve this but neither did she completely trust it. In reality when she tried to envision a future as near as tomorrow, let alone the idea of actually living in that big old house, the picture was unclear. Like a television screen covered in snow, she knew a program was running but she had no reception.

The last night in the apartment she packed their photos. Slowly, almost robotically, she sat at the kitchen table wrapping each frame in tissue and carefully placing them in a box. As usual, Buck led her back into the present moment by being thoroughly awake to the situation at hand. He ran from room to room, his nails clicking on the bare floors. He sniffed the stack of boxes by the front door with great care. Finally, he stood in front of her and wagged his tail. She could see he was anxious. *I am too!* She hadn't even recognized the obvious in herself until she saw it in Buck's dear face. She patted her lap and he leapt up into it so forcefully he almost shot off the other side. He put his two paws on her chest and covered her face with kisses.

That night she had a dream about Sean. She had never dreamed about him. Even in the early, hideous, raw days, the days when she felt like she literally could not continue to live, she didn't see him in her dreams. She wished he would come to her, even as a figment but he didn't. In the dream she woke up and Sean was sitting on the side of the bed looking at her.

She smiled up at him. A big happy smile. "Sweetheart! You're back! I knew you were going to come back."

In waking life this was not the case at all. He had always seemed to her to be thoroughly gone. But in the dream the truth of her words was irrefutable. She started to cry from relief and joy. The nightmare was over, finally. But as she stared into Sean's eye, he shook his head slowly, no. He moved toward the bedroom door. She got up, compelled to follow him.

Next, in the sudden way that dreams change, they were riding on his motorcycle. It was getting dark and the town they motored through was unfamiliar to her. She held him tight and they flew through the murky twilight past tall houses that seemed to lean over them as if eavesdropping. She put her head against his back. Now she realized she had moved into his body and she could feel her hands on the handlebars, could feel the knobbly grips. And then there was a surprise, a sharp pain that passed almost immediately.

Abruptly, she was back in bed and Sean was standing by the door. He said no words but she understood perfectly the message in his deeply sad eyes: *I have to go now and I won't be back.* With absolute clarity she understood that his sadness wasn't about the loss of his life, but the pain of loss he saw she still carried.

14

It was early on a blustery April morning when Addie and Buck left the apartment for the last time. She lifted Buck up on to the rental van's passenger seat, neatly arranged with his pillow and blanket. She got herself situated in the driver's seat, coffee mug in the cup holder, purse close at hand, cell phone in the other cup holder, key in the ignition. There was no one there to wave goodbye. She felt a tug of self-pity even as she recognized it was her doing entirely.

It was she who had slowly but surely drifted away from the friends she and Sean used to see regularly. She thought of her mother and father, hundreds of miles away in Tucson. They barely knew her anymore. Addie recognized that, just like her lost friendships, she had neglected to feed and water the relationship with her parents. She knew they worried and she tried her best to let them know she was fine, fine, fine.

Leo had offered to bring her breakfast and help her pack the van. She had said no thanks. Now, looking at the blank face of the apartment building, she regretted whatever impulse had caused her to turn Leo away. She wished he was here, someone to look at in the rear view mirror as she and Buck drove away. Someone to affirm she would be missed. Buck sat up, looking expectantly out his window, waiting for things to start whizzing by. She turned the key, released the brake and shifted into drive.

Addie's larger possessions, the bookcase in the living room and most of the books, the king size bed and frame, the couch, she had put in to storage. She had purchased a twin bed and had it delivered to Pen House. It was in the dining room, still wrapped in plastic. The van was filled with everything else. Not much, as it turned out.

She was going to drive to Pen House, unpack, bring the van back to the rental office and return to the house in her car. Leo had offered to drive with her but in the end she had said no to this as well. Again, she wasn't sure why. At the time he'd made the offer it had seemed like she needed to do this alone. Now it only felt preposterous to have said no. She could have had help, could have felt less afraid. Buck startled her by giving a proprietary yip at a French bulldog tugging his owner, a woman about Addie's age, down the sidewalk.

"I can always count on you to be excited, buddy. Excited to leave, excited to return. Buddha Buck." He wagged his tail and barked again, a dog smile on his face.

15

It was a long day and when Addie finally got back to Pen House it was nearly nine. She was starving and she realized she had never seen the house in anything but broad daylight. Mike had met her there earlier with his teenage son and they had helped her unload the van. Everything she had brought fit into the front entryway with room to spare. Mike offered to help further but she didn't know how she wanted things arranged and wanted the freedom and time to consider it once she knew the house better.

She had gone slowly down Orchard Avenue, afraid of missing her landmark, the rusty mailbox. No streetlights out here, just a quarter moon popping in and out behind the clouds. She had her brights on and they played over the firs that were bending and shivering in the strong breeze coming off of the bay. When she saw the mailbox she realized it was hers now. She would walk down the driveway with Buck and they would collect her mail. She idly wondered what time the mail was delivered.

She first saw the house not under the glare of headlights, but off to her left, in a slice of moonlight. Why hadn't she thought to leave a damn light on? But then she noticed a little warm glow emanating from the right rear of the house. Mike must have switched a light on and, thankfully, forgotten to turn it off. It didn't help much for getting in the front door, but it was a lot more comforting than a house wrapped entirely in blackness.

She climbed out of the car and stretched. The wind had abruptly died away and the air was still and stingingly cold. She let Buck out and predictably he relieved himself immediately. Once he was done he faced the house and started to bark. The quiet had been so profound that this shredded it more violently than she could have imagined.

"Buck! Quiet! No barking!" Then, more quietly and kindly, "It's ok buddy, I'm scared too. Let's just go in together and we'll be fine. Before you know it, it'll be morning."

Buck growled but followed her. She walked past the barberry and up to the front door. She fumbled in her pocket for the key, stuck it in the lock and undid the deadbolt. She went to turn the handle but it remained frozen in her hand. A childhood memory popped vividly into her head: She was chasing a visiting cousin of similar age through the house. He would run into a room, slam the door and then hold the knob as tightly as he could to keep her out. Then he would let go and she would tumble into the room, both of them laughing. She tried the brass handle again. This time it turned easily, quietly. She reached in and turned the porch light on as well as the switch that controlled the six wall sconces in the entryway.

"Come on, Buck, we're home." She waved him in. He didn't balk at entering but he was alert.

"Hello Pen House!" She called out, "We're home!" Her voice was met with a small echo, then stillness. Buck looked up at her as if to say, *Are you out of your ever-lovin' mind?*

"Let there be light!" she announced, this time in a conversational tone that caused Buck to wag his tail halfheartedly.

She walked first into the dining room and turned on the chandelier. It was brighter and warmer than it had appeared in daylight. She continued into the kitchen, turning those lights on as well.

"We're sleeping with the lights on tonight, buddy. We can do what we want, right?" She reached down and gave him a scratch and then picked him up and held him to her chest.

"I love you, Buck." Buck gave her a big lick on the face.

Addie walked on through the pantry, into the back hall, turning lights on as she went. Buck was sniffing the floor and looking confident and curious again, which felt absurdly reassuring to Addie. As they passed the door to the basement she shuddered at the thought of the dark rooms down below. She noticed for the first time that there was a sliding lock. She immediately slid the bolt home and felt a little better. She got to the little back bathroom, pushed open the door and flipped the light switch. *This is the bathroom I'll be using*, she thought. She took this opportunity to pee, hoping she wouldn't have to get up in the night and knowing if she did that Buck would be required to accompany her. She noticed that the mirror was back up and felt grateful to Mike for taking care of that.

Completing the circle, she made her way into the living room. The moon was still visible and by its light she could make out the silhouette of the big tulip poplar beyond the west window. She saw by the movement of its bare limbs that the wind was up again. Soon there would be no moon at all. She flipped on the wall sconces and noticed they were the same as those in the entryway. Each sconce comprised a pair of tarnished brass candlestick holders, each holder complete with the dish to catch the non-existent drips and the shellacked cardboard faux-candles into which were screwed the bulbs shaped like little teardrop flames. There were eight sconces, and half of them were burnt out. A few of them still had the little half-round ivory-colored shades clipped to the bulb. Each shade was painted with the entwined vines that were the decorative hallmark of Pen House. Addie could see the ornate plaster circle on the ceiling where a chandelier once hung. At its center was a badly done plaster patch, discolored by a long ago leak.

Back in the dining room Addie felt her exhaustion again. She had a bag with some snacks in it. She laid them out on the sideboard; crackers, a few carrots, a container of hummus, two bottles of water and a cookie. There was also a can of dog food and a bowl.

"First things first, huh Buck?" she said, noticing Buck's attention was fully on her.

She dumped the food into the bowl and then scrounged around

in a box until she found his water bowl. She filled it and set the bowl down next to where Buck was wolfing down his venison with sweet potatoes. She sat with a crunch on her plastic covered mattress and ate. Looking at the sideboard, she sent another grateful thought toward Mike. The beetle was gone.

Addie didn't have the energy to find the new set of twin sheets that were somewhere out in the stacks of boxes piled in the entryway. She pulled the plastic off of the mattress and box spring, rolled out her sleeping bag and tossed both of her pillows on the top and called it done. She found her bedside lamp, plugged it in and turned it on. Then, hoping it wouldn't make the space too dark, she turned off the chandelier and the entry hall lights. She opened the front door for Buck and he ran out, peed on the birdbath and ran back in.

Addie snuggled into her down sleeping bag knowing it would only take a couple of minutes to warm up. Buck nosed his way in and down to his favorite place by her feet. She tried to read but found herself reading the same paragraph over and over again. Finally, when her book fell to the floor, she switched out the bedside light. She was glad to see there was light seeping in from under the kitchen door and from across the entryway in the living room. As she was drifting away into sleep she remembered the light she had seen when she had first driven up. And then she remembered going room by room turning on the lights. She was quite sure, positive, none of the lights had been on. It was a measure of her fatigue that as strange as this was, sleep still captured her entirely in just a couple of minutes.

16

Addie woke with a start, thinking she'd heard the upstairs neighbors tromping around. It took her a few seconds to realize she wasn't in her apartment and she had been dreaming. The sun was up and coming through the window, spilling over the floor and her bed. Out in the garden and beyond masses of birds were singing and talking back and forth. The sky looked cloudless from her vantage point.

She nudged Buck with her toe and he growled grumpily. Addie wriggled out of the down bag and sat up. She picked up the wristwatch that was lying on the heap of her clothes. Nine o'clock. She couldn't recall the last time she had slept so late. She stood up and stretched. Buck poked his head out of the sleeping bag.

"Are you trying to kill me with cute?" she said, sitting back down to give him a comprehensive belly scratch.

When Buck had had enough he hopped down to the floor, stretched, walked to the front door, sat and looked at her expectantly.

"Me first," Addie said, heading through the kitchen and to the bathroom.

"Brrrr, Jesus it's freezing back here," she said to no one. Tee shirt, undies and no shoes was definitely not the way to travel in this house.

A slice of sunlight was coming in the kitchen's east window but the room was cold and still felt dark. She realized the light she had left on was now off. She looked at the switch and it was in the down position. No wonder they were going to rewire the house, something was certainly screwed up. There was a disquieting feeling in her that something more than an electrical problem was afoot. Surely a switch was something that had to be manually flipped? Could they just fall down? She needed to check that all the locks on the outside doors worked properly and that the windows couldn't be gotten into.

She suddenly felt naked in her underwear and hurried toward the bathroom. She opened the door and had to immediately stop herself from stepping on broken glass. This was so surprising, she only vaguely registered that this light too was switched off. She was actually relieved to see that it was the mirror that had fallen and not a broken window. A reflecting mosaic of glass, mostly large chunks, but a lot of nasty shards as well, covered the floor. She looked around reflexively, making sure Buck was not about to walk in, and pulled the door closed. How had she ever slept through the crash that must have made? She ran back to the dining room and pulled on her jeans and dirty socks from the day before and stepped into her clogs. Buck, now managing to look both reproachful and desperate, had again positioned himself by the front door.

"Ok, buddy, you first after all." She opened the door and Buck ran out into the morning sun.

The sky wasn't completely cloudless after all but what was up there was puffy and harmless looking. There was a sprinkling of glittery dew on the grass and the air smelled unfamiliar, rich and complex. Buck took his time and she realized she didn't have to stand there and wait for him; she could go use the upstairs bathroom. She left the front door open and took the stairs two at a time, turned down the hall and almost shrieked when she saw herself in the hall mirror.

"Damn it!" she cursed, angry to be fooled again.

After a breakfast of coffee with no milk and crackers spread with a little hummus, she swept up the broken mirror pieces and even picked out the stray bits still left around the edges of the frame. She inspected where the mirror had been hung. There was a gaping hole in the plaster where the nail had pulled itself out under the weight of the mirror. The nail itself was small and inadequate for the job. *No mystery why that fell down*. She opened both the back and the front doors and let the clean fresh spring air waft through the house. Buck was particularly happy to be able to wander in and out at as he pleased.

Addie spent several hours slowly going through her things and arranging them. She got her CD player hooked up and put on a disc that opened with Mozart's Serenade No. 13 for strings in G. The music filled up the house, exalting the space in a way it never had in her apartment. She imagined the sweet strings to be a kiss both energetic and lingering and the house, like a princess under a curse, waking slowly out of her hundred-year sleep.

After she got the bulk of her things in order, she put a grouping of photos of Sean on top of the sideboard. "Best for last" she said out loud to the arrangement of frames.

Somehow, in the apartment, the pictures had made narrative sense to her. But here they looked like a shrine that was gloomy as well as disconnected from any sense of fresh feeling. She thought of the shoeboxes of random old photos she had seen in secondhand stores. All of those people were once someone's somebody and now they were just faces staring out into nothing.

Sean was her somebody. Could she really keep that idea vital forever? No. Someday she'd be gone too and then what? She didn't really believe she'd be joined with Sean after death. Not in any corporeal sense. There seemed to be something so wasteful and unjust about their two lives, like vines, becoming entwined. They had depended on each other for structure and strength only to have one vine ripped out by the roots. This left the other vine swinging in midair, casting around for something to hold on to. She turned away from the dark sideboard, consciously shutting off that line of thought.

After a thorough cleaning of the tub, she showered in the upstairs bathroom. There was a gush of rusty water but then the shower proved to have good pressure and, eventually, plenty of hot water. Next she went in to Sutton Bay to buy the food and household items she'd been jotting down on a list throughout the morning.

The sun was dropping quickly toward the western horizon, fingers of golden light coming through the trees, when she and Buck returned to the house. She was glad it was not quite dark yet and hurriedly unloaded her groceries and the cloth she'd bought to make a simple curtain for the front window of the dining room, now her bedroom. Buck growled at the front door, which opened without the sticking she'd experienced the day before.

The house was cold. There was no trace of warmth left from the sun that had so generously spilled in the windows all day. Even the smell of the house was fusty and withdrawn. Mike had told her she could simply turn the thermostat up and the furnace was ready to go. The truth was she had been afraid to turn it on, afraid it wouldn't operate properly; afraid she'd have to go down to the basement. Realizing there was nothing she would know to do if it didn't work except call Mike, she set it at sixty-eight and then immediately nudged it up another five degrees. The sound of it rumbling to life in the basement was immediate. The radiators creaked and popped and released a smell like a hot iron left too long on a cotton shirt, almost burning, lifted away just in time.

Standing by a gradually warming radiator, Addie looked out the living room window and saw the orange and pink sky reflected in the deepening blue of the bay. "Spectacular", she whispered to herself. She had the wonderful kind of fatigue one feels when a comfy bed and no other obligations are all that's left of the day. She looked forward to sleeping in her fresh new sheets, cuddled up with Buck in the place she was falling in love with. It was this night, however, that forced Addie to admit that something was seriously wrong with Pen House.

17

Addie took her flannel pajamas to the bathroom to change. Tomorrow she planned to sew a curtain to hang up over the front window of the dining room. The room felt frighteningly exposed even though she was quite alone down a long driveway that could barely be found in daylight. She noted that Buck was following her everywhere and she was glad to have his constant company. Face washed, teeth brushed, pajamas on, Addie opened the door to leave the bathroom and paused, trying to decide whether to turn the light off or leave it on. She opted for on. "Now stay on, damn you!" She spoke out loud.

Suddenly Buck growled, startling her. As she looked down to where he was standing, halfway between where she stood and the pantry, he faced the back door and broke into a bark. It wasn't a simple yip but a series of barks with growls separating each one so the sound was constant and surprisingly ferocious. With each bark his entire compact body jerked forward toward whatever it was that was frightening him. The barking was full-throated, as if someone stood right in front of him, and when he growled his lips were curled back exposing his little pointed teeth.

Addie looked down the hall. Nothing. She found herself hoping to see something like a mouse or even a rat. Nothing. Frozen to the spot, she was afraid to go forward, afraid to stand where she was. Afraid. A frigid draft blew over her flip-flop shod feet and bare ankles. Had a door blown open?

"It's OK buddy, there's nothing there, shhh, Buck, it's OK."

His barking slowed and then stopped but his lips were still curled back and his growling continued. She could see the shiny pink of his gums. Then, abruptly, he stopped. He came back to where she stood and put his paws up on her. OK now he seemed to say. All clear. And she felt better, relieved. Slowly, she started down the hall. She had only gone a couple of steps when she heard a click behind her. Barely daring to, she turned back and saw that the bathroom light had gone off. She felt light-headed with apprehension. Buck, however, seemed back to normal. *Thank God*, she thought. She trusted Buck, knew he was focused in a way that wasn't possible with mere human skills.

It seemed like an inordinately long walk back to the dining room. Paranoia caused the walls to seem taller and more closed in and any evidence that just hours earlier the house had been filled with light and fresh air was now erased. Along the way she checked the doors and windows. She didn't want to and she fought off the image of a strange face looming on the other side of the glass. But she knew that the best way to deal with what was unknown was to look at it with as much thoroughness as she could muster. How else could she weigh her options? Simply running to bed would end in her lying there for hours imagining terrifying scenarios.

The windows were shut tight as were the doors, everything fastened and locked, as it should be. She got into bed and pulled the bedclothes up around her and Buck, grateful for the weight of her winter comforter. She wanted to pull the covers up over her head, employing the child's logic that if she could not see anything, she also could not be seen. She remembered her cell phone in her purse and was able to lean over to where it sat on a chair and fish it out. Who would she call? The police? She commanded herself to be still.

The house was utterly silent, even the radiators, now toasty warm, only hissed occasionally. If there were a person sneaking around the house, Buck would know it. She put the phone on the little bedside table and lay absolutely still. She had a dilemma: leave the bedside light on or turn it off? She did not want to be in darkness. And yet, with the light on, she was lit up like a store window. As much as she tried to keep the image at bay, she could not entirely banish the thought of someone, the murky animus of nightmares, peering in at her through the window. Experimentally, she turned the light off. The sconces in the living room were on, as was the overhead in the kitchen. There was plenty of illumination, enough so that she still had some of that exposed feeling. She knew one thing for sure; she wasn't getting out of bed until daylight. She thought it quite likely she would be awake all night. What had she been thinking to take on this house out in the middle of nowhere? Buck was lazily licking her toes. As was normal, the licking slowed, then stopped and soon after she heard the sound of his sleep breathing, deep and relaxed. She listened, her body rigid. She breathed and focused on relaxing, starting with her feet and moving upwards. The house was quiet. She fell asleep thinking it would be impossible to do so.

18

A door slamming woke Addie and Buck in unison. He barked and barked again as he made his way up and out from under the bedclothes. Addie's eyes opened and she could see the room around her. It took her a minute to realize that the only thing casting light was the sickly glow of the moon trapped behind a thin veil of cloud. As far as she could tell the house lights were utterly extinguished. She whispered, "What is it Buck?" Buck sat on the end of the bed, ears cocked, body forward, every part of him concentrating. She couldn't hear anything, but there was a sense of suspension, as if the door slammer was waiting and listening too. Addie squeezed her eyes shut. *Go away, go away, go away.* She repeated the words over and over in her head and then, in a seamless transition, she found herself whispering them aloud. Then, in another invisible transition, she realized a voice not her own was echoing back to her faintly, softly mocking, almost playful, "go away, go away, go away." Buck had made his way up next to Addie's face and stood staring at the dark space that was the entryway. He was silent and afraid.

The sense of being taunted became unbearable and Addie shouted, "stop it right now!" She had tried to make her voice sound big and authoritative but it had simply sounded ragged, and verging on hysterical.

Now there was quiet, and the echo her outburst left behind seemed to linger as if it was caught in the thick, cold air. The quiet stretched out unnaturally in front of Addie and Buck. Like blowing up a balloon, one rhythmical breath after another stretching its wall ever closer to exploding, the anticipation of something inevitable made Addie want to cover her ears and hide.

There! Finally the wait was broken. Something was smacked down hard on the sideboard and there was the crunch of breaking glass. Buck immediately started barking more aggressively than ever before. Addie carefully reached out and held Buck by his collar. She was afraid he might jump down and go after whatever it was. At the feel of her hand he sat down and stopped barking. But he was shivering and so was she.

In this insanity Addie sensed a pattern. First there was an event. The event was followed by a hideous pause. So she and Buck paused again. This one lasted only seconds and then there were footsteps walking away from them, across the floor and up the stairs. It wasn't a heavy footfall and neither was it rushed. On the contrary it seemed hesitant, like a child dawdling on the way to bed. The footsteps paused on the steps and Addie prayed for them to continue upwards. She heard them overhead in the upstairs hall starting and stopping. And then, strain her ears as she might, she heard nothing more.

Finally Addie knew it was over. There was a sense of peace as if a tremendous rush of new air had scoured the house. Buck stood for quite awhile up by Addie's head. She stroked him over and over, both of them needing the contact. He licked away the tears of relief that had silently run down her cheeks. She heard the unmistakable half whistle, half cry of a killdeer. And that sound, which had always struck her as eerily sad, she now found deeply comforting. It was the sound of life. Of normalcy. After several minutes, Buck nudged the covers with his paw. Addie lifted them and Buck made his way down to her feet. Each of them settled uneasily into their preferred sleeping positions.

19

The sound of rain woke her. She opened her eyes and the room was in gloom. She got up and walked to the front window. The sky was solidly gray. The rain was dense and steady. The trees, unmoved by even a breath of wind, looked defeated. She opened the door and let Buck out. While she waited she turned and looked up the stairs. What the hell had happened last night? She was deeply shaken, but she did not doubt the veracity of what she, and Buck, had heard.

Buck ran in and shook the rain out of his coat and onto the bare oak floor. Addie went back to the dining room to get a towel. On the sideboard, face down, was one of the framed photos she'd set out the day before. This is what she'd heard being slammed down and shattered. She was almost afraid to touch it now, as if it was a fallen power line sizzling with high voltage. She lifted it up and the broken glass underneath was still holding the shape of an orderly rectangle. The photo was one she'd taken of Sean not long before he'd died. She remembered the morning. She'd just gotten a new camera. She'd called his name and snapped it when he'd glanced up at her from across their kitchen table. She loved the picture, one of those lucky shots that caught someone at their best through no skill of the photographer's. She stared at it. Had he always looked so sad? She remembered the dream she'd had the night before leaving the apartment. He had looked just like this. How had she never noticed it? It passed through her mind that he had been last night's visitor. Perhaps angry with her for leaving? But no, she knew she was just making that up. Sean's visage, even in anger, would have been a relief. The truth was that she had recognized immediately that the goodbye Sean conveyed in the dream had been loving and final. Her melancholy remembering of the dream was quickly crowded out by the sickening mystery of the night before.

Addie didn't think she could stay another night alone in this house. She felt heavy and more fatigued than she had felt since Sean's death. Buck too seemed restrained. He was back up on the bed, curled up, and watching her as she pulled her clothes on.

"We have a serious problem here Buck and I'm not sure what to do." Buck eyed her, listening.

She had given up her apartment; there was no going back there.

She thought again of calling the police. But what did she really have to report? That she, a woman alone in a big empty house, had felt terrified in the night but hadn't seen a thing? That she heard something that wasn't there? Whatever had happened it didn't feel like a police issue. She was definitely going to call Mike. Did he know anything about the house that he had held back? She thought he almost certainly did. She felt angry and duped.

Stunned at the turn of events, she went over the night's occurrences as well as all the things, prior to that, that had struck her oddly. It took being halfway through a second cup of strong coffee before Addie felt prepared to do anything but sit on the foot of the bed and stare out at the rain pelting the barberry hedge. When she finally roused herself, the first thing she did was clean up the broken glass on the sideboard. She removed Sean's picture and threw out the frame. She put the photo in the bedside table drawer, barely able to glance at the sadness that seemed to be oozing out of the photograph. She placed it face down in an attempt to blunt her pain.

She made herself eat some toast. All the while she was aware of the rain coming down, its patter echoing through the empty rooms. Underneath the sound was the peace and stillness of Pen House. *Do I feel afraid? Right now?* The answer was a clear no. But beyond that there was no clarity at all.

Once it occurred to her to call Leo, she couldn't believe she hadn't thought of it earlier. Since Sean's passing Addie had let friendships lie untended. She noticed there wasn't any heroic attempt on the part of her friends to intervene either. There is only so much one can say in the face of loss. There is only so long one can keep saying it. There was no drama, no sudden shift that lead to the loss of her friends. There was merely a quiet and steady erosion. She could feel their awkwardness and

103

impatience with her. And she pushed them away too, angered, despite her better self, by their easy happiness. When she thought of Leo it was as if her oldest and dearest friend had come to mind. She smiled. He was the oldest. And though she knew him only a little, he seemed as precious as a handful of diamonds. She ran into the dining room, grabbed her cell phone, scrolled through the contacts to his number, and hit the call icon.

"Be there, Leo," she said into the phone. But Leo's number didn't ring through. She looked at the screen and saw the words, *no service.*

She cursed, "shit, hell, damn." Rattled but undeterred, she grabbed her hoodie and her car keys. Buck was off the bed and at the door before she could call him. She would drive until she got service.

She was prepared to drive into Sutton Bay but all the bars on her phone had popped up once she was in the car. She took the old towel she kept on the backseat and rubbed the water off of Buck. The rain, now heavier, was pounding on the roof as she re dialed Leo's number.

"Hi, you've reached James and Sarah's machine. Leave your number, we'll call you back." She plunged ahead with a message. "Leo, it's Addie, Adeline...I need you to call me." She started to relay the number when Leo picked up.

"Adeline! Don't hang up. I have dough all over my hands. Hold on a sec." She heard him put down the phone, walk to the sink and run the water. The thought of him in that warm kitchen filled her with hope. She scratched Buck behind the ears, passing the good feeling on to him.

Leo picked the phone back up. "How are you? I wondered if

you were going to call." His tone was light and conversational causing Addie a moment of panic. Was he going to think she was crazy? Was he going to find a reason to politely say goodbye and never pick up again if he heard her voice on the message machine?

"Leo, something's wrong. Can you talk?" Her voice sounded calm. Good.

Leo was immediately responsive. "What's up, honey? You sound awful."

So much for calm. She didn't know how to tell the story so she let it come out in a jumble, jumping back and forth between events. Leo was quiet, letting the whole thing unfold. She came to the part of the story where she was in the car calling him.

"What do you think's going on Leo? I can't stay. I have nowhere to go. I'm so disappointed, I love the house, or I thought I did."

She looked out the car window at the house. The rain had let up a little but the darkness of the day hadn't. The house seemed to be hunkered down, waiting it out as it had through many such days for over a hundred years. *What a beautiful place it is, even on a day like today.* It seemed as much a part of the landscape as the tall firs dripping rain and the gray water of the bay to the north.

"I'm coming over." Hearing Leo's words, Addie was beyond relieved. In some way she felt like he could fix the house. Make it all right for her.

"I can't come today, I don't have my car. I loaned it to the kids because theirs is getting serviced." Then, before Addie could express any disappointment at the delay, he went on, "don't stay there tonight honey. Get a room in Sutton Bay. I can come over in the morning, meet you at your motel and we can go from there."

Addie, feeling like a child needing extra clarification, asked, "go back to the house?"

Leo chuckled gently. "No honey. Not if you don't want to. I just meant in the morning we can look at your options."

A couple beats of silence followed, long enough that Addie reminded herself to slow her breathing, then Leo said, "call me when you find a room and then you can tell me where to meet you."

"I'm so sorry, Leo. I would never call like this if I wasn't really...concerned."

"Sorry? Are you kidding? This is an adventure. And I like the feeling that you think of me as someone who might be able to help."

Addie asked one more question before they hung up, "what the hell do you think is going on, Leo?"

Leo answered matter-of-factly, "same as you do. I think you have a ghost."

20

After she hung up, Addie sat in the car staring at Pen House. Buck, tired, had curled up in her lap. Ghost. The word sounded preposterous. She didn't believe in God or ghosts.

But Pen House loomed up in front of her daring her to come back inside. There could be no doubt that she had been terrified the night before, too terrified even to reach out and use the phone. There wouldn't have been any service anyway. She would have had to climb out of bed and go out into the night, searching for a signal. She blanched at the thought. It occurred to her that this intruder had a curious lack of intention. Surely someone breaking in would have had an aim? Robbery or, she shuddered, rape? But how would she understand a ghost's intention anyway?

She agreed with Leo that the best thing to do was to get a room in Sutton Bay for the night. Tomorrow she would have her friend here with her, someone who could help her sort through what was going on and what her options were. She needed to go back inside to get her bag, some toiletries, a change of clothes and Buck's leash. She opened the car door and Buck stayed curled on her lap. "Come on buddy, we just need to go in for a couple of minutes." She had to swing her legs out and begin standing before he consented to hopping down on to the drive. Together they went to the front door. Buck stopped there and sat down to wait. Addie reentered the house.

She quickly gathered her things and turned the heat down to sixty-two. She thought of turning the furnace off but didn't want to lose all the lovely warmth. And turning off the heat seemed so final. She forced herself to check that the backdoor was locked and that all the lights were off except those in the front hall and over the porch. Then she double-checked that those lights were in fact on so that she could create a firm memory of what she had done.

Buck, waiting just outside the front door, wagged his tail, knowing they would soon be leaving. He trotted out into the front garden. The rain had stopped but a large smudge of charcoal-black clouds was smeared across the sky inland from the bay. The lighter clouds overhead were a sickly greenish gray. Any minute now it was going to start again and rain buckets. She set her bag down and grabbed the handle to pull the front door shut. From the other side it was pushed closed so hard she almost lost her balance. Buck started to bark loudly and insistently. With shaking hands, Addie got the key into the lock and locked the door. She felt like running to the car but made herself keep to a brisk walk.

"Buck! Hush! It's nothing." Buck stopped barking and ran to the car, waiting for her with tail wagging as if waving at her to hurry the hell up. At her back, like an icy gust of wind, she could feel the intense conviction of whoever had just pushed her out the door.

The rain started as she was turning the key in the ignition; big fat, widely spaced splats on the windshield. By the time she was turned around and heading down the driveway it was coming down in sheets and required the wipers to be set on high.

21

Addie had been worried about finding a motel that would allow Buck, but it proved to be no trouble. She made her way to the room, clutching the magnetic key card and the little bag of dog biscuits the plump, blond clerk had handed her with a professionally friendly smile. In the other hand she gripped Buck's leash. On her back was the small daypack she had quickly crammed with the rest of her stuff. Though the rain had eased off a little, she was soaked by the time she made the small exposed trek from car to room.

The first thing Addie did was to strip off her wet clothes and get in the shower. The showerhead's flow was frustratingly weak but the water was hot and she began to feel soothed. Using the provided soap and shampoo she washed from head to toe. It felt good to put on dry clean clothes over her clean skin, as if signaling, finally, that a fresh approach to the puzzle she faced was now possible. Conversely, her wet jeans and shirt dripped into the tub from where they hung on the shower curtain rail, a jarring reminder of the last twelve hours. She shut the bathroom door and immediately realized she was starving. Telling Buck to stay and that she'd be back soon, she fished her wallet out of the daypack and went out looking for lunch.

She found a café on the main street through town and went in. It was a few minutes past noon but the lunch crowd, if they ever had one, wasn't there yet. The waitress seated her at a booth. It was quiet, comfortable and private, perfect for the call she was going to make as soon as she ordered.

With coffee in front of her and a B.L.T., fries and a salad on the way, Addie called Mike's cell phone. He picked up on the second ring, "Addie, how's everything going?" Were her nerves shot, causing her to imagine things, or did Mike's voice sound worried, like maybe he had been expecting a call?

"Not that great, Mike. Actually, I just booked into a room in Sutton Bay for the night until I figure some things out."

She could hear his intake of breath, knew he was getting ready to say something, but she jumped in ahead of him, unwilling to let him take control of the conversation. "Mike, you need to tell me what's up with the house. Something's not right and, frankly, I'm feeling like you weren't totally upfront with me." She finished and there was silence on the line. She could hear Mike breathing, realized that for some reason she was feeling sorry for him, for the position he was in right now.

Finally he spoke, softly and slowly, "I'm sorry Addie. You were by far the most squared away person I talked to regarding the caretaker job and I guess I hoped…"

She cut him off again, "that I wouldn't be affected by a house that appears to be…" she stopped, unwilling to use the word haunted. The further she distanced herself from last night, the more ludicrous it sounded.

He laughed sadly. "I can't tell prospective caretakers that people say Pen House is haunted; I'd sound nuts and they'd run away so fast it'd make your head spin. I can honestly tell you I have never had an incident of any kind in the house. It's true, there has always been talk, but this is a small town and if I bought in to all the talk…"

They both let a little silence and air into the exchange. "Ok," Addie said, "I understand you represent the owners and I'm sure as a real estate agent you're used to putting the best face on things,"

"Ouch," Mike interjected. She pictured his face, like a dog after a thorough scolding.

"But what about human to human? I'm a woman alone out there for Christ's sake." Addie felt anger tightening her throat and making her free hand clench.

"Where are you, can I take you to lunch? I have an appointment I can easily cancel."

She looked at the café's name, backwards, on the front window, "I'm at Della's. I've already ordered."

"I can be there in about twenty minutes. Can you wait?"

"Ok. I agree it would be better to talk this over in person. I'll be here."

Addie hung up and immediately called Leo. He answered as if he had been waiting for her call. "Ok," she said, "I got a room at the Bay View. Are you still up for coming over tomorrow?"

"I've already let James and Sarah know I'm going to take off. Sarah wants to do some research into the house, find out about the architect, any interesting tidbits she can pick up."

Addie experienced a rush of resentment. It sounded like Sarah, whoever the hell she was, thought this was a lark. Picking up on the frost in the air, Leo said, "I told her to go ahead since it might be a help toward understanding the house."

"I'm sorry, Leo. It's fine. If I hadn't had the bejeezus scared out of me last night I'd be interested too. The thing you have to know is that I am incredibly grateful that you are willing and able to come over here."

"I know, honey and I didn't mean to sound blasé about what's going on." They wound up the conversation after settling on meeting at Della's at ten the following morning.

22

Mike showed up when Addie was about halfway through her lunch. He stopped and said hello to the waitress, whom he obviously knew. He ordered and then walked back to where she was sitting.

"Thanks for agreeing to meet with me."

"It's ok," she said, "I have no idea what I'm going to do. I can't even really believe I'm here meeting you about a "haunted" house." Addie made the sign of quotation marks with her fingers. She continued, "and sitting here, away from the place, I wonder did I whip myself up into some kind of frenzy because I was alone in a big, unfamiliar house?"

Mike spoke thoughtfully, "but you didn't did you? Something scares people in Pen House. Who knows what it is, maybe not a ghost...subterranean waters?" He smiled sheepishly, but Addie's face had no hint of lightness in it and Mike adjusted his demeanor accordingly. He asked her to tell him the whole story and she did. He didn't interrupt but let her get all the way to the point at which she drove away this morning before he spoke.

"I didn't hang the mirror back up." He sounded incredulous, almost as if he were speaking to the air and not to her.

"Did your son maybe do it?" Addie knew he didn't the moment it was out of her mouth. But she couldn't help but ask sanity to throw her a lifeline.

"No, he only came out the day you arrived, the day you met him. I wish it was him or someone I could think of but, unfortunately, it wasn't Cooper and no one has the keys besides you, me, and the owners."

Addie wished it too. How did something with no body pick up something, move something, hang something? There had to be a sensible answer. Maybe there had been, was, a human intruder.

"Do you think it's possible that there is someone holed up in the house?" Addie shuddered. That thought was hair-raising as well.

"I think before anything gets decided, we should search the house from top to bottom. I guess it's not impossible that someone could be in there. It's a big house. Have you looked around the basement?" Addie looked at him, saw it was a serious question.

"Uh, no, Mike, I haven't. The thought of going down there by myself is…" She struggled to find the word that adequately described her feelings, "…unimaginable at this point."

"Well we need to go through the house, top to bottom. When did you say your friend will be here?"

"Tomorrow morning. We're meeting here for breakfast at ten."

"Can I meet you at the house later, sometime after noon?" Addie thought about it and realized there was something still unspoken.

"That's fine. Leo wants to look around. You want to look around. But I don't know what is happening in my life right now. I gave up an apartment and work to be here. I love the house. I'm disappointed. Afraid." She realized she had gone beyond the arena in which Mike could help but she couldn't stop herself yet. "You said something about Pen House scaring people and that makes it sound like this *problem* with the house is old and possibly intractable. Where do I fit in to all this? Was I just supposed to breeze through this? What happened at that house anyway? And what about the new owners, are they aware of the house being…*off*? Addie stopped, breathed, took a mouthful of water.

"The owners have never stayed there. They have heard a few stories. I believe they find the thought of a ghost somewhat charming and see it as something that will attract people to stay there if they turn it in to a B and B."

"That's just bullshit, Mike. There is nothing charming about what goes on there. It's painful. Sad. Angry." Addie heard her own assessment and realized what she had said was true. There was personality to the energy in the house. She had the odd and fleeting sense that as a therapist she might be able to help. *Ex-therapist.*

"I'm not saying *I* find it charming," Mike spoke a little defensively, "I'm just letting you know what the buyers have said to me. Honestly, and I feel like a jackass admitting it, I haven't given any of it credence. I am in empty houses all the time. They feel weird sometimes but I've never concluded they're haunted."

Addie broke in, "Mike, I don't believe in ghosts. This isn't just a *weird* feeling. Give me a little credit." She heard the imperious tone in her voice and added, "sorry."

"No apology necessary. I told you I thought you were by far the most straightforward applicant I had. I thought the other couple bolted because they heard some rumors in town and just let their imaginations run wild. I guess I don't believe in ghosts either." He hastily added, "but I believe you, Addie. Totally."

"Thanks. I want this to work out but it's hard to see how I can stay alone there. Thank God for Buck." She felt a stab. She should get back to the motel and let him out.

"I've always heard that dogs can sense haunted places."

"Me too. I guess it makes as much sense as any of this does. They are so much more aware than we are. I think they are tuned in to the nuances. In a way I felt like Buck was my Seeing Eye dog last night. When he relaxed, I relaxed. The down side is that when he was alert or actively growling and barking, I didn't have the luxury of thinking it was all his imagination. And it was unnerving, to say the least, thinking he was picking up something so strongly. Something I couldn't see or smell."

"You heard it, though, didn't you?"

"Yes. I think I did. I heard a voice." Addie felt a sense of wonderment. "I heard a voice mimicking me. Or did I just hear me?"

"How can a ghost really hurt someone?" Mike's question sounded innocent. Childlike.

"I assume that's a rhetorical question and not one I'm expected to answer." Mike looked at Addie, saw there was a little bit of a smile in her eyes, and smiled back. "I'm just saying that in all the scary movies and books it's always the person's fear that ends up hurting them."

"Well," Addie said, "you could inadvertently step on glass that was on the floor because some ghost broke a mirror there." Addie was smiling now and it felt like something warm at her core was finally making it out to her extremities. She could move and breathe. She was fine, in actual fact. Not a hair on her head harmed.

"True," Mike agreed, "but I guess I'm suggesting that we look around with an open mind, with a little curiosity even."

"Are you curious?" Addie was abashed to realize that she was mildly flirting with this man.

That's two really unexpected guys who have shown up in my life; an old man who's an amazing cook, great listener, and apparently has conversations with his dead wife, and a slightly overweight and strangely appealing real estate agent who is probably ten years older than me, married, with kids, and living in the sticks.

She brought up Sean's face in her mind and instantly felt chastised. Beyond that she discovered a new guilt: that she had somehow newly abandoned Sean, left him alone in Pen House. Face down in a drawer no less. Addie found herself back in more familiar territory, circumspect and self-critical.

Mike's voice broke in, "I am curious. I really am. I feel awful that I didn't say something right in the beginning. I feel awful about what you went through last night. You could have called me. If you ever need to call it's ok. Anytime."

"Thanks, Mike. I can't say I'm more curious than scared yet, but I do feel willing, in broad daylight and in the company of you and Leo and Buck, to really look the entire house over."

Mike nodded. A shy silence rose up and Addie quashed it almost immediately. "Did something happen at that house? What's the history?"

"I have a folder full of info about the various owners, year it was built, etcetera. I can tell you that Laura Davies lived in the house her entire life and was only moved to a nursing facility after she fell and broke her hip and a wrist. She couldn't do anything for herself and never improved enough to be on her own again. She didn't want to move and used to call her home phone and leave messages begging to be let out, saying she was imprisoned. There was no one in the house to hear the messages. I heard about them from the people who originally bought the house from her estate. They said there was a message machine with the entire tape filled with her voice, pleading to be taken home."

"Jesus, how dreadful. Who was she pleading to?"

"Don't know," Mike said simply.

"The voice I thought I heard didn't sound like an old lady at all. And the energy felt more childlike." Addie could hardly believe she was having this conversation, quantifying a ghost's tone of voice. "When did Miss Davies die?"

"The late eighties, early nineties at the latest. I think she was in care nearly a year before she passed away. It's hard to imagine how someone in so much misery can hang on to life." *And how easily they can go when they have everything to live for*, Addie thought.

"What I heard was that about a month before she died she just stopped eating and then, finally, she even refused water." Mike shook his head slowly.

"If it's her haunting the house, it sounds like dying was the only way to get back there." Addie had meant it to be funny but somehow the words sat between them, making an odd sense. Mike looked at his watch and Addie immediately spoke up, "I have to get back to the motel and take Buck out. He's probably about to burst." *He's probably fast asleep on the foot of that king sized bed.*

"It's nearly two if you can believe it," Mike said. All the booths and tables were empty. Addie could see the waitress out on the sidewalk smoking a cigarette and hear the swishing of a dishwasher in the kitchen. "I'll walk with you back to the motel. I'm parked that way. When do you want to meet tomorrow?"

"Leo and I are getting together here at ten. Can you join us?"

"I have appointments until noon. I can meet you after that."

"Why don't you meet us at the house, then? We'll just see you when you get there."

Mike left money on the table to cover both their lunches and a generous tip. Addie argued but Mike said it was the least he could do after what she'd been through. They walked out into what had become a glorious day. The heavy rain of earlier seemed like ancient history and there was more blue sky than cloud. The heat of the sun quickly settled on the crown of her head, making her feel drowsy. Waking up at Pen House that morning seemed impossibly long ago. And going to bed last night seemed like another lifetime, a woman different from today's Addie. She still didn't know how this was going to be resolved but she relaxed, knowing she had a room for the night and wasn't going back to Pen House alone.

23

Addie woke up just as it was getting light. She had fallen asleep early, slept soundly and woken up energetic and ready for the day. The thought that she had over four hours until she met Leo made her antsy. She tried going back to sleep which proved to be a total failure. She lay on her back, eyes dutifully closed, trying to watch her thoughts without becoming involved in them. In the end her thoughts were too alluring and she chased them down so many paths that she finally gave up and got out of bed. She peeked out through the vinyl-backed curtains and assessed the weather. No rain. A few orange-tinged clouds were scattered across a mostly blue sky.

"Buck, you wanna go for a walk?" Buck came out from under the covers wagging his tail. He hopped down onto the dark green carpet, did his stretching routine and looked up at her as if to say, "Ready!"

She laughed at him, "We haven't even cuddled yet and I'm still in my PJs." Buck hopped back up on the bed, rolled onto his back and made himself convenient for a belly rub, which Addie gladly gave him.

Addie put on her clothes from the day before, now rumpled but dry. She stood in front of the bathroom mirror to dress. She looked in the mirror, really looked, something she almost never did anymore. She put her thick brown hair behind her ears. "I need a hair cut." She said to herself in the mirror. Buck wandered in since he had the only other pair of ears in the motel room.

"What do you think, Buck? I know I don't have a tail and my ears aren't fluffy." Buck wagged his tail.

"You're just saying that because you want a walk." At the word "walk" Buck's ears raised involuntarily.

Addie had turned forty in March. A Pisces. The fish. When she was in college her roommate's older brother had cast her astrological chart. All she remembered was that she was a Pisces with a Leo moon. There was a lot of meaningful tut-tutting on his part about the disagreeable mix of fire and water. Everything else he'd said was long forgotten. She hadn't given a lot of thought to the milestone turning forty was supposed to represent. Standing in front of the mirror she had the distinct sense that she had been, and still was, somehow absent from her life. She looked at her face, into her eyes. Sean used to say they were muddy green, which he smilingly insisted was a compliment. Her driver's license listed them as hazel. Despite some new lines, she still had the face she was familiar with. Straight nose with freckles splattered across it. Large, nicely spaced eyes, pale lips that needed color to stand out, a somewhat small forehead and a streak of gray hair at her left temple that had been there since her late twenties.

Her body, unmarked by pregnancy and childbirth, was still athletic looking. Her legs, while not particularly long, were shapely. Her breasts were neither small nor large; "perfect" Sean had called them. Her arms, like her legs, were nicely muscled. In her hands she could see her father's hands. Long fingers and large nails, which she kept cut short and unpainted.

She applied coral tinted lip-gloss and decided against any other makeup.

"I look fine," she said to the mirror, " I look like me". The cloak of widowhood had made her feel invisible for years and standing now at the mirror she was genuinely surprised and pleased to see herself again.

She and Buck walked up and down the streets of town, stopping at a drive-up espresso stand for a cappuccino. Addie thought the shots tasted burnt but Buck enjoyed the dog biscuit he was given. They walked down residential streets and finally out into countryside when the town petered out. They headed toward the bay, reaching it in about twenty minutes. There was a small county park on the bluff with picnic tables and a path down to the beach. Addie looked over the bluff and saw that the beach was just a narrow stony strip, almost swallowed by the tide being in. A great blue heron stood statue still at the water's edge, staring into the gently lapping waves, ready to strike. She watched the bird until something prompted him to take to the air. Following his flight she turned and let her eyes travel the shoreline south and west. She suddenly wondered if she could see Pen House from where she stood. She felt unsure even where to look. She saw a few houses on the bluff but behind them the land was thick with fir trees. She saw a place where smoke rose up and experienced a moment of panic that the house had somehow gone up in flames. Maybe she should have turned off the heat. She startled herself further by entertaining the bizarre notion that the house had set itself on fire. She calmed herself by noticing that the smoke was a simple thin column curling upward, a fire in a fireplace and nothing more. She realized she was excited to return to the house. She was looking forward to seeing Leo, sharing this with him. There was also a murky and unfocused anticipation that Addie barely registered: she was looking forward to seeing Mike.

24

Leo got to the restaurant before Addie. She saw him waving at her as she came in the door. They hugged warmly.

"Fear and adventure has put a bloom in your cheeks," Leo commented, "you look lovely this morning."

"Buck and I went for a long walk. That's what put a bloom in my cheeks. Believe me, the house drained my color entirely."

"Be that as it may, I stand by my observation." Leo gestured for her to sit then slid into the booth across from her.

"Have you ordered?" she asked, looking over the menu.

"No, I was waiting for you. Are you having coffee?"

"I had a bad cappuccino already so maybe I need to chase it with some weak diner coffee."

Leo got the waitresses attention and ordered two coffees and cream. They studied their menus in silence for a couple of minutes. Leo pushed his away, "I already had a little something to eat at home. I'm going to go with this somewhat embarrassingly titled 'Senior Heart-Friendly Special'. You don't qualify."

"I'm starving. I'm thinking about going for this also somewhat embarrassingly titled 'Lumberjacks' Pig Out'."

Orders placed, they each sipped their coffees. It was surprisingly good, strong without bitterness and freshly brewed. Leo started the conversation,

"What's our agenda for the day? I admit I am really looking forward to getting out to see the house." He looked at her to see if his excitement was ok with her. Addie saw the concern, felt a surge of gratitude and moved to reassure him.

"I can hardly believe it but I'm looking forward to it as well. I woke up at the crack of dawn. I tried to go back to sleep but couldn't…I couldn't stop thinking about the prospect of looking the house over with you. Yesterday, when I drove away from there, I didn't know if I would ever be able to come back." Addie paused a minute and then added, "I don't know exactly what we're supposed to find or do with what we find. I mean, it's hard to imagine being there alone again, regardless."

"Maybe we'll be able to come to a better understanding of what is actually going on there. It's possible you won't need to feel afraid of the house if we can figure out why it's so, shall we say, energized."

"Leo, I can hardly believe I am having this conversation. If what had happened to me had been any less compelling, I would have been able to write it off mentally. But I can't do that. For one thing it would be intellectually dishonest. But, more pragmatically, I need to figure out what I'm going to do now. Become homeless?" Addie felt the darkness crowd in on her again and consciously fought to regain the hope she had woken up with.

"I understand that you are a level headed and completely sane woman. No one could doubt it. And, the reality is that something has happened that is asking you to open up to some new understandings."

"You make it sound sensible. What it felt like was that I was inside someone's insanity."

"Perhaps you should think of the house from your therapist's perspective. Maybe the house is communicating some kind of pain that is caught in its four walls and needs a deeper understanding." Addie grimaced at the therapist reference.

"I don't think I am a particularly good therapist, Leo. And it's a house for Christ's sake. A house!"

Leo addressed her frustrated annoyance, "I think perhaps your methodology as a therapist isn't reflecting the wisdom you've gained over the last few years. It's not surprising you have been finding it so dissatisfying." They both paused in the conversation while the waitress delivered the food.

"Explain."

"I just get the sense that you've had some personal experiences that you haven't integrated into your work yet and that's making your time with clients feel rote or inauthentic."

"Whose the friggin' therapist at this table?" Addie asked with mock grouchiness.

"Me, I guess," he answered with mock resignation.

She smiled and shrugged to concede the point. "Let's go back to what you said about the possibility that the house is trying to express something. What do you mean? I don't buy that a bunch of lath and plaster has some kind of compulsion that drives it to scare the shit out of people."

"No, no of course not. When I say the house, I mean the energy that is apparently embodied in the house. The energy that is so identified with the house that the house appears to be haunted."

"Do you understand this stuff because you talk to your wife?" The minute the words had escaped her lips she worried that she had gone too far. "I'm sorry, Leo, I didn't mean to sound flip."

"Not at all, dear. In the beginning I missed Teddy so much I wished she would haunt me." Leo paused, his eyes thoughtful. "I talk to her but she *is* gone. I knew it in my heart of hearts almost immediately." Addie nodded. *Yes*, she thought to herself, *I knew that about Sean, too.*

"We were married for forty five years and all that memory has a life of its own. I can ask her for advice or share something I'm excited or worried about and she answers me. She has a hell of a lot of wisdom too."

"But how can that happen if she's gone?"

"I don't know any way to explain it that wouldn't sound nuts. Maybe on some level beyond a corporeal one, we aren't ever really separated. Maybe that sense of separation is only a trick of the body."

"So what is the distinction between what you sense with Teddy and something being haunted?"

"I think of a haunting as usually associated with a place, as if whoever it is that died can't seem to leave the place behind. Something I never felt with Teddy or you with Sean."

"Does it have to always be scary?" Addie realized her questions sounded like a child's. An uncomfortable feeling.

"No. You hear about playful ghosts and about people who adjust to the ghost in the house...creaky footsteps, the movement of a small item now and then."

"Like a dead beetle?"

"Was there a dead beetle in the house that got moved?"

"Yeah, but it might have been Mike. Remind me to ask him." Leo surprised Addie by taking a small notebook and pen out of his jacket pocket and jotting it down.

"Have I thanked you lately for coming over and for not dismissing me?"

"Not for several minutes." Leo looked at his watch. "We should get going."

25

Leo followed Addie and Buck out of town and to the house. Once they turned onto Orchard Boulevard, Buck put his paws up on the window. Addie put the window down enough so he could stick his snout out into the sunny midday air. She looked in her rearview mirror and was comforted anew at the sight of Leo's car right behind her. Up in the sky it was cloudless and still. As much as she often found a blowy, wet spring day invigorating, she was grateful that this day was both calm and temperate.

Addie switched on her blinker to warn Leo that the driveway was imminent. She looked at the car clock: almost straight up noon. It was too early for Mike to have shown up. Damn, she thought, realizing she liked the idea of the three of them going in together. They bumped down the drive through the fir trees, took the last bend and there was the house. It sat in the full sunshine looking a little unprepared, like an old lady without her lipstick and rouge. Addie looked beyond to the bay's glassy cobalt waters. This was truly a magnificent place, she thought.

Leo pulled up behind Addie and climbed out of his car. Buck, who had been the first out ran back to greet him as if it had been weeks rather than minutes since their last encounter. Leo crouched down and greeted him with the same enthusiasm.

Addie said hopefully, "Buck doesn't seem too concerned to be back here. Maybe that's a good sign?" Maybe this entire episode would have some explanation that would make them all laugh later. She doubted it, however.

"I'd say Buck lives in the moment and at the moment there's nothing to worry about." Leo had his hands on his hips and was gently arching backwards, working the kinks out of his tall frame after being cooped up in his small car.

"Adeline, this place is stunningly gorgeous. I don't know what I imagined but this is more than whatever it was."

"Any first impressions of the house? Aside from it being beautiful?"

"It looks like it's in great need of love. Persevering, tender loving care." He paused, then added, "I don't think that's a very deep or meaningful observation, however. Anyone can see by the general shabbiness of the exterior that the house hasn't been tended to for some time."

Addie nodded, "Did you see the bay view?"

"Yes, and isn't it interesting that the front of the house faces away from the bay?"

"There's a lovely view of the water from the living room window," she said, pointing to the left side of the house, "and in a way I think it was more dignified, not so greedy to face the house the way they did." She paused, trying to figure out if she actually believed that last statement and if so, why.

"I agree," Leo said, "and when company calls, how ungenerous it would be to have your friends and relations greeted by the back side of the house." Leo and Addie laughed at the unintended double entendre.

"I forgot to ask, did your daughter-in-law find out who the architect was?"

"She's going to look into that today and call me on my cell phone. She doesn't think she'll have any trouble. They have an excellent library at her firm and she's a great researcher. She was quite taken with the idea of a haunted house."

Addie had the urge to shush Leo. "I realize I have trepidations about the house overhearing you. What do you suppose that's about?"

"I think you're intuition is telling you we should approach this in a dignified and respectful way. I agree. It seems from your description of events as if there is some kind of residual pain or anger or both here and it would be unwise to appear to be taking it lightly." Addie nodded.

"Having said that," Leo continued, "I think we can be forthright in our discussions. Maybe a reassuring honesty will help clear the air here and allow for the energy to move along to a freer place."

"You kind of lose me with the metaphysics, Leo. But I want to understand. I want to open up to the possibility that there is still something I can learn." She had said the last with a little bit of humor in her voice. But it was true. Since Sean's death she had felt like the big experience of her life was now behind her and she was in neutral, unengaged, coasting. At first she had known it for the pain it was, but what was it now other than a strange attempt at keeping Sean close to her?

Leo broke in on her thoughts, "let's go inside. Do you have any tea or coffee? I'd love a cup of something and a chance to just ease into meeting the house."

"I have both so you can take your pick." They each moved to get their things out of their cars.

"My stuff is going to take an extra trip."

Addie was glad to see that Leo had included an airbed, pillow, and sleeping bag since there was only one bed in the house. They hadn't talked about sleeping arrangements and she hoped he would be ok with sharing the front room with her. She didn't want to spend another night alone.

As they approached the front door Addie said, "here's a good sign, the front porch light is still on. I made sure as I locked up that this light and the lights in the entry hall were left on."

Addie put the key in the lock and it turned obediently. She pushed the door open, "entry lights are on too."

Addie suddenly remembered Buck. She went back to the front porch and called, "Buck, come!" She felt a wave of panic. How could she forget Buck? Leo had also turned back toward the front garden. Before her panic could escalate, Buck came running around from the rear of the house.

"Good boy, buddy. Where'd you go?" And then a second later, "Buck! What's in your mouth, drop it!" Buck dutifully dropped the shiny black beetle, unmarred from its journey in a dog's mouth, at her feet.

Addie looked at Leo with a shrug that was on the verge of morphing into a shudder, "It begins."

26

After they had piled all their respective stuff on the floor of the dining room Addie took Leo back to the kitchen where they put on a kettle and got out tea things. It was a measure of the outside temperature that the house felt chilled to her. She looked at the thermostat, still registering sixty-two degrees. She bumped it up to seventy and immediately heard the rumble of the furnace adjusting. The radiators began to creak and groan.

Addie saw that Leo's face had an intent expression, not unlike Buck when he heard a noise or expected a knock at the door. She quietly set out the tea and cups and came to sit with Leo at the table.

"Well," her voice sounded huge in the yawning silence of the house, "what do you think, any impressions?" Buck put his paws up on her and she patted her lap to indicate he was welcome up. He jumped up effortlessly and made a cursory inspection of the table for a smidgeon of something tasty. Finding nothing he curled up comfortably on her lap.

Leo nodded slowly, sipping his tea. "The house seems awfully quiet."

"What do you mean? Weird quiet?"

Leo laughed, "yes, weird quiet. Like someone trying to be so quiet they are holding their breath. Like when a child hides behind a curtain."

"Yes!" Addie said excitedly. "I felt that the other night between events. But I don't understand the feeling. The house is empty, it should be quiet." They both sat without conversation for several moments, then Addie added, "except the radiators, man those are loud."

"I like that sound," Leo said, "reminds me of any number of apartments I've lived in. Tell me about this Mike guy," he continued, changing the topic entirely.

Addie described him. She started with her first impression, which she admitted had been unfair. "It was Buck who got me to open my mind a little bit. He seemed to like him right from the start even though Mike actually asked if Buck was a poodle."

"Maybe it was an awkward attempt at conversation, sometimes that can come out pretty stupid sounding."

"Leo, I need to take charity lessons from you. Seriously though, he's a good guy. I like him. I was really angry at him yesterday, I felt like he threw me to the wolves. But I don't feel that way anymore. I still think he should have mentioned there were rumors, no matter how wacky, that the house was, um, problematic. And he's decent enough to agree that he should of too. He apologized, said all the right things. And I believed his apology, I really did."

A door slammed and they both jumped. Buck who had been sleeping soundly sat up. He was befuddled only momentarily before he started to bark.

"Mike?" Addie called out loudly. This caused Buck's barking to become louder and more insistent. "Buck, hush!"

She looked at Leo, watched him stand and walk toward the front door. "I don't think it's Mike," he said.

"Where are you going?" Addie said, coming along behind him.

"Just out to the entry. Wasn't it the front door that shut?"

"That's what it sounded like to me. Did we leave it open? Maybe it blew closed."

Leo slowly shook his head, "I closed it and I turned the deadbolt as well."

The door was closed but the deadbolt was no longer locked. They looked up the stairs. Both sets of eyes came to rest on the top of the newel post where the shiny black body of the beetle lay face up.

"Now *that* is impressive," Leo said.

Addie, who was hugging herself, nodded, "I don't know which is stronger in me, fear of what's going on or relief that you're here to witness this stuff." She looked down at Buck and he wagged his tail, seemingly unconcerned. "Buck seems fine."

"I think it's important to recognize that nothing has happened that is actually dangerous. A door has slammed and this little dead beetle has traveled to a new spot." Leo opened the door and looked out on the front porch where Buck had dropped the beetle. Addie came up behind him, knowing exactly what he was checking for.

"Are you surprised that there is no beetle where Buck dropped it?" Leo asked and then, without waiting, continued, "because I'm not. We are apparently looking at the same beetle. And I'll say it again...that is impressive."

They both looked up at the sound of a car crunching over the gravel drive. Mike waved out his open window. Addie waved back, glad to have the ratio now three humans to one ghost. In any case, she hoped it was only one.

Mike walked over, introduced himself to Leo and shook his hand. He turned to Addie, put his hand out to shake hers and then gave her a quick hug instead.

"Have you been here long?" he asked.

Leo, who had watched Addie and Mike's brief embrace with interest, looked down at his wristwatch, "about an hour and it's already gotten interesting." Addie and Leo filled him in.

"I'm really sorry about this Addie. I..."

"It's ok. I think we just need to go forward from here. I want to tell you both what my most immediate concerns are. Let's go make fresh tea"

They decided to take their tea out onto the back porch in the strengthening April sun. Buck stretched out on his side on the concrete patch at the bottom of the steps. Addie, Mike and Leo, after Addie laid down a bath towel, sat on one of the wide wooden steps. For a couple of minutes they sipped their tea and luxuriated in the heat of the afternoon. The bay was calm and they watched a tanker and a tug pass their line of sight through an opening in the fir trees.

Without preamble Addie broke the peace of the moment, "I feel great sitting here with both of you. But the reality is that I have agreed to be the caretaker of Pen House for a full year and I don't know if I can take one more night alone here. The two of you won't be here with me and I need to look at the situation keeping that in mind."

"I wouldn't hold you to any agreements, Addie, in light of what's happened. Happening."

"Thanks, Mike. I appreciate that and, to be frank, I figured I could wiggle out of this deal. I guess my problem is more existential."

Leo jumped in, "You want to be here. You want to be able to come out on this porch all summer long and drink tea and look out at the bay. This is where you want to consider what's next for Adeline."

"Yes. Despite all that feels wrong about this house, something feels right. Something has gotten hold of my imagination. And I am having this quiet crisis trying to reconcile these two very powerful impressions."

"Maybe you don't have to decide yet," Mike said. Addie and Leo both looked over to where he sat, legs outstretched, back against the railing. The sun was caught in his tangle of red-gold hair making it look like the tousled head of someone just a moment after getting up in the morning. *He's strangely hot for someone so totally not my type,* Addie mused. And then: *I have a type now?*

"Mike has a good point, Addie. I have no plans other than a doctor's appointment next week sometime. I'll need to call James and have him check the calendar for me. Anyway, I can stay; in fact I'd like to if it's ok. There's no real reason to force a decision right now."

"I can stay here when Leo can't or whenever," Mike added. Addie noticed he didn't meet her gaze and that his cheeks had reddened.

"The more the merrier, strength in numbers and all that," Addie said, trying to shoo away the little cloud of shyness that hung in the air between them. "If I knew I didn't have to be alone here for the next few days it would give me some time to see how I feel and to determine what my options are. In other words, it would be great. Thanks. Thanks to you both."

Mike turned to Leo and said, "you seem to know something about this kind of thing. What do you suggest we do?"

"I don't really know anything. I think what I bring to this is that I'm seventy-five years old and I'm not afraid to die. When you're not afraid to die it frees up the mind to think about things that are otherwise too frightening to ponder. Like the idea that life energy, unhappy life energy can stay behind in a place after the body has expired."

"Does it have to be unhappy?" Mike asked.

"That's a good question. I suppose not."

"But," Addie added, "a ghost does seem to suggest that someone was unable to accept the next phase of, I was going to say life, I'll just leave it at 'the next phase'. And I wonder, does a ghost, I wish there was a more dignified word, spirit perhaps? Anyway, does this left-behind energy know it's scaring me? Does it intend to scare me? Or am I as invisible to it as it is to me?" Addie smiled at the next thought. "Am I haunting its house?"

There was a pause, they all looked out at a song sparrow in one of the barely budding apple trees, its melody pleasantly filling the air. Buck was dreaming, legs twitching and a little whiney growl in his throat.

"When you can't accept the next inevitable thing it suggests a kind of rigidity," Leo said. "I suppose this entity could see itself as still embodied and in that case we could seem like intruders."

"Maybe whoever it was died unexpectedly, too young..." Mike stopped as if mid-thought. Knowing Addie had first hand experience with someone dying when life was just getting rolling, Leo looked over at her, his eyes said: "you ok?" She nodded.

"Go on, Mike, what's your thought?" Leo prodded gently.

"Just that if you had life taken away when you were young, it might feel pretty unfair, you might feel cheated, angry even." He stopped, seeming to collect his thoughts. " The thing that is blowing my mind right now is the implication that it would matter."

"What do you mean?" said Addie.

"Well, up until a day ago I would have said who gives a rip how you feel about your death. When you're dead, you're dead. What we're talking about is that something stays alive, for want of a better word, and it's either able to accept the new situation it finds itself in or it's stuck."

"Yeah, I am definitely experiencing some cognitive dissonance...I mean, the situation at hand is absolutely bumping up against a lifetime of contrary belief."

"I suggest we go forward with the situation at hand," Leo interjected. "Let's investigate. Addie says you had some information?" Leo looked over to Mike.

"I have a folder of stuff out in the car. I glanced through it. Most of it seems to be maintenance receipts, furnace upgrades, that kind of thing. But I haven't given it a super close inspection."

"Well, we'll do that first, don't you think?" Mike and Addie nodded.

Leo continued, "and Sarah, my daughter in law, is supposed to be calling me on my cell phone with information about the architect and any other house tidbits she digs up. I don't know why she hasn't called yet." Leo looked at his watch.

"Maybe she has." Addie said. "I couldn't get any service in the house, although I did get it out in front when I was sitting in the car."

"If we're going to stay out here," Leo said, "I need a sweater." All three looked out at the bay, the direction from which the new cold breeze was traveling.

27

Addie, Leo and Mike walked around the side of the house to where Mike's car was parked. He got the folder off the front seat and together they went back in through the front door. The beetle was on the newel post. Mike reached out and turned it over onto its belly making it appear as if it was just pausing rather than dead. "I'll be damned," Mike muttered to himself, "that is amazing."

They moved three chairs into the living room. The sun was getting low and there were long streaks of golden light on the oak floor. The trees were tossing in the wind that had come up and the water in the bay had lost its glassy appearance and was dotted with white caps. Leo went back to the kitchen to put together something for them to snack on. Mike set the folder down on the empty chair. "Let's wait for Leo."

"Absolutely," Addie agreed. They sat in a fading pool of light and looked out at the garden, the line of firs that fringed the garden, and beyond that to where the sky was turning from blue to pink to orange. The sounds of Leo in the kitchen provided a comforting background noise.

"It's really great to hear sounds in the other room and know I am not alone in the house hearing it."

"Yeah, I can imagine. It's interesting to be in the house as a visitor. I mean I'm always a visitor when I'm here but now I'm not on company business." Then, flustered, he added, "well I guess I am on company business."

"No, I know what you mean," Addie said, trying to give him a hand out of his predicament. "You've taken an interest. You're doing more than is strictly called for. We could have just arranged to cancel the agreement but...." Now she felt her own minor predicament and Mike held out a branch to her, "the whole thing is so intriguing and I'd much rather have it work out so that you can stay."

Leo came in the room, tray in hand, Buck the beggar following at his heel. Addie turned to Mike, "Did I mention that Leo is a retired baker and all-around miracle worker in the kitchen?" She took the folder off the chair so Leo had a place to set the tray.

"I'll go get another chair, since we seem to be using this one as a table," Addie said and took off for the kitchen.

When Addie returned with the chair Leo gestured toward the tray, "Here's what's on offer this evening: first and foremost, three shots of Laphroig. I think it's just the thing for investigation. A bit of courage." He passed each of them a glass with a generous finger of the smoky single malt. "To Pen House!" he toasted. They clinked glasses, "To Pen House!" Mike and Addie echoed.

"Next, we have two kinds of bread, wholegrain French and a dill rye. This spread" Leo pointed, " is liver pate, this cheese is a raw milk Swiss and that stinky one is a blue cheese I am very fond of." Leo paused, "the apples and carrots are self evident and this sad little tub here is a spot of leftover hummus I rescued from the fridge. Dig in."

As they snacked they looked through the folder. Mike had been right, it was filled with random receipts mostly from the original owners. Addie put them in date order as they went.

"Well," she said, "it's mildly interesting seeing a receipt for chimney cleaning from nineteen thirty-two, but I'm not seeing anything that feels pertinent. How about you guys?"

"You know what I think is interesting," Leo said, "I think it's interesting that all three of us are widowed." Before Addie could recover from this surprising statement, Mike said, "so was old mister Davies."

In his hand he held up a death certificate, stained brown with age and bearing two deep lines where it had been folded in thirds. He read aloud, "Elizabeth (Thomas) Davies, born eighteen seventy-one, died Nineteen oh-one. Cause of death: Childbed Fever." He added, "I can't believe I never saw this before. What is childbed fever?"

Leo answered, "A bacterial infection, puerperal fever. It came from not having sterile conditions during delivery. My great grandmother died from it when my grandmother was only a couple of days old."

Addie's head was spinning, a little from the Laphroig but mostly from the information that Mike, too, was widowed. Leo must have quizzed him in the short time she'd been off getting the chair. She felt as if she was sitting a little bit away from her body, away from Mike and Leo. She agreed with Leo, it was interesting. But when she asked herself why, her thoughts came back to her like headlights reflected in fog.

"Adeline, didn't you tell me that the Davies' only child was born in the eighteen nineties?"

Mike answered for Addie, "Miss Davies lived here until she had to be put into care, shortly after which she died. She was born in eighteen ninety-four. I don't know about any other kids. Maybe there's another death certificate." As he spoke he started to flip through the remaining papers, handing Addie the receipts so she could continue putting them in order.

Leo excused himself saying, "I'm going to get that bottle of whiskey. This house definitely has history and that calls for a splash more alcohol."

Addie and Mike kept looking through the folder. "Here we go," Mike said, handing Addie a similarly aged piece of paper.

"What is it?" said Leo, walking into the room with the green bottle and a plate of replenishments.

Addie looked it over and said "It's a death certificate for *baby boy Davies.*"

They compared the dates between the two death certificates. Mike said, "he died when he was three days old and never even got a name." They sat pondering the double-barreled loss the Davies family had suffered over the course of three days more than a hundred years previously.

Addie was the first to break the silence, "I'm starting to get a feel for the sadness in the house."

"But death was a common visitor in the days before penicillin," Leo said and Mike picked up his thought, "yes, and every house of this age and older would likely be haunted if that's all it took."

"I agree," Addie said, "we don't know the whole story." But as a therapist she also knew that people had wildly different reactions to similar experiences. Some people were broken by circumstance. Others could weather hardship and heartbreak, weaving the storyline into something rich and meaningful.

Leo refilled their glasses and they sipped and perused the rest of what was in the folder. When they had made their way through the stack, they put the death certificates on top of the receipts and closed the folder. It was completely dark out now and the living room, no longer basking in the gloriously warm sunset, was shabby and dim.

"Let's move out of here," Addie said and wordlessly they picked up all their things and moved through the entry hall and into the dining room. The beetle sat right side up on the newel post.

Addie didn't like nightfall. Leo, sensing her increasing anxiety, put an arm around her, "there's nothing here to hurt us." His voice was firm and she gladly, greedily took the solace he offered.

The dining room was cozier. Addie turned on the chandelier and two of the lamps she'd brought with her. She bumped the heat up a little.

"I need to take Buck out. Either of you guys care to come?"

They both followed her to the door. Mike went to open the door and Addie could tell immediately that he was getting resistance, that feeling that someone was holding the handle on the other side.

"Problem?" Leo said.

"It's that thing that happened to Addie. Here, you try it," he said, letting go and stepping aside.

Before Leo could get his hands on the knob they all felt a gentle but unmistakable rush of air brush their faces. Buck immediately began to bark. They turned in the direction of the stairs and saw that the beetle had fallen or been knocked to the floor. Buck stopped barking and went over to sniff.

"Leave it, Buck," Addie commanded and Buck turned away from it and went back to the front door.

The door opened easily and they stepped out into the cold starry night. Buck ran beyond the barberry, the cold and change of pace making him frisky. "Not too far, Buck," Addie warned.

"Is anyone else a tiny bit freaked out?" Addie asked. She realized they stood in a close knot and knew this largely answered her question.

Leo didn't answer but threw another question out, "do either of you have a sense of what that was? I mean if you had to put a body around it, what would the body look like?" Mike and Addie considered.

"It reminds me of when my cousin and I used to chase each other around the house. We'd slam a door in the other's face and then hold the door knob to keep the other one out." Addie looked at them to see if her analogy was resonating with either of them.

"Kind of bratty boy stuff?" Mike asked.

"Yeah, sort of." Addie answered hesitantly. Something about the characterization wasn't completely spot on.

"How about you, Mike, any impressions?" Leo rubbed his hands together and they all moved in a little closer to one another.

"I don't know. I don't know what to think."

"But what do you feel?" Leo persisted.

"It scared me. I admit it. But in a way it seemed pathetic, like…" Mike floundered, unable to come up with an apt example.

Addie jumped in, "I agree with the word pathetic. If it wasn't so goddamned scary I think I would feel sad or sorry for whoever, whatever it is." Buck had come back and taken off again while they stood there.

"What about you, Leo?" Mike asked. Both Mike and Addie looked at him expectantly.

"The energy feels childish but I wouldn't say for sure it's a child." They both nodded. He continued, "I'm fascinated by the strength it takes to hold that handle. Or to move a beetle for that matter."

"How about moving a mirror, for God's sake?" Addie asked, shuddering at the picture in her mind of a mirror seeming to levitate itself up onto the wall.

Buck came back and put his paws up on Addie. Just as she bent down to scoop him up, the quiet night was blown apart by the piercing blast of what Addie at first thought was an explosion but quickly realized was the furious sawing and blasting of an orchestra's strings and horns. Someone, some *thing* had turned her CD player up to full volume. She screamed reflexively and was immediately drowned out by the near-deafening trombones. To Addie they sounded like the cruelest kind of laughter, laughing at the shock and fear of the stunned little group huddling in the dark. The sound of a percussionist remorselessly striking a wood block drove the music like a giant doomful clock.

The music surged out into the night as if every window had been thrown open. Addie felt sure this was much louder than her modest system was capable of. She hugged Buck close, covering his exposed ear with her hand. He shook convulsively against her chest, which felt constricted with alarm. She couldn't organize her thoughts and, looking back on the event later, it struck her as a sort of miracle that Leo spoke only moments after it began.

"I'm going in to turn it off!" Leo had to shout and gesture to be heard. "Stay here, I'll be right back." He turned and quickly made his way to the front door and opened it apparently without any resistance. Mike had put his arms around Addie and Buck in a move that seemed to both give and seek solace. Leo didn't waste a moment getting to the system and only a few more seconds passed before the music stopped as abruptly as it had started.

"Sweet Jesus." Mike's voice came to her sounding full of wonderment and horror. He had released her and they both stood dumb on the lawn. Leo came out of the open front door and stood under the porch light. Mike and Addie, Buck still in her arms, reluctantly reentered Pen House.

They filed into the dining room. Addie finally set Buck down. He jumped up on the bed and looked at her expectantly. They laughed in unison, the laughter sounding more than a tad hysterical. "Looks like someone's inviting you to hide under the covers with him," Mike observed. Addie walked over to Buck and stroked him behind the ears. "It's ok buddy, it's only a ghost." This started them laughing again. Buck wagged his tail but his heart wasn't in it and he plopped down, head resting on his front paws, eyes watching them. He was still shivering but there were increasingly longer pauses between each ripple that seized his little body.

"What the hell was that about?" Mike's tone maintained the same sense of awe.

Leo held up an empty jewel case, reading its title aloud, " Cinderella Suite."

Addie looked down at the scattering of CDs on the table. She picked one up and, attempting to take the horror out of what they had just experienced, said, "it could have been scarier, it could have been Charles Ives."

"Who's that?" Mike spoke but both of them looked at her.

"He was this American composer, very disconcerting. This was Sean's CD, I've hardly ever listened to the it…" She trailed off and tossed the CD back on the pile, realizing her effort at lightening the mood sounded flat and false.

"Had you been listening to this Cinderella Suite earlier?" Mike asked.

"No. I hadn't been listening to any of this stuff. They were all still in one of the boxes."

Mike picked up each of the CDs and recited, "Jane's Addiction, Beethoven, Chet Baker, The Beach Boys, Soundgarden, Mozart…"

Addie interrupted, "I *was* listening to Mozart."

"And you hadn't played the Cinderella one?"

"No, but I do love it and I've listened to it a million times. That little snippet we were just subjected to was *Midnight*, the part of the story where Cinderella has to get away from the ball before all the magic disappears and exposes her."

Both men were silent. Did they not know the story of Cinderella? Addie continued, now slightly embarrassed, "you know, she runs off and loses her glass slipper?"

Mike deadpanned, "I've seen the movie."

Leo imitated his tone, "I've read the book and my experience is that a movie never matches up to the book."

Mike assumed a haughty posture, "Well I've done both and I assure you, the movie was awesome."

"Why this one, I wonder?" Addie said, ignoring Mike and Leo's repartee. "Is it just coincidence or a message or what?"

Leo picked it up, "Let's think about it, who was Cinderella, anyway?"

Mike, a model of succinctness, summed up, "A girl who lost her mother and was treated like shit by her stepmother and stepsisters."

Addie added what she considered important details, "Her stepmother and stepsisters were greedy, cruel and vain and she was innocent and pure hearted and didn't rebel against them but just toiled away night and day. In the end Cinderella gets the big prize, i.e. the love of the prince."

Mike sat down on the edge of Addie's bed and absently scratched Buck's belly. "Laura Davies' mother died when she was only a little girl. But I don't think old Mister Davies ever remarried."

Leo said, "it seems like we don't have enough information to figure this out."

Addie noticed his face looked fatigued and she moved to change the subject to getting some rest. "Well, I'm not drunk anymore. I guess that's what they mean when they say scared straight. I don't know about you guys but I'm wiped out."

Mike spoke, either not getting or ignoring her hint, "the real danger here is in being startled. I mean, loud music, in and of itself, isn't dangerous, except to your hearing. But that kind of surprise could give someone a heart attack." Both Mike and Addie looked at Leo.

"I'm ok, but you're right Mike, being startled like that does have an element of danger in it. If this ghost is simply playful, it has a pathetic grasp of the concept."

"There's that word pathetic again," Addie said almost to herself.

Mike looked at her, "I'm amazed you were here all night by yourself." He seemed to be sizing her and the situation up from scratch.

"Me too," she agreed. "Is it any wonder that I am completely exhausted? What are you going to do tonight, Mike?" She was pretty sure her hope that he would stay with them was written all over her face.

"If you want, I can stay here. I need to call Cooper and see if he's ok staying alone tonight." Addie nodded. She could feel her stomach muscles relaxing.

Because there was no service in the house, Mike went outside to make his call. Without discussion Leo and Addie trooped out with him. Leo pulled out his phone as well and dialed home. Addie listened to Mike's conversation. It was short, ending with *I love you* and she assumed the little pause that came after was filled with *I love you, too*. Leo didn't get any answer but he did have a message from Sarah left several hours earlier.

"What did she find out, anything?" Addie asked as they walked back in through the open front door.

"The architect was quite well known at the time. He designed several prominent houses in the area. His name was Edward Thomas and he was also Elizabeth Davies' brother, the uncle of Laura Davies. I'll call Sarah back tomorrow. She said she had more tidbits." As potentially interesting as this news was, Addie was too tired to open up a new conversation and only nodded in acknowledgement that she had heard what he said.

A little awkwardly the newly acquainted trio worked out the sleeping logistics. Addie insisted that Leo take her bed. She and Mike set up the airbed Leo had brought and laid Addie's down bag on top. Mike, assuring her he'd be fine, rolled out Addie's foam mat she used for camping and Leo's sleeping bag. Together they went to the bathroom, taking turns while the others waited in the hall.

After they turned out the light, Addie could hear Mike and Leo rustling a little, getting settled. Buck had wiggled down to the bottom of her sleeping bag and was lightly snoring. She heard the killdeer crying as it circled over the house.

28

Addie woke up to the sound of Leo's voice. She was disoriented for several moments as she listened to him in the dark.

"Go on now," Leo whispered gently, "you've already frightened the living daylights out of us. We're tired. Go now."

Addie came fully awake. "Leo," she whispered, "what's going on?" Down at her feet, Buck growled, first sleepily, then with full attention.

"It's ok Addie," he said soothingly, "we have a visitor in the room. I can hear breathing and I think it's gotten a little cold in here, don't you?"

Addie realized she had pulled the down bag up to her chin and was curled in an almost fetal position. The ambient room temperature felt like a snowy December night with all the doors and windows left open. She strained to hear the breathing Leo mentioned but all she could hear was her own, which sounded loud and ragged. Each exhalation made a cloud in the frosty air.

"We want to understand, we want to help," at first Addie thought Leo was talking to her and then realized he was addressing whatever it was that was capable of lowering the temperature thirty degrees, "but we're tired and need to rest as do you. So go along and rest now. Tomorrow is a new day, we'll become better acquainted then." Leo's whispered voice was calm and measured, as if he were talking to a child who'd just had a tantrum.

Addie inched the bag up to her nose not wanting to draw any attention to herself. Why wasn't Buck more upset? He had stopped growling and Addie now wondered if he'd just been warning her not to mess with his comfort level by getting out of the sleeping bag.

Leo continued, "go on now, we need to rest and so do you. Go on now." Addie marveled at the quiet authority in his voice. There was a loud melodramatic sigh that echoed as if they were in a space far more cavernous than the Pen House dining room. Whatever it was quite audibly gave up. As it left the room it pulled the cold out in its wake, as if it were dragging a big blanket.

Mike's voice, not loud, but conversational, was surprising, "it's going, I can feel the air changing."

They lay quietly listening to the creaking of the stairs. Mike whispered, "that's pretty hokey, don't you think?"

140

Addie put her hand over her mouth so great was the urge to laugh out loud. Suppressing the laugh made her want to cry. Something inside her needed to give way. A few tears ran down her cheeks.

Leo said, "wait for it."

No sooner were the words out of his mouth, one of the upstairs doors was slammed hard. The sound reverberated angrily throughout the empty house. The most startled this time was Buck who began to bark ferociously. Addie reached down and grabbed his collar, shushing him firmly. She didn't want anything to bring that energy back into the room. Buck slowly quieted and grumpily got resituated.

"I didn't know you were awake," Addie said to Mike.

"I was the one who woke Leo, or as I like to call him, the ghost whisperer, up," Mike answered.

It seemed like they were going to erupt into conversation until Leo wisely directed them elsewhere, "let's try to get back to sleep." And they did. First Mike. Then Addie. And just a few minutes before first light, Leo finally dozed.

It was nearly eight o'clock when Buck woke them all up by jumping down off the bed to go stand by the front door. Addie climbed out of her bag and up off the floor, feeling stiff, a little hung over and not very rested. She also felt shy getting out of bed in her long johns in the presence of two men she barely knew. She glanced over at Leo who had his arms folded behind his head and was staring up at the ceiling. He turned his head toward her and smiled. "Morning. I was just about to get up and get the coffee going."

"Coffee, yum." Mike sat up in his sleeping bag. He added, "I won't get up until you go out with Buck seeing as I'm only in my boxers." He added, "you don't need any other frights."

Addie looked over at him. "Ha, ha," she said, wondering what he looked like in his boxers. Her cheeks flushed as if he could read her mind. A voice in her head, the one she was coming to view as a scold, suggested she was somehow cheating on Sean. Impatient with herself, she yanked a hoodie on over the long sleeved shirt of her long johns and slipped on her clogs. "C'mon Buck," she said unnecessarily, since Buck was still patiently waiting by the door.

She walked with Buck down the driveway, her pensively plodding, him running off for ten or fifteen yards and then back to her. The morning was thick with fog and when she looked back at the house it was indistinct, more like a study in gray watercolor than a real house. She shivered with the damp and thought about what it would feel like to pack up Buck and her things and simply take off from this place for good. It would be a terrible disappointment. She prodded herself further. What about if Leo and Mike weren't in the mix? Hmmm. That was a much more difficult scenario to penetrate. In a way, listening to Leo last night, ghost whispering, as Mike had said, had changed her idea of what might be in the house. Maybe it was something that could be communicated with. Maybe she didn't have to be scared witless at every incident. She might even become accustomed. But no, she had to admit it wasn't a reasonable expectation even though the idea of being unafraid, of going it alone, appealed to her. She questioned herself again. What was the appeal of going it alone? Her eyes filled with tears and a couple spilled over making cold tracks down her face. If I can go it alone, she thought, I don't need anyone, and if I don't need anyone no one can leave me. It was psych 101 and yet it took her by surprise, both because she had been blind to this timeworn truth and because it hurt so badly.

When she reached the road she called Buck and turned back to the house. He came out of the trees and raced past her, his spirits high. *I'm glad someone is rested and not hung over*, she thought. She noticed as she had a thousand times before that it was impossible not to be positively affected by Buck's embrace of whatever the present moment tossed his way. Buck ran around the corner yipping and wagging his tail. As Addie rounded the bend she met Mike coming toward her carrying two cups of coffee. Buck bounced up on Mike's legs, causing coffee to bloop over the edge of the cup.

"Don't spill my coffee, Buck!" Addie called out, then added, "one of those is for me, right?"

Mike held it out to her and she took it gratefully. "Leo makes great coffee."

"I know," Addie agreed, "everything he touches in the kitchen hums."

"He's pretty amazing with ghosts, too."

"Yeah, he is. Weird night, huh?"

Mike nodded, "one of the weirdest. And that includes all the acid-tinged days of my misspent youth." Smiling, she readily agreed, "way weirder than that."

They walked slowly back to the house. The thought came in to her head that she would love it if this man would put his arm around her. This time she didn't banish it like a parent scolding a naughty child, but instead let it sit quietly inside her. *No big deal*, she thought, *no big deal*.

"So, I need to take off pretty soon. I am meeting clients for lunch and then driving them around to a bunch of properties. I have to go home, shower, shave, put on clothes that haven't been slept in." Addie looked over at him, his shirt was badly creased and he did need a shave. His hair, never very obedient, was verging on wild.

"I can't tell you how much I appreciate all you've done," Addie started but Mike broke in, "I'm coming back. I mean, if it's ok with you? I want to know what's going on."

Addie didn't hide her pleasure, "more than ok, I would love it."

Mike added, "and I think the three of us make a good investigative team."

"Me too. You know your way around the house cold, excuse the unintentional pun; Leo is calm and seems like he can actually communicate with him. Or her. I'm not sure what I'm bringing to this yet but I know it's got me totally hooked."

"Are you kidding? You're a psychiatrist." Addie interrupted him with a correction, "therapist."

"Sorry, therapist. Anyway, you're going to understand what makes this ghost tick and how to help it."

Addie wanted to laugh at him. This felt dangerously like a Scooby Doo cartoon to her. But his face was serious and yes, the respectful tone of voice was genuine. She let herself think about what he said. Before she had formed a response Mike said, "what do you think about the fact that the three of us are widowed? Do you believe in coincidence?"

"Yeah, I do. I guess the thing that separates coincidence from synchronicity is how the three of us relate to it. Does it feel meaningful?"

"It does to me," Mike said. "I feel stupid, but what exactly is synchronicity? Is it just a woo-woo coincidence?"

"Kind of," she laughed. "It's the occurrence of seemingly unrelated events that on another level one knows to actually have connection." Addie had a sudden memory. "And interestingly, Jung, who coined the term, had his first aha about synchronicity after he saw a beetle." She wondered if she was sounding school-marmish but a look at Mike's face told her he was waiting to hear more. "He had a patient who reported having a dream about a scarab beetle. As she told him the dream he saw a beetle crawling along the ledge outside the window of his room. He recognized that while there was no reasonable explanation that tied the two events, he knew they were connected."

"How?" Mike asked.

"How. That's a great question." She thought about it. They had reached the front door where they lingered, a little saddened to have this time together end. "I think he believed there was a reality that transcended our nuts and bolts, cause and effect world. A reality in which there was the unseen hand of not only our personal subconscious but a collective one as well."

Mike said with great sensibleness, "that seems to be right based on what's been going on here. We need to pay attention to that beetle."

"Leo said he thought we should look into the symbolism of the beetle," Addie said, "and I agree it may be enlightening."

"Does Leo know about this thing with the dream and the beetle?"

"Do I know what?" Leo called from the living room, then added, "come and have breakfast."

Breakfast was a plateful of buttered toast, grapefruit and orange slices, scrambled eggs and more coffee. Addie and Mike recounted their conversation as the three of them tucked into their food. Leo had never heard the story but also found it relevant. He reiterated his opinion that exploring the symbolism of the beetle might deepen their understanding.

Mike left at about nine thirty, saying he would be back between six and seven that evening. He also asked Addie and Leo how they would feel if Cooper came along. He explained that leaving him alone for one night felt ok, but not more.

"I think the question is how will Cooper feel?" Addie asked.

"I think he'll think it's an adventure. If he's really opposed I'll see if he can spend the night with a friend. But I kind of doubt he'll turn down the offer. We'll bring dinner with us."

Addie was sorry to see him go but it was tempered knowing he'd be back. In any case, she and Leo had a lot to do and the day was going to race by.

29

Addie washed the dishes and Leo dried. "Let's go poke around upstairs, I'm dying to see the rest of this place."

"I know. I can't believe I haven't taken you up there yet."

"All in good time," Leo said. "I like Mike. He's a solid citizen." Addie smiled at Leo's characterization, recognizing the truth of it.

"Yeah. He is." She dried her hands on the dishtowel Leo held out to her.

"Mike asked me when we were walking Buck what I made of the fact that all three of us are widowed. That's how we got on to talking about the beetle and synchronicity." She paused for breath and slipped her wedding ring back on. She always took it off to wash dishes. And she always put it back on as soon as her hands were dry. "Anyway, I never answered his question. What do you think about it?"

Leo turned it back to her, "You first, what do you think?"

"I think a few days ago I would have pretty aggressively defended the position that it was coincidence only. But now?" She looked out the kitchen window where the morning sun had finally managed to pierce the fog and even feel warm on her face. "Now I'd say I have no idea why but it feels like the three of us have found each other for a reason. Maybe just for friendship, I don't know."

"That seems true, regardless of what else may be so. The fact that we have all lost a spouse is something we have in common with old Mister Davies..." He looked at her. She nodded.

"And?" Addie coaxed.

"I guess my thought is that people who have lost someone know what it feels like and might be more likely to empathize, to understand."

"Are you saying the house chose us?"

"No, not really. But doesn't it feel like a bit of both? A little bit of the house choosing and a little bit of us?"

Addie considered. "It doesn't make sense but I am still thinking about Jung and the beetle. I was never a particular student of Jung because in a way it all seemed beside the point of sitting and listening to people with a sympathetic ear, which is about ninety percent of what I've felt I really had to offer as a therapist." She considered again, "and not paying a lot of attention to Jung was a weird kind of rebellion I mounted in college. Don't ask me why. Now it just seems juvenile and silly I didn't pay more attention. I am looking forward to becoming much more familiar with his work." She smiled, "I think I am digressing."

"Not at all, Adeline. Your sense of yourself as a professional listener is pertinent here. It seems to me your existing ideas are being challenged here. And why not let it happen? You were unhappy with how your practice felt to you. So, the house or the inhabitant of the house I should say, needs some help with moving to new territory and maybe that help will be reciprocated."

Addie realized she felt a little defensive, singled out. Was she here because *she* needed help?

"What about you, Leo? What is your connection to all this?" She regretted her tone, which had been sharp. Leo seemed to note it and not take it personally.

"I suspect I also am in need of a shake up, some kind of deepening experience"

The word *deepening* seemed to echo in Addie's awareness. She felt a surge of gratitude for Leo, for his willingness to open himself up to this mystery and by so doing give her the courage to do the same. Ever since the day she'd met him he had been like a lamp lighting up her interior corridors. *What a gift*, she thought.

She gave him a quick hug and said, "I apologize for being snippy."

"No apology necessary. Let's go exploring."

30

They walked thoughtfully around the circuit of rooms that comprised the ground floor. Leo had seen them all but he asked Addie to indulge him by walking slowly through each one again. She spent time in the bathroom showing him where the mirror had once hung and retelling the mysterious tale of its journey from window seat in the pantry to being remounted on the bathroom wall and finally falling to pieces on the floor. Buck walked all around the room, nose to the ground, busy with his own investigation.

"Our ghost seems young and vital to me," Leo commented.

"How is that possible, Leo? Aren't those attributes associated with physicality?"

"Yes, of course. But if we are dealing with energy that is stuck, then how the energy views itself must color the way it manifests."

Addie thought about it as they stood on the tiled floor of the bathroom. Through the window she could see the sun glancing off the trees. It wasn't the confident sun of summer but the skittish light of spring. It had a fresh quality, direct and pure. To Addie's mind, its most springlike attribute was its changeability; every few minutes it was obscured by the bullying clouds that were delivered on winds still carrying the sting of winter. It was a beautiful morning.

"So a little old lady ghost might make hardly a peep. All you'd ever hear was the sound of a cat food can being opened or the clicking of her knitting needles."

Leo smiled and shook a finger at her, "terrible ageist stereotyping Adeline. But you get my drift."

They moved down the hall toward the pantry. "Seriously Leo, it makes sense. I can feel that there is a kind of pathology that motivates this and, like everything else, it makes sense at some level."

Leo nodded, "that pretty much sums up my hypothesis. Where does this go?" Leo indicated the basement door with a little wave of his hand.

"That's the basement and furnace room. I haven't been down there yet." *And I don't want to.*

Leo pulled the little sliding lock back and opened the door. The fusty smell of windowless space came up into their faces.

"The light is here," Addie said, reaching in and turning it on. The single bulb, which was nearly overhead, lit up the steep wooden steps and smoothed railing. "Mike says there are lots of lights down there. Shall we have a look?"

Leo walked down first, Addie close behind him, Buck taking up a cautious position in the rear. He didn't like the stairs, which had an open back. Addie could feel the warmish air hitting the back of her ankles. She watched Leo's hand on the banister. It was covered in liver spots and the veins were prominent and ropey. She noticed again how his fingers were slightly deformed from arthritis. Leo walked cautiously, taking each step carefully. *He's old*, Addie thought. *I forget about that.* She suddenly felt worried about him. What had she gotten him into?

"Sorry I am going so slow," Leo said, seeming to Addie to be reading her mind. "At my age they warn you continually about the danger of falling down and breaking a hip."

"These stairs are steep, I don't want to fall either." They reached the bottom and stood in the last of the light.

"There may be a lot of lights down here," Leo commented, "but these eyes can't see a thing. Do you have a flashlight?"

"I do. Do you want me to go get it? Do you mind standing here while I run up and grab it?

"Not at all. I'll be right here when you get back."

Addie turned and started back up the steps, "It's in one of the boxes but I know which one it is. I'll be back in just a minute. Buck, you stay." She took the stairs two at a time.

She ran back to the pile of boxes in the front hall, trepidation driving her pace. She remembered the childhood fear that unseen hands could grab her ankles in the dark. Pen House wasn't dark and there was not much furniture under which groping hands could emerge to grab her. But the fear was the same: fear of surprise, fear of mysterious events springing up without warning. *Like a motorcycle crash.* This last thought seemed spoken out loud, beyond the borders of her body. It was as if it had been whispered into the air. In the front hall she saw that the beetle was no longer on the floor and had been returned to its newel post perch, again placed on its back. She somewhat defiantly turned it back on to its belly.

Addie found the flashlight easily and even though she knew the batteries were fresh she tested it. The beam looked weak in the daylight but that was to be expected. She loped back through the living room and to the hall. The basement door was closed. She knew she had left it open. Her guts did a sickening little somersault. She turned the knob and was grateful to the point of weak knees to feel it turn normally. She pulled open the door and heard Buck growling. She could see Leo's back. He was sitting on the bottom step, holding Buck by the collar. Buck twisted around and looked up at her, His tail wagged a couple of times perfunctorily. "Leo, you ok?" She started down the steps, flashlight gripped ridiculously hard in her hands.

Leo's voice came back quietly, "yes dear. Just fine. Our host is with us." He added in a light, quiet voice that was quite alarming, "hold the rail, the stairs are steep." She understood the back message: *We don't know how rambunctious this guy is. He may be into pushing.*

Addie got to the bottom, Leo stood up slowly. Buck kept up a low level growling but wagged his tail vigorously this time. She reached down and patted him. "It's ok buddy, we're all just fine." *What a liar I am.* Buck agreed and kept up his guttural warning.

"What happened?" Addie was whispering.

Leo turned to her with the same unnerving calm, smiled and said, "Buck and I were sitting here and we heard the click of the door closing. I think it's a little chilly down here, don't you?"

Yes. It was chilly. Not like the night before but not toasty like it had been when they'd first walked down the stairs. The cold air carried the stale earthy odor of the basement overlaid with the smell of concrete. It felt like the furnace hadn't been turned on for months. Addie listened for any telltale sounds that the furnace was on and heard nothing. The quiet between them was strained, as if they were psychically leaning into the unknown to hear whispered words. Even Buck had stopped growling and was simply sitting at her feet looking into the dark.

When Leo broke the silence Addie's shoulders twitched with surprise.

"Buck seems wary but not overly so. I've certainly seen dogs make more of a to-do when the UPS truck shows up." Addie nodded in agreement.

"I trust Buck," she said, "he doesn't have all of our preconceived notions. He calls it like he feels it."

"Agreed," Leo said, still using what Addie was coming to think of as his Mr. Rogers tone. She wasn't knocking it; it was definitely helping her maintain her equilibrium.

"Maybe our host likes dogs?" There was a rush of cool air, as if someone, arms outstretched, was spinning around right in front of them.

"I'll take that as a yes," Addie said, emulating Leo's well-modulated voice. *This is nuts*.

"I'm glad you're here," Leo said and Addie thought he was talking to her but he wasn't.

He continued, "we are so curious about the house, which is lovely by the way. And we hope to get to know you as well..." Leo seemed like he was about to go on when Buck jumped around growling and snapping, lips retracted up above his gums in fear and ferocity.

Addie reflexively bent down to scoop him up. There was a spot on the middle of his back that felt as if an ice pack had been on it. "Jesus, Leo, feel Buck's back." She was aware that her voice was stretched and distorted. Leo ran his hand lightly over Buck's curly back. "I think our host may have tried to pet Buck which was a bit much for him."

The air had warmed around them a little. "Sorry about Buck," Leo called out gently as if speaking to someone in the next room, "he's wary of strangers. He doesn't mean any harm." Turning to Addie, he said, "click on that flashlight and let's have a look around." Addie found herself in a curious position; afraid to turn the flashlight on for fear of what she might see in front of her and afraid to turn around and head up the stairs because of what was unseen at her back.

"Go ahead, Adeline, it's fine to switch that flashlight on."

She clicked it on and immediately saw a light switch not three feet in front of them. She reached out, flipped it on and they were seemingly flooded in light. She clicked off the flashlight and followed Leo and Buck into the space where the piercingly bright bulb hung from its chunky brown Bakelite ceiling fixture.

"That's got to be a three hundred watt bulb," Leo said in a completely normal voice. Addie realized her abdominal muscles were sore and she consciously took a few deep and measured breaths. *Something I advise my clients to do when they're freaking out*, she told herself wryly.

"Is it gone?" she said, still whispering.

"I believe he is," Leo answered. He had moved to a long wooden shelf that ran along one wall. It was bolted sturdily into the concrete and had beefy four by four legs at each of its two outer corners. There were several mason jars of various sizes lined up haphazardly. The lids looked rusted on and many were empty. Addie could see that some held nails now rusted and useless. One jar was full of an assortment of washers, red and black rubber, cracked with the fatigue of age. On the wall were several hooks, and someone had carefully drawn black outlines where tools were meant to hang.

"Do you think whatever it is is male?" Addie asked, as she picked up a jar with a little bit of brown oily liquid in it. She sniffed and caught the unmistakable whiff of paint thinner that had been dipped into with an oil paint-filled brush.

"I guess I do," Leo answered.

"Why?" They both turned toward the sound of the furnace cycling on.

"It seems boy-like to me, not exactly sure why. Slamming doors, playing with bugs, blasting music, none of it very ladylike."

"I've known plenty of girls who do all of those things," Addie said reasonably.

"Yes, but if this person passed a long time ago, social mores would have been different. I think these things might stay consistent since, once again, we are hypothesizing that this is energy that has frozen in time, someone who doesn't realize they're dead."

"How did he know how to turn on the CD player and crank the volume?"

"Good question." They walked to the back of the room which went around behind the staircase. There was a broom lying on its side under the stairs. Nearly all its straws were broken or worn down almost to the stitching. There was also a cheap plastic nightlight, the glass of its shattered bulb swept into a tidy pile. Addie squatted down, switched on the flashlight and shone it under the stairs.

"Anything?"

"An old broom and a broken nightlight." She added wryly, "no doubt the one Mike told me he would put down here so I could see where the light switches were." *Am I getting used to this?*

"Maybe it's like a dream state," Addie said, setting aside the broken nightlight and attempting to answer her previous question. "Maybe he sees and feels everything as if it is simply waking reality. I mean, no matter how twisted the details are, unless and until the dreamer becomes conscious that he is dreaming, the dream reality is the only reality. So a CD player, even though it wouldn't have been a part of his reality when he was alive, unless he died fairly recently, made some kind of sense to him."

"Yes! And he could operate it just like I have dreamed of picking up a violin and playing a tune on it when in fact I've never even held a violin."

"Right," Addie nodded enthusiastically. This was the first time in this entire strange affair when something made deep sense to her.

"I was going to say how dreadful it must be to be caught in a dream for God knows how long. But I guess if you're immersed in it the dream is all there is and you don't know anything else. Shine that flashlight over here, Adeline, let's see if there's another light in this next room."

Addie shone the light. Now they were again at the foot of the stairs and she directed the beam toward Leo's waving hand. Off to the left was a doorway and they could see the light bouncing off the walls of the next room. They walked through.

"There it is." Addie pointed. She walked over and flipped the switch. Nothing. She aimed the flashlight at the ceiling and saw another brown fixture, this one with a broken bulb in it. She checked the floor carefully for the glitter of broken glass, thinking about the possibility of Buck cutting his paw, but the floor was clean.

"Look over here," Addie said, directing the beam to an ornate dining room chair with a reddish-brown leather seat. It was obviously meant to be at the head of the table because it had arms. "I think it's a match to the sideboard in the dining room. Must be papa bear's chair."

Addie caught Leo's smile in the half-light as he walked in the direction of the chair. "Looks like someone had a bone to pick with papa bear."

He tipped the chair forward toward Addie to show her a neat diagonal slice across the chair's seat, revealing what looked like horsehair filling.

"Doesn't look like normal wear and tear to me," he added, setting the chair back down.

Leo put a hand on each of the arms and rocked the chair gently. Deciding it was sturdy enough, he sat down. Buck, who had been following them room to room in a desultory way, immediately hopped up on Leo's lap. Leo laughed, surprised. He stroked Buck gently and Buck rolled to his side making his stomach available for scratching.

"Are you ok Leo?" Addie was surprised at how easily she could go from fine to near panic in this place.

"Yes, dear. I am a little tired. I'll sit here and you give me the flashlight tour. I'll be right as rain in a couple of minutes."

She looked at him in the strange shifting light, but without turning the flashlight directly into his face, she couldn't see his coloring.

"I'm fine, Adeline. I just need a couple of minutes. I'm old, remember?"

"I have an idea," Addie said brightly, "let's finish poking around down here and then let's go into town and get lunch, my treat."

"Sounds good. And we'll bring your laptop and do some beetle research."

"And you can call your daughter-in-law and see what she's found out." The idea of being outside of the house seemed exotic to Addie and she realized she now wanted to be done down here, away from this claustrophobic and depressed space.

"What's your sense of this place, Leo, the basement I mean." Addie trained the light on the wall to the right of where Leo and Buck sat and began to move it methodically around the room.

"Well it looks like someone had their shop down here at one time…" Leo trailed off, then, after a longish pause, answered Addie's question, "I feel exhausted down here."

Addie nodded. "Ditto."

This had obviously been the laundry room. There was a large, double concrete utility sink. Addie walked over and turned on the tap. There was a small explosion of released air and a gush of brown water. She turned it off immediately. Leo chuckled from his perch. "I guess we could have called that."

Addie shone the light into each side of the deep sink. Curled up on the right side was a pair of washing machine hoses. For a couple of startled seconds she thought she was looking at coiled black snakes. She hoped Leo didn't notice her sharp intake of breath and the quiver of her shoulders. She was too embarrassed to tell him. She moved the light along the concrete wall and wasn't surprised to see an outlet suited for plugging in a dryer. Metal conduit exited the outlet, ran along the wall and ended at a large gray metal fuse box.

Addie walked over and opened it. Each of the fuses had a yellowed label next to it. The writing was small and exceedingly meticulous. The ink was fading. She could see the writer had used a fountain pen because of the telltale dark spots where letters had been completed and the ink had pooled as the pen had come to a brief rest.

Addie reported to Leo as she held the light up to the panel, "this is handy, it's all labeled." The labels fascinated her, arguably the most personal thing she had yet witnessed in Pen House. She went one by one, reading them aloud, picturing each place in her mind. Leo interrupted her, "are they typed or what?"

"No, they're all hand written. Beautifully hand written. It looks like a woman's writing." And then, "yeah, this one says *Papa's Room*. None of the other ones have that personal touch." She read each one out loud; kitchen, scullery bathroom, northeast bedroom/front, and so on, until she reached the bottom.

Addie stared at the last one trying to remember the little bit of Davies genealogy Mike had relayed to them.

"What's it say?" Leo asked impatiently.

"Well, it did say *attic*, but there's a line through it and above it is written *Chas*. Was that Mr. Davies' first name?"

"No," Leo came back immediately, "his name was William, wasn't it?"

"Oh, yeah, you're right. Who the hell is Chas?"

Leo hoisted himself up out of the chair, dumping Buck rather unceremoniously, and came over to look for himself. Buck had a shake, sat down and lazily scratched an ear.

"Hard to tell if the writing is by the same person," he said. "Whoever wrote it looks like they were about a jillion years old." Leo was right. The writing looked as fine and fragile as the exposed filament in the broken bulb above their heads. It looked as if the writer had barely had the strength or control to keep the pen firmly in contact with the paper.

"It must have been Laura, the daughter. Who else would have called that room *papa's*? She must have crossed out this last one and written above it a lot more recently than the original ones. The ink is darker for one thing and the writer's hand looks pretty old and shaky." The furnace cycled off, this time startling them with the sudden quiet. Addie wanted to be done. The labels had delighted her, giving her a feeling that they were finally seeing signs of the lives once lived inside the walls of Pen House. But seeing the last one had brought back the sick feeling in her stomach. She wondered if there was something bad in the air down here that could be causing the feeling.

"It's creepy, Leo. I don't know why it should be, but it is."

"Come on, let's finish looking around and go to lunch."

The only room left had a weak overhead light but it did work. It was the room that housed the furnace, a big metal box with ducts sprouting off of it like rectangular arms. There was a small access door on one wall. Leo opened it and Addie flipped on the flashlight to illuminate a large dirt crawl space.

"Not going in there," Addie shuddered, "that is spider heaven." She shut the door firmly. They made their way back to the stairs, both of them ready to be in the daylight. On the top step was the beetle. Addie nearly stepped on it. They placed it back on the newel post, right side up, in the front hall.

31

Addie and Leo were mildly discomfited to see that the day had clouded over completely and a soft rain was falling. They found a booth at the back of a coffee and sandwich place that touted its Internet access. The coffee had come as Leo was placing a call on his cell phone to Sarah. Addie ordered for both of them and then tried to ascertain, without much luck, what Sarah was telling him.

"What about a lawsuit?" Addie asked, as soon as Leo had disconnected.

"According to a biographical sketch about Edward Thomas that Sarah found, there was enormous acrimony between Thomas and Mr. Davies. Apparently Davies brought a lawsuit against Thomas that he lost but in effect it ended Mr. Thomas' career." Leo sipped his coffee and reviewed the notes he had jotted down as Sarah talked to him.

"What was the lawsuit about?"

"She said there was hardly any detail. Davies accused him of fraud but it didn't say anything specific."

"Whatever happened to him?" Addie saw the waitress coming their way with food and she scooted her coffee cup and water glass to the side to make room.

"No idea. It gave his birth and death dates as eighteen sixty-one to nineteen oh-two." Leo shut his little notebook and tucked it back in his pocket.

Addie did the math. "He was young. Only forty-one. I wonder what happened?"

"He made it longer than his sister," Leo observed. "Didn't she die at twenty-five or thirty?"

"I don't remember exactly, but something like that. I do remember she died in 1901. That means her brother only outlived her by a year."

"Tonight, when Mike gets to the house, I think we should make up a little family tree to refer to. Hey, I have a question I keep meaning to ask." Addie looked over at him as she sipped a spoonful of Mulligatawny soup.

"Mmm, the soup is good, you want to try some?" Leo nodded and dipped his spoon into her bowl.

"When are the contractors due to get started? That's good but it needs salt."

"Soon. Mike said early May. They want to re-roof in May which is usually a pretty reliably dry month."

"I wonder if their presence will be upsetting for our friend? Or maybe it will be like you suggested earlier."

"What did I suggest?" Addie asked.

"That the state he is in is dreamlike."

"Oh. Right. I did say that. Well, if that's true, he'll continue to absorb these twists of reality unquestioningly, as the passive dreamer does."

They quit talking and finished eating. "Split a cookie?" Leo asked.

"Yep. And I want more coffee too." Addie opened her laptop, waited for it to come out of hibernation and then did a search on beetles and beetle symbolism.

32

Addie and Leo stopped at the store on their way back to Pen House to get salad fixings. Mike had called Addie to find out what kind of pizza they liked and confirmed that he and Cooper would be at the house by six-thirty or so. Addie let him know that she and Leo would make a salad and not to bring any bread because they still had plenty of the loaves Leo had brought with him from home.

"So, Cooper was ok with coming along?" Addie asked.

"Definitely. He's excited. He's been hearing crazy stories about Pen House for years. And you know how kids like to scare themselves and each other with morbid stories." Mike laughed, "he's packing for us, he's totally into it."

"But, did you warn him that this is for real?"

"I told him what I had experienced and I told him honestly that I was frightened." There was a pause between them. "I don't know what to tell you. He wants to come, no hesitation." Mike added, "he's really a good kid, he won't do anything stupid."

Addie jumped in to reassure him, "I'm not worried about that, I mean I hope *I* don't do anything stupid. I just wanted to make sure I wasn't involving him in something that might give him insomnia for the rest of his life." She worked to keep her tone light but she was pretty sure it only sounded strained.

"I wouldn't bring him if I didn't think he'd be fine."

"Great," Addie jumped in, wanting to end an exchange that felt clunky and self conscious, "it's actually reassuring that there will be four of us in the house tonight."

"Five, actually. Four reassuring, one not." They both laughed and the conversation felt adjusted.

It was still light out when Addie, Leo and Buck got out of the car at Pen House. Despite the continuing rain, the air was soft and filled with spring. There was an abundance of late afternoon birdsong and everywhere around the house was a mass of vibrant new green. Addie noted again how grumpy the barberry looked, forced into a rectangle guarding the empty house. She stood looking at it, grocery bag in her arms, while Buck relieved himself against the birdbath. It wasn't a bad plant, the leaves were delicate, the thorns almost elegant and the color attractive. It just didn't belong here.

Leo had walked up to the front door and Buck ran up to where he stood waiting for Addie, who had the key. Buck started to bark at the front door.

"I'm coming," Addie said, "keep you're curly shirt on." She looked up from fumbling the key out of her bag. Leo had his finger up to his lips. Addie immediately put her groceries down on the porch, lifted Buck up and shushed him. He wouldn't stop barking and even when she lightly held his muzzle, he continued to growl. Leo took his hand and pushed lightly on the door. It opened easily. Addie had to hold Buck, now barking wildly, to keep him from leaping out of her arms. "Jesus," she hissed, "quiet!"

The entry hall was cold enough to make the outside temperature, somewhere in the mid to high forties, seem balmy. There were blankets, sheets and sleeping bags strewn around the floor where they had been dragged from the dining room. A box of art and craft supplies had been tipped over, apparently with some force and the floor was strewn with pastel crayons, tubes of paint, glue sticks, scissors, and paper.

"Why?" Addie said, looking at Leo. Buck had calmed down almost as suddenly as he had become so agitated. Addie noted without surprise that the dry chalky cold was ebbing and the room was warming up.

"I don't know," Leo said.

"It looks like a tantrum." Addie's voice was hushed as if she stood in a foreign church, uncertain of the etiquette and awed by the strangeness. Leo nodded in agreement. He pointed to the beetle lying calmly on its back on the newel post.

"Did I do something, do you think? This is all my stuff." It chilled Addie to think that a personal animosity could be forming in this odd boy. That's what she thought: *odd, sad boy.*

"Well, there's no one else's stuff to hurl so I wouldn't jump to that conclusion. Let's put the groceries away and get this picked up."

Wordlessly they both set to work, first bringing in the groceries, putting down food and a fresh bowl of water for Buck and then clearing up the entry hall and tidying up the bedding.

"Let's turn the heat up a little and put on some music," Leo suggested.

Addie thought she caught Leo's drift and agreed entirely. If this thing, *God, I wish I could give him a name*, had indeed had a tantrum, regardless of the reason, it made sense to create something that felt normal, enjoyable in the house. Addie bumped the thermostat up from sixty-five to seventy-two. The Cinderella Suite still sat in the CD player. *Not that*, she thought with a shiver, unsure whether that piece of music would ever call to her again. She pulled out something completely different; Malini Rajurkar singing Raga Bageshree. She noted wryly that Buck took to the new mood instantly. He came trotting out of the kitchen, wiped his chops along the edge of the bed, and hopped up on her pillow for an evening nap.

In the kitchen, Leo was washing lettuce and had laid out a fennel bulb to chop and a beet to grate. Addie had offered to make the salad but ever-perceptive Leo had heard how halfhearted the offer was and said, with a smile, that he felt like doing it and would she just keep him company.

As she watched Leo work, the singer's gorgeous voice and the accompanying tanpura, tabla, and harmonium wafted in from the other room with a sound both exotic and familiar. The fact that Buck was snoozing it up on her pillow meant the house was, at least for now, blissfully at peace.

Abruptly a longing for Sean sideswiped Addie, triggered first by hearing a CD they had listened to together countless times and quickly followed by a sense of alarm that the last few days had gone by with only a trace of the familiar ache of missing him. Confusion shoved its way into the reverie she had only just fallen into and crowded out the provisional peace of moments before. She felt that her memories of Sean were disappearing. No, that wasn't quite it; she felt the *weight* of the memories lessening, a weight, until now, she had gladly carried. It was all she had left of him and now, apparently, even that was going. She didn't notice the tears rolling down her cheeks until she tried to hide them when Leo turned toward her. He walked over and folded her neatly in his arms. She let the tears come down. Not a lot of them as it turned out, just enough to leave a small wet spot on his shirt. She was even ready to talk, tell Leo about her guilt that maybe she was forgetting Sean, ask him how it had been with his wife. But Buck was barking again.

Mike and Cooper were at the door. Addie, Leo and Buck met them in the entryway. There was a tremendous friendly hubbub and quietly, without her noticing, Sean again slipped out of her thoughts.

33

Addie helped them in with their gear; airbeds, pillows and sleeping bags, a duffle bag of fresh clothes and a couple of large pizzas. Mike and Cooper set about getting their bedding rolled out in the living room.

"Come on you guys, let's eat." Addie had come through the back hall and into the living room where Mike and Cooper were inflating their mattresses. "Leo put the pizzas in the oven but they won't be good if we wait much longer."

Addie caught Cooper looking at her. *Checking me out, wondering who the hell this woman is that his father is tangled up with in this weirdness.* Addie smiled at him, trying to reassure him with her eyes that she was ok. Embarrassed at being caught looking at her, he smiled crookedly and looked away.

"We're coming right now," Mike said, rising, smiling. He was glad to see her, Addie could tell, and the feelings his smile engendered in her were both sweet and scary.

Leo had pulled one of the pies out of the oven and put the salad on the table. He was pouring wine and asked if Cooper was allowed to have a small glass.

"You want some, Coop?" Cooper nodded and Mike indicated to Leo *just a little* with his thumb and forefinger.

Addie tried to imagine by looking at Cooper what Mike might have looked like as a young man. They shared the thick red-gold hair but Cooper was slender in a way that Addie thought Mike had never been. His eyes, unlike his father's blue, were a somewhat startling fawn color. His lashes were long and girlish and his features were delicately handsome. He was tall like his father, maybe even besting him by an inch. She thought that he must look like his mother and that she must have been pretty.

Sitting at the table both Addie and Leo asked Cooper about school, what he and his friends did for fun in a small town and, finally, what he had heard about the house. Buck, sensing the possibility of a fresh prospect had seated himself next to Cooper's chair and was watching with rapt attention as Cooper's hand moved back and forth from plate to mouth.

Addie noticed, "No begging, Buck!" Buck ignored her and kept staring devotedly at Cooper.

"Everyone says the old lady who used to live here haunts the house." Cooper handed Buck a little piece of crust and Addie decided to let it go.

"You mean Miss Davies?" Leo asked.

Cooper looked at his dad to confirm that was the correct name. Mike nodded.

"Yeah."

"What's that based on?" Leo asked. "Was she one of those mean old lady types who hates kids?"

Mike shook his head, "actually, she was a nice old lady. She died the year Cooper was born so no one his age ever knew her. I used to work for a lawn service when I was a teenager and we cut her grass here a couple of times a month in spring and summer."

Cooper looked at his father for a long moment then said, "you knew her, Dad?"

"Yeah, well I didn't know her but she used to always have cookies and juice for us. She was nice in a kind of formal, upper-crust way." He picked up the last piece of pizza on the tray and Addie got up to pull the other one out of the oven.

"The thing was, in her last few years in the house, she became more eccentric and I think that's when the rumors started to build about her."

"Why?" Addie asked, "what'd she do?"

"She didn't really do anything. She just looked crazy, for want of a better word. She came into town and her hair was this tangled mess like it hadn't been combed for years. And no matter what the weather was, she always wore those wooden Dr. Scholl sandals. Her feet were gnarly, let me tell you." He paused and Addie could see him collecting the memory together.

"Part of the reason I never bought into the whole haunting thing was because she was this nice, really proper lady and what happened to her, her letting herself go like she did, was sad. I was an adult by then of course, but I'm sure to all the kids seeing her wandering around town she looked scary and the stories just built up around that."

Leo, who had been listening quietly to this exchange, said, "I don't think she haunts this house for what it's worth."

"Why?" Cooper asked. Addie could see his eyes were bright with curiosity, excitement.

"Adeline and I discussed this, was it just this morning, dear?" Addie nodded, remembering their investigation of the basement which did seem like another day altogether.

"Anyway, to me the energy seems male, possibly about your age, Cooper." Leo continued, telling Cooper about their investigation of the basement.

"Dad told me about the other night. I can't believe the bug keeps moving around. Where is it now?"

"Last place I saw it was on top of the newel post at the foot of the stairs in the entry hall." She added, "that seems to be its default place."

Mike said, "it seems like the way he tells us he's here and sees us."

"Right," Leo said, " it's a way we're staying in touch."

"Why a dead beetle?" Cooper asked.

"We're not really sure," Leo said. "Adeline and I did a little bit of internet research on beetles today." He pulled out his notebook and consulted it. "From the pictures we saw, it looks to be a Predacious Ground Beetle, also called a carabid. It is known as a beneficial beetle because it eats other insects that are pests. It lives near water. It's attracted to light at night." He looked at Addie and she took over.

"There's a lot of symbolism associated with beetles. What I found most interesting was that the Egyptians considered the beetle to be sacred. The beetle that turns up in their art is the Scarab, which is a type of dung beetle. It sounds gross, but they eat the dung of animals. The thing is they also bury it and all this provides nutrients for the soil and I guess it aerates it as well. So you can see why they, the Egyptians I mean, saw it as a positive symbol, a symbol of renewal." She looked at Cooper and seeing he was following her, continued, "the hieroglyph image for a scarab meant transformation, coming into being."

Leo looked at his pad and added, "renewal and resurrection. And the scarab was associated with the god of the rising sun, whose name, Khepri, literally translates as *he who has come into being.*"

"What do you think that means?" Mike asked.

"I'm not sure. Maybe our friend was an amateur entomologist or Egyptologist. Maybe he's asking for something or trying to send a message." Buck had given up on any more morsels coming his way and had put his paws up on Leo who was absently scratching his ears.

"Is it ok if I go look at it?" Cooper asked Mike. Addie saw Mike pause and knew it was a measure of the fear he had of the house that he was reluctant to let Cooper out of his sight.

"Sure, but let's save looking at the rest of the house until we all go together." Cooper nodded and got up from his chair.

Addie stood up and started clearing the dishes. Mike got up to help her.

"I'm going to let you two do the work. I feel pretty tired." Addie looked over at Leo and saw that he looked drawn. Buck had jumped onto Leo's lap and curled up. Leo gently and methodically ran his palm over Buck's back.

"Are you ok, Leo?" We can bail on this thing anytime." Mike nodded his agreement.

"No, I wouldn't dream of it. I just need to pace myself, that's all" He smiled at her, "I'm fine. Remember what I told you earlier? I'm old."

Addie didn't think Leo would flat out lie to her but she wasn't entirely convinced. Something about his color, did it look a little gray? She noticed he hadn't even finished his first slice of pizza and half his salad still sat in a limp pile on his plate.

"Are you warm enough?" Mike asked, "I could turn up the heat."

"No, no. I'm fine. Really." Then, changing the subject he said, "Adeline and I thought that maybe our friend threw a tantrum this afternoon and that's what caused him to toss all that stuff around."

"It sounds like he was freaking out about something," Mike agreed.

"Maybe he wants us to go away," Addie said. She looked out the window into the night. The moonless black held the house in its fist.

"Maybe he missed you while you were gone." Mike was smiling at her. She laughed. "I'm going with your take on it."

Cooper came back into the room. "It was there."

"Right side up or upside down?" Leo asked.

"It was on it's back," Cooper answered. "What's up with all the scribbling on the wall?"

34

Addie's stomach did a queasy tip. They all exchanged looks.

"Where were you, did you go upstairs?" Mike's voice was sharp with concern even though Addie could tell he was trying to keep the accusatory tone, brought on by fear, out of it.

"No," he shook his head, "just to the bottom of the stairs."

Leo stood up. He lifted the sweater he had hung over the back of his chair and hurriedly shrugged into it. "Show us," he said simply.

"Haven't you guys seen it? It's all over the staircase wall." Cooper's voice cracked with excitement and his cheeks flushed with embarrassment. Addie thought she also heard fear in his voice. *Smart kid.*

"Nope," Leo said, "it must be new."

Mike said, "let's all stick together."

Addie laughed but it sounded more like gargling in her throat, "no way, I want to strike out on my own and look around."

"Ok. I guess that was a dumb thing to say. What I meant is, Cooper, you stay with me, with us."

They walked out of the kitchen and through the dining room. Addie grabbed the flashlight off of the sideboard. Leo nodded at her approvingly. Buck ran out in front of them, wagging his tail but when they moved toward the front hall, Buck hung back. His reticence increased Addie's tension.

"Go on, buddy, get up on the bed." He jumped up obediently and gave her a look that seemed both anxious and hopeful, the lets-get-into-this-comfy-bed-and-cuddle look. Addie smiled and stroked him lovingly. "You stay. I'll be back soon." He looked at her with disappointment then dutifully lay down, head on front paws, eyes alert.

Addie was tremendously relieved that the temperature appeared to be holding steady. Mike clicked the lights on at the base of the stairs, illuminating them and the upstairs hall. But even before he had done so they had seen the senseless black scrawl that traveled up the wainscoting to the left of the staircase.

"What the hell?"

"What is it?" Leo asked as Addie ran her finger over it.

"I think he used one of my sticks of charcoal." She held up her finger, which was smudged with black.

The line looked idle, as if someone had dragged the implement lazily up the wall as they climbed the stairs. Every couple of feet there would be a loop or scribble as if the writer realized what he was doing and put some effort into it.

"Let's go upstairs and look around," Leo said.

Mike and Addie both exchanged hesitant looks.

"Yeah, let's go upstairs, dad."

"Aren't you scared?" Mike seemed surprised by his son's eagerness. Addie nodded as if to say, *yeah, good question*.

Cooper shrugged, "I'm more excited than scared, I guess."

Leo, responding to Addie and Mike's hesitation, spoke up. "I think the key here is to treat these incidents with compassion and respect. There is nothing our friend has done that is any more than what a small child might do. Make a mess, play with the volume dial, draw on walls, and so forth."

Leo's comment shifted Addie out of fear and back to a more analytical frame of mind and she was forced to agree that nothing really dangerous had happened. "What's made this so frightening for me is how far it deviates from everything I've ever believed. But in a weird way, a really weird way, this reminds me of meeting a new client and trying to assess what it is they need and want from me. When I calm down enough to think about it I can see that."

"Jesus," Mike interjected, "are all your clients this weird and indirect about what they need in therapy?" Before Addie could answer, Mike continued, "and if a client wrote on the wall what would you say he wanted or needed?" They had started to mount the stairs slowly, looking closely at the drawing as they went.

"I don't know. I have no context. A young child could easily write all over the walls and it would simply be an impulsive act, even a creative one, albeit one requiring some educational follow-up on the parent's part. In other words, apart from being a pain in the ass for the parent to clean up..." She trailed off.

"Does this look creative?"

Addie considered. She shone her flashlight on a jagged squiggle that interrupted the meandering line. "Well, if this entity is trying to talk to us, it seems pretty ingenious to dig around in one of my boxes and find something to draw with." They stood on the first landing. Addie looked at Leo to see how he was doing. He caught her glance, smiled and winked.

Cooper looked up from scrutinizing the wall. "I don't think it's a little kid, they were pressing down too hard." They all peered more closely in light of Cooper's observation. The line was heavy and, regardless of whether it was semi-straight, looped or jagged, there was a remarkable consistency to the weight of the line.

"Good eye, Cooper," Addie said. "It would be much too hard for a small child to maintain such even pressure. And am I crazy or does the line seem strangely confident?"

"Raise your hand if you liked the idea of the ghost being a small child better," Mike said, lifting his own hand up.

"I know you're joking Mike, but seriously, it is scarier thinking it's an adult."

"Why, Adeline?" She had asked herself that question even before Leo got it out of his mouth.

"I think," Addie said slowly, wanting to really try and nail the fear down, "it's because the older one gets the more..."

"The more fucked-up they can be," Mike jumped in with a loud whisper. They laughed quietly.

"Well, I wasn't going to put it that way," Addie said, looking over at Cooper who rolled his eyes in response to his father's bad language, causing her to smile, "but, yes. The hurts sustained in childhood, when never understood or properly acknowledged will almost certainly color and twist one's adult behavior. In other words we find ways to adapt to pain that never gets attended to. The longer one stays stuck in their adaptive behavior, the harder it can be to open up to new ways of thinking and feeling." She heard her own voice and felt embarrassed, worried that she might be coming off as a know-it-all. She was also struck with the recognition that since Sean's death she had become pretty handy at her own adaptive behavior. No one else seemed to take any notice.

"Why do you think the ghost had a painful childhood?" Cooper asked. Addie loved the directness of his question. She could see that Mike's confidence in his son, his assurance to her that Cooper would do ok in Pen House, was well founded. He had a thoughtfulness that seemed both mature and guileless.

"I have no idea, really." Everyone was quiet and Addie heard their collective breathing. She continued, trying to answer with the frankness it deserved, "we don't know who this person was. We seem to at least informally agree it's not old Miss Davies. Could it be her father? Her mother? The mother's architect brother, what was his name, Thomas? I think we have all been making an assumption, one we haven't really discussed, that some sort of painful pathology is the only explanation for why a person, or the energy of a person would remain so stuck after death."

"Yeah, it doesn't seem like a happy thing to do," Mike added.

"Oh my God! Check this out." Cooper, who had walked up a few stairs ahead of the other three, was pointing excitedly at the wall. The line had come to an end at a drawing of a beetle. It was about three inches high and an inch or so across.

"It looks exactly like one of the drawings we saw online today." Addie was awestruck.

"It's weird how messy it is going up the stairs and then this cool little drawing." Cooper's voice was soft with wonder.

"Maybe the contrast is the point." Mike said.

"What do you mean?" Cooper asked.

"I'm not sure. Just that by showing one thing and then the other, it's like saying, *you may think I'm this, but really I'm that!*" Mike made a grand gesture toward the scarab.

Leo nodded. "It certainly seems to suggest we shouldn't underestimate him…as if we have."

"This morning in the basement, Leo and I were speculating about what the experience of this guy might be. Something made me think it might be similar to what it's like to be deeply absorbed in a dream…" She paused, looking to Leo to jog her memory.

"We were talking about how he was able to work the CD player."

"Right. So what if, maybe, he drifts in and out of a sort of lucidity. The line up the stairs seems pretty unconscious and then suddenly, this. As if he comes to for awhile and says, *I'm here, I exist.*"

"I know the CD thing was weird but why is it any weirder than carrying a dead beetle or a mirror around? Or slamming doors? Or an invisible hand scribbling on a wall?"

"Great point, Cooper. I guess I was assuming he died a long time ago and that made me wonder how he would know how to turn the CD player on, put a CD in and press play. Leo compared it to dreaming you can do something which you can't really do. His example was playing the violin." Addie had lowered her voice for fear that whatever they were dealing with might not know that it was disembodied. She didn't relish the idea of being the one to break the news.

Cooper persisted, "but he really does do stuff, it isn't like a dream where you just think you do it. Maybe he learned by watching you do it."

The foursome became quiet, all of them facing the extraordinary little drawing. Addie now recognized that it was not simply accurate but that it also possessed an assuredness. The artist saw and captured the essence beneath the hard black exoskeleton. It looked as if it was about to scurry down the wall and across the floor. Addie shivered, her body actively rejecting the last image. She spoke, "I realize the dream thing doesn't translate exactly but there's something about it that feels true to me. Somehow he is suspended in time like the dreamer is but he also has moments of real volition and the ability to interact with the physical world."

Leo picked up Addie's thread, "He's a sort of hybrid character. He is apparently without substance but still able to, at least sometimes, make himself known by manipulating a door handle or a piece of charcoal."

"I still don't get why a beetle?" Mike asked, shifting the conversation's focus. "I mean he could draw a flower or a smiley face, but he seems kind of obsessed with beetles. I realize it was a symbol in ancient Egypt but I still don't get what it means to him, or for us."

"I used to draw unicorns, Dad. All the time; remember?" Something in Cooper's tone sounded a little defensive. Addie thought he might be sticking up for the ghost's right to draw whatever he wanted or maybe he thought his dad's comment was dumb. Addie didn't know what it was about but she recognized the electricity of familial current running between them.

She said, "maybe it's as simple as that. Maybe he just loves to draw beetles. Why did you like to draw unicorns?"

Even in the dimly lit stairwell Addie could see Cooper's cheeks redden. "I was really in to them being magical. I used to draw them and think about all my dreams coming true. Seriously and totally coming true. But then I just grew out of it. Now it seems completely weird that I was ever into it." Addie saw a sort of surprised sympathy in Mike's eyes. Chances are, she thought, he'd never heard Cooper explain it before.

"Ok," she said, "so the unicorn was a symbol for you of the possibility of dreams coming true, right? You grew out of that symbol but I'm suggesting that this beetle still resonates pretty powerfully with our friend."

Is that what I'm suggesting? Addie was winging it now and she knew it.

"I'm guessing that when he has these lucid moments, the drama that caused him to be stuck here in the first place, whatever his central predicament is, comes back to him pretty powerfully. So powerfully that he somehow conjures up the ability to interact with the waking world. I would say the beetle is a familiar and forceful expression of his sense of self."

"What do you mean by his central predicament?" Cooper asked.

Addie had the strange feeling that she and Cooper were suddenly alone. Cooper's hunger to understand the point she was making seemed to be a bright circle of light beyond which Leo and Mike stood in shadow. She looked at them to shake the feeling. They appeared to also be waiting for an answer. She couldn't remember a time when it felt so important to give the right answer and have it come from her heart.

"What I mean by the central predicament is the repeating question or questions each of us has about our lives that seem to point, if we can only answer them, to a deeper understanding of who we are." Sean came into her mind, barged in and took up space in a bullying way, momentarily scrambling her thoughts.

A silence fell between them. She could hear each of them breathing and the house was breathing along with them. Addie thought Cooper was going to ask another question but he didn't. The quiet began to feel stretched and unnatural. It wasn't awkwardness between them but something that felt bogged down in the space.

Finally Leo spoke, "either we need to keep going or I'm going to have to sit down." Addie had the disquieting feeling she had just popped awake out of a nightmare in which she had been trying, hopelessly, to yell for help.

"You want to go hang out with Buck? He'd love the company."

"Maybe in a few minutes, dear. I'm too curious to turn around yet."

Cooper started up the last few steps and turned to the right. Before anyone could warn him about the mirror he braked and drew in his breath sharply, "Jesus!"

"Sorry Coop, I always forget it's there."

Three white glass globes, each surrounding a single forty watt bulb, comprised the hall lights. Addie thought the pools of light looked like three small dimly lit stages in an empty theater. The mirror caught a little of the light and threw indistinct images back at them.

"What's on it?" Cooper, again out in front, asked.

Now, nearly to the door, they could see the mirror had been drawn on as well. This time the artist had used red pastel. The lines were faint because the glass was a poor substrate for the medium. But faint as they were, it was still unmistakable: a life-sized drawing of a human figure. A man. Cooper was the first to approach closely. He stood facing the mirror, fitting his own body into the mirror image. They were remarkably similar in height and body shape.

"He traced himself," said Mike, "unbelievable."

"It's not a child," said Addie, "it's a full grown man. Look, you can even see the line of his hair. And he looks to be just a little shorter than you, Cooper. How tall are you?"

"Six two."

"Well, I'd say our friend is at least six feet," Leo said, then added, "and slender by the look of it."

Mike said, "I've seen a photograph of the old man. They had a picture of him in the paper when Miss Davies died. He wasn't skinny. He was definitely portly."

"What about the architect? Mister Thomas?" Addie asked him.

"No idea. I didn't even know he was related to the family until Leo found that out."

Cooper said, "he can see himself." The foursome stared into the mirror and then laughed as they all saw themselves. "I wonder how he sees us?"

Mike pushed open the bathroom door to their right and switched on the light. The room felt cold. He went over and touched the radiator, which had clearly not been on anytime recently.

"It's cold in here but I think it's just because the radiator is off." He walked back out and pulled the door closed. Cooper tried turning the glass knob on the mirrored bedroom door. "It's stuck. It feels like someone's holding it."

 Mike said, "let me try," but Cooper gave it a strong jerk and it turned.

They walked into the room and it was markedly colder than the hall. Unlike the bathroom, the cold in the bedroom was odd. Their bodies registered immediately that the temperature was somehow wrong and couldn't be explained by the temperature of the night air.

 "It feels like a refrigerator in here," Leo said, "cold, yes, but also stale like a big walk-in fridge."

Addie went over to the wide-open double hung window that overlooked the front garden. Almost whispering she said, "I don't suppose either of you opened this?" No one answered, knowing it wasn't really a question but simply and expression of bafflement.

Addie looked out. The rain had stopped and she could hear the sound of the trees dripping and smell the perfume of spring. The air was both fresher and warmer outside. Was he also standing here, feeling this lovely air wafting around the empty room? Or was he caught in some other season, some other time of day, surrounded by people no one could see anymore? She pulled the window down and secured the latch.

"Whose room was this?" Cooper asked.

They looked around at the large empty space. Their voices echoed and their shoes squeaked on the hardwood floor. Cooper opened the closet door and pulled the little chain that dangled from the overhead light. "Ick, this closet is smelly and it's bigger than my bedroom." Addie walked in.

The closet was large and the smell of the cedar-lined walls was still vaguely detectable. Stronger was a smell of mothballs. Addie pulled open each of four large built-in drawers. They were all empty except for a lining of rose-patterned shelf paper. The smell of mothballs increased.

"This must have been Miss Davies' room. A man probably wouldn't choose such a flowery shelf liner. I bet this is where she kept her sweaters." Addie realized she had said this to nobody as Cooper had walked out and joined the other two in the main room.

"Addie, check this out." Mike called to her. She walked out of the closet, turning off the light and shutting the door.

"What?" She saw Mike, Cooper and Leo all standing around the radiator.

"It's off too, isn't it?"

"Just come here and check it out," Mike persisted. Addie joined them.

"Ok," Mike said, "keep your hand about a foot away from the heater and then move it slowly toward it." Addie obediently followed Mike's instructions aware that all eyes were on her. She held her hand, palm facing the radiator, and moved it slowly forward. At about six inches distance she suddenly, very suddenly, felt the full warmth of the radiator. She moved her hand slowly back and forth several times. There was no question; her hand passed through a very specific though invisible barrier beyond which the heat of the radiator could not penetrate.

"He's here with us right now," Addie said. They all turned back, away from the radiator and toward the center of the room. Addie whispered, "Empty. Empty and cold." They were all silent for a moment and Addie could not only hear their collective breath, she could see it floating out in front of them. It wasn't cold enough outside to see one's breath but it was in here.

"Maybe it's the cold that we need to think of as his presence. In that way, he isn't invisible at all. We are all feeling him and rather intensely at that." Leo embraced himself in a warming hug as he spoke.

"It's too damn cold for you to be here, Leo. You're already tired. This is too much." Addie waited for his return argument but he surprised her by saying, "You're right, Adeline. I need to do this when I am fresh from a night's sleep. I'll go down and keep Buck company."

Suddenly the air around them was alive as if someone was moving frenetically in front of where they stood. All four of them remained still, each touched by wonderment and fear at the bursts of cold air, enough to ruffle their hair, enough to make them reflexively blink.

Leo said, "I need to go downstairs. You seem agitated. I'm sorry if we've said something to upset you." Everyone understood immediately whom he was addressing.

Cooper spoke up next, "We should all go back downstairs and stay together." Mike looked over at his son as if seeing something in him he'd never seen before. "I agree, Cooper." He put his arm around Cooper's shoulders and Cooper didn't shrug him off. Addie nodded. Despite their agreement that they needed to go back downstairs, they all stayed huddled in the spot where they stood.

"He's not moving anymore." Mike whispered.

Leo's voice was measured and reasonable, "we're all tired and we're going to turn in for the night. We want you to continue showing us around the house tomorrow. For tonight, however, we're just hoping for a nice quiet sleep."

The stillness of the room swallowed up Leo's words. Taking this as assent, they moved in unison for the still-open door to the hallway. The door lazily swung shut and a little frigid breeze touched their faces.

"That's ok, let's not make a big deal out of it." Leo's voice had maintained its calm and everyone fell into line behind him.

The handle turned normally but just as Leo was pulling it back open they were startled anew by the sound of tapping on glass. It was light, like the sound of a fingernail striking the surface. Turning and staring at the west-facing window, they saw a face, unmistakable, reflected in the glass, looking out as if the eyes could see something in the distance beyond the black of night and the reflection of the room. The eyes were large and curiously lacking in an expression that any of the four, all crowded at the door's threshold, could make out. The face was that of a young man, no more than twenty or so. He was gaunt, his cheekbones unhealthily prominent. His nose was slender and his lips full and slightly parted. He had a deep dimple in his chin and his coloring was both translucent and sickeningly pale, almost the color of mold on white bread. The smoothness of his skin wasn't quite waxy but neither did it bear any resemblance to the living.

He slowly shifted his infinitely sad eyes, as if it took great energy, until he had met each pair of eyes staring at him. Addie was reminded of flying through clouds. When she tried to get a fix on him he grew more faint. When she loosened her analytical grip a little and let herself feel the extraordinary image in the glass, the visage sharpened. She found him terrifying and achingly beautiful. Time didn't seem to pass so much as hang like a frozen sheet in the bitter cold air.

Later, they all agreed they'd felt hypnotized by his dark eyes, which, paradoxically, they collectively described as both distant and intensely present. All of them had tried and failed to properly see his body or what he wore. What they remembered was the face, the awful hue, and the dark curly hair framing it. Only Cooper saw a stiff white collar at the base of his slender neck and the shadowy outline of shoulders. As the face faded they all tried to hang on to it, to him, but he was as ephemeral as a rainbow. Without any of them being able to recall the exact moment it happened, he disappeared.

Addie quietly shut the bedroom door behind them and they filed down the hallway and to the stairs, the house growing warmer with each step.

After Buck had been taken out, after everyone had washed up, done their teeth, completed the soothing rituals that lead to sleep, Addie lay in bed going over the evening's events knowing that Leo, Mike and Cooper were doing the same. It was almost as if they were talking to each other though the house was as peacefully quiet as Addie had ever known it to be. They had all hugged each other goodnight with the same reverence they had maintained since coming back downstairs.

Addie had just entered the state where thoughts wander into dreams when she heard a door upstairs close, and then creak open. This repeated at a measured pace for maybe twenty iterations. Addie knew without a doubt that Leo, Mike and Cooper all lay like her, still and listening. The door wasn't being slammed. It sounded like a bored child, unready to give up and go to bed. If not for its preternatural quality it would have been annoying. After the last closing click echoed back to them the house became quiet and one by one they all fell into sleep. The house stayed quiet and no one woke until daylight was filtering in through the windows.

35

Addie could feel the gentle heat of the morning sun on her eyelids before she opened them. She lay on her back savoring the sleep she had just come out of. Leo snored lightly. She could hear Mike and Cooper talking in the next room. Arguing? They were speaking quietly but there was intensity behind it, each voice cutting in on the other before the other's words had been completely spoken. She listened. But they had stopped. She nudged Buck with her toe, scratched his belly with her foot. He growled at first then stretched out to give her better access.

She climbed out of bed trying to be quiet so as not to wake Leo. Buck, however, scooted out from under the covers and did a full body shake, jingling his metal tags noisily.

"Morning, Adeline."

"Sorry to wake you, Leo. Try and go back to sleep. I'll get some coffee going."

"No, I've just been dozing off and on since first light. I'm ready to get up."

"Quiet night, huh?"

"Absolutely glorious. One of the best sleeps I've had in months."

176

"Me too. And I had serious doubts after the excitement of last night. I thought for sure I wouldn't be able to turn my mind off, but go figure, I don't even remember dreaming anything." Addie slipped on her hoodie and clogs. Buck, taking the cue, ran to the front door.

"Wrong door, Buddy. We are going out the back door via the bathroom." Buck wagged his tail with ok-with-me abandon. Leo was already sitting up on the edge of the bed, stretching his arms up over his head.

"I'll get that kettle going." He called out as Addie and Buck headed through the kitchen and to the bathroom.

She took stock of how she felt. Warm. Safe. Happy? Happy. She reflected on how her life had taken such an unanticipated turn in the space of a few short weeks. And now she was in a house, sometimes terrifying and sometimes wonderful, with three new friends. Three male friends at that. She reminded herself that there was a fourth man in the house, one she hoped was friendly, or at least not acrimonious. She sent him a peace-be-with-you thought and halfway feared a rejoinder or a cold rush of air, a slamming door. But the house felt warm and the only sounds were Buck's nails on the hardwood floor and the sound of running water in the kitchen. She saw with satisfaction that the bolt on the basement door was in the locked position, just as she and Leo had left it yesterday.

She met Cooper coming out of the bathroom as she was about to head in.

"Good morning." She said, smiling. He smiled, said hello, but didn't meet her gaze. Instead he looked away shyly and ducked back down the hall toward the living room. She thought she understood. There had been a deeply intimate quality to last night's experience. Like watching a baby being born, seeing that reflection had been amazing and deeply moving. No wonder, in the light of an ordinary morning, a boy his age would look away. She felt the same shy urge.

Addie stood outside and took stock of the perfect spring morning that was unfolding in front of her. Buck ran around the fruit trees, sniffing, lifting his leg once for a good long pee and then several times more just to let the world know that Buck was back in town. The sky was a crisp blue with a few fat, happy clouds cruising slowly across it. There was a breeze but it was gentle, carrying no bite. The fruit trees were in various stages of blooming. Some already had masses of white and pink flowers, many of which had dropped and now carpeted the grass. Others were loaded with pregnant buds, each bud suggesting a hint of the color that was about to emerge. Addie had a pleasurable sense of anticipation about being at Pen House and watching each season unfold. She filled her nostrils with the sweetness of the blossoms. The air carried a woody perfume from beyond the garden's boundary. In the distance, the water of the bay was rippled but unbroken by whitecaps. Addie looked to see if there was a view of the town from where she stood. All she could see were some distant columns of smoke coming up out of unseen chimneys.

Buck ran in past her and down the hall to the kitchen. She followed his little dew-sopped footprints to where he stood greeting everyone in the kitchen.

"Good morning. Have you guys seen what an amazingly beautiful day it is?" Addie could see they had been in the middle of a conversation. Cooper sat at the table drinking a glass of orange juice and eating a piece of toast. Mike was leaning against the counter next to where Leo, bless his heart, was cooking an omelet in one of Addie's cast iron skillets.

"How's everyone this morning?"

Mike answered, "we've been having a discussion about our day. Cooper and I had a little difference of opinion about school."

"What about school?" Addie asked, watching the omelet form itself in the hot pan. "Damn, that smells good, Leo." Leo reached out and patted her on the cheek, smiling, "my biggest fan."

"Well," Mike continued, "I said I was going to drive him in to school, which starts in fifteen minutes, so there's no way he's going to be on time." Addie glanced around the room reflexively, looking for a clock.

"It's seven forty-five." Mike said. "Anyway, I said I was going to take him to school and he said he thought, in light of the," he waved his hand around the room, "unusual circumstances we find ourselves in, he should be allowed to take the day off."

Addie nodded. It sounded like a reasonable argument to make. And she found that she hoped Mike would relent. She wanted them all to be here.

178

"Then Leo here piped up and said he agreed with Cooper. He argued that this is more educational than anything he can imagine they have planned for today at school." He smiled broadly and Addie thought that smile must sell a lot of houses. "And I had to admit I agree." Addie looked over at Cooper who was smiling behind a mouth full of toast. She gave him a thumbs up.

"What about you," Leo asked, "can you hang around today?"

Mike shrugged, "I think so. I need to call in to the office and let them know I won't be in, but other than that I don't have anything going on. I need to keep my cell on because I am expecting a call from those people I drove around yesterday."

"There's no service in the house," Addie said, hoping this wouldn't make him change his mind.

"I know. I'll just go outside once in awhile and check for messages."

"While we are talking scheduling," Leo said, deftly flipping the omelet over, "I have a doctor's appointment in town tomorrow so I'll have to drive home sometime later this afternoon. I could leave in the morning but it feels like a bit much."

Addie nodded. She knew he was thinking if he stayed the night and things were active, he might not get any sleep. "That makes sense, we wouldn't expect you to stay." We? She felt her cheeks redden and hoped that one word had slipped by unnoticed. She added, "are you going to ask them about your fatigue?" and then immediately followed that with, "none of my business, strike the last question."

"Actually," Leo said, "it's just routine. My son has convinced me it's smart at my age to get regular check ups. You ready for this Cooper?" He sliced the omelet into two pieces and slid one of those onto Cooper's upheld plate. "But I have felt unusually tired the last couple of days so I guess I'll mention it. Might as well give the doctor something to do."

"Good for your son." Addie said. "It's probably nothing, but why not find out for sure?"

"Would you like some omelet, Adeline?"

"You go ahead," Addie answered.

"No. I'm just having toast and coffee."

Addie looked at Mike, "want to split it with me?"

Mike and Addie divided the rest of the omelet and Addie put more toast in and poured juice all round. The sun had made it up and in through the east-facing window and it illuminated the little foursome as grandly as sunlight pouring in through the stained glass of a cathedral.

36

"Let's talk about our day," Mike said, tipping down the last of his coffee.

Cooper said, "I think we need to start where we left off and explore the rest of what's upstairs."

"Mike, you've been up in the attic, right? What's up there?" Leo was filling the kettle for a second pot of coffee.

"I went up there with the latest buyers when I showed them the house. There's one of those staircases you pull down."

"Cool," Cooper interjected.

"I remember it being a pain in the ass to pull down so I'm glad you're here to help," Mike said in an aside to Cooper, then continued, "we were only up there for a couple of minutes. It was in July and it was an oven up there. I didn't notice much. One or two chairs? And maybe some other furniture. Not a lot whatever it was because my main impression of it was hot and empty."

"I wonder where our companion was?" Leo asked.

"I've told Addie this and it's the God's honest truth, I have never felt anything in this house until Addie came, and I have always completely written off the stuff I've heard over the years. And I can't kick myself too much for that because all I've ever heard is that it was the old lady who haunted the house." Cooper was nodding in agreement.

Leo returned to his unanswered question, "I wonder where our companion was?"

"We certainly could have used his air conditioning," Mike joked.

"I just have to say this," Addie said, "did we really see that young man's face in the window?"

Everyone nodded. Cooper spoke first, "who is he?"

They reviewed the little bit of history they knew. Mike drew a sketch of all the people directly connected to the house. A surprisingly small number.

Leo asked, "what about the people who owned the house between Miss Davies and the current owners? What happened to them, why did they sell?"

"The Ralston's," Mike said, jotting down their name and drawing a line from Laura Davies to them. "They bought the house from the estate in ninety-one." They were a young family. They had one kid, a little boy about three and Mrs. Ralston was pregnant with their second when they bought the house. They moved up here from somewhere in the Bay Area. He had money that he'd inherited but he was also a lawyer. He'd just left some big firm in San Francisco. I think the idea was that they were going to remodel the house and open a Bed and Breakfast. Same idea the current owners have. Mrs. Ralston, Kit was her name, was an interior designer."

"So what happened?"

"I'm not exactly sure. I heard all this secondhand. I started handling the house when the Ralston's sold it to the next guy. But I do know that she had a problem pregnancy and they never had a chance to get started on the house. The baby, another boy I think, was born with serious problems that required all kinds of surgery. They ended up moving to Arizona, which is where her parents lived. The feeling I got was that they were never able to settle down here and after the baby was born with all the problems it just seemed like the wrong place for them, like they never got off on the right foot."

"Considering what we've witnessed here, it certainly doesn't seem like a place to have a calm, healthy pregnancy." Addie said, inwardly recoiling at the notion.

"No," Mike agreed. "I am rethinking every part of the sequence of owners in light of what we know now.

Leo added, "and small children and babies on the way could be especially upsetting."

"Why do you say that, Leo?" Addie didn't necessarily disagree, but wanted to hear his thoughts.

"Not exactly sure. I guess it seems like a happy little family is a very private, very exclusive club." She nodded and picked up from there, "and someone on the outside of that system, an unhappy someone, might feel jealous and angry. Jesus, he could have bedeviled them no end."

"Who bought the house next, Dad?"

"That was Jake Knight. I was the agent on that deal and, like I said, that's when I got involved in the house." Mike jotted this name down and drew another connecting line.

"The Ralston's had already moved to Arizona, the house was empty and we dealt with each other long distance. This guy Jake was a character. He hardly looked at the house, paid with cash. When I showed it to him, it was the first time I'd been in there since mowing old Miss Davies' lawn as a teenager." Mike put his hand over the top of his cup when Leo went to pour more coffee, "no thanks."

"Tell us about that guy," Cooper said impatiently.

"He seemed like a total bullshitter to me. He told me all these ideas he had for the house. He wanted to make some kind of resort here. Wanted to dig a pond and stock it with trout. The house seems to have that effect on people. Anyway, I was stunned when he made an offer and then paid with cash."

"Where did he come from?" Leo asked, "was he a local?"

"Not exactly but not too far away. He lived in Woodside. He owned a company that owned and leased out heavy equipment. Anyway, not long after he bought the house he rented it out to a group that turned out to be some kind of religious cult. They were all real clean-cut and polite. There were about ten of them sharing the house. They were all in their twenties and early thirties. The guys always had on white shirts and ties and the girls looked sort of old fashioned. The general consensus in town was that they were creepy and couldn't be trusted.

They never really did anything that I know of. I met them on and off in town and they were friendly but I never had the feeling they saw me. There was something robotic about their courtesy, you know? They were just kind of off somehow." Mike held his palm face down and canted it to the right.

"Anyway, not too long after they moved in, this guy Knight petitioned to have the zoning changed so he could create a center for this group. He wanted to build extra dormitories and a meeting hall. The town felt kind of hoodwinked by the guy and people raised a big stink. People were mad at me. They thought I knowingly turned over the property to some religious nut who wanted to take over our fair town." Mike shook his head, remembering. "It was awful for awhile. Anyway, the mayor and the council were against the zoning request and it died, thankfully."

"When did he sell?" Addie envisioned the Ralston's and then Jake Knight and the clean-cut cult. She felt sorry for the house, as if it were a friend who kept falling on hard times.

"That group was here for several years after the zoning change was denied. They got pretty frosty after that. Went out of their way to not shop in Sutton Bay, that kind of thing. Knight ended up being forced to sell because he was indicted for tax fraud and needed to raise money for his legal bills. There was a lot about it in the local press.

"I remember that," Cooper said, "we used to call them the space cadets when we'd see them in town. They never did anything, they were just super nerdy and weird."

"I remember that too. Apparently they thought the house was this ideal place to have a center. And when I say ideal, I mean, you know, *God* told them that. It always seemed so strange that this hard-nosed heavy equipment guy, Knight, was mixed up with them. He always seemed like someone on the take."

Leo commented dryly, "apparently Uncle Sam agreed with you." Mike nodded and Leo continued, "do you think the reason this group thought Pen House was so ideal is because they were able to incorporate the strange goings-on here as proof of their beliefs?"

Mike shrugged. "Honestly, I never heard about anything strange, except the group itself, and they kept to themselves completely. They didn't talk to anyone in town, especially after the town turned against them with the zoning thing."

Addie thought she detected a defensive tone and she jumped in to save him. "You are a fountain of information this morning, Mike. I realize I didn't know much about the house at all until this morning." Mike grinned his thanks at her and she grinned back.

Cooper, catching the flirtatious exchange between his father and this attractive younger woman, intervened to get things back on track.

"Ok, so they moved out and then the current owners bought it. When was that?"

"That was just over a year ago. This is a married couple, no kids that I know of. Their name is Jiao. They're Chinese. Real nice people, don't believe in aliens or anything." Mike smirked. "They also have plans to remodel and have a bed and breakfast. They live in Vancouver and Hong Kong. I've never figured out why they want to do this thing here or if they even plan to live here or turn it over to someone to manage."

There was a little pause in the conversation. Everyone seemed to be listening to the house. The air was warm with the heat of the radiators and the sun, which was high enough now to be hitting the upper half of the windows. The house was quiet and Addie had a powerful conviction that they were being listened to. When she shared that feeling with the three men around the table they nodded in unison.

"I think that's more likely than not," Leo agreed. "In a very real way we are recounting a piece of his history. Everyone likes to hear their story being told."

"I wonder what his impression was of all those people coming through here?" Cooper asked.

Addie looked around the room, "in a way it feels as if the house has been essentially untouched by any of these people. They are transients. Strangers passing through and leaving the house unmarked."

Mike reflexively followed her gaze around the room as if to catch sight of what she was seeing. "I've definitely had that feeling too. Even after that group was here for so long, nothing ever seemed different. It's like the house is immune to change."

"Where do we fit in?" Cooper asked.

37

"That's a great question." Leo pushed his chair back and stood up. Buck, curled up on a sunny patch on the floor, let out a startled bark at the scrape of the chair. "I think we should make a move upstairs and continue the conversation as we go."

"I realize as we've been talking, that I've felt like I needed to almost whisper, for fear I will say something to rouse this guy." Addie pointed up toward the ceiling. They were all standing, stretching a little. Buck, too, stood, stretched and then wagged his tail with the anticipation of whatever was next.

"We should put on something warm," Mike said. Everyone nodded and headed in the direction of their respective rooms, Mike and Cooper through the back hall and into the living room, Leo and Addie through the kitchen and into the dining room.

"Adeline, I heard what you said about feeling like you should keep your voice down. I've also noticed myself wanting to make sure I don't piss this guy off. I'm wondering how you would approach him if he was a disturbed client and if he wasn't," Leo smiled and shrugged, disembodied?"

Addie had pulled on a thick pair of socks and was putting on a long sleeved shirt over her tee shirt before she put her hoodie back on. She took her time thinking about it and finally said, "I guess, as long as I felt sure I was safe, I would tell him what my honest sense of him was, but really take care and be gentle. I don't know yet what his problem is," Addie said, again pointing toward the ceiling, "but I would assume it's something that requires a lot of empathetic listening."

"I agree."

Cooper and Mike joined them. "Agree about what?" Mike asked.

"We were talking about Adeline's impulse, and mine too, to not do anything we perceive would anger this entity."

"And Leo asked me how I would handle it if he was client of mine. I said I don't know what his problem is, what's made him unable to leave the house, but that since he's been here for several years at least, we can assume it's a deep problem, one that he can't seem to resolve on his own. So I said I would approach him with honesty but also be gentle."

185

"No shock therapy?" Mike said, "like he gives us?" He was smiling but Addie took the question seriously.

"No. I think we should take the position of listening as closely as possible and try to find out any history that might lead us to unraveling the mystery of why this young man is stuck here. Can we contact any of the people who were here, like the Ralston's or even someone from the religious group?"

"I could probably find the Ralston's pretty easily. I don't know about any of that group. I wouldn't know where to start."

"Maybe that wouldn't matter so much," Leo said. "The Ralston's were the first people here after the old lady died. They would be the most likely to have come across something left behind. The presence of the original family was so much fresher when they moved in."

They had started up the stairs, taking the steps slowly, fascinated again by the black scrawl along the wainscoting. It looked different in daylight, both messier and less frightening. Why was that? Nighttime fear just seemed hardwired into the human brain. She supposed it was something as basic as not being able to see in the dark. Electric lighting had ostensibly done away with the problem. The reality was that powerful traces of primal fear remained.

"So, is what we are doing here trying to figure out why the ghost is unhappy and make him feel better so he can stop haunting the house?" Cooper's words lingered in the silence of the other three considering his question. This was the kind of obvious question that Addie had been feeling nervous about asking. But she had to admit there was a kind of relief to having it so plainly and innocently stated. Before anyone could answer he added, "and what does it hurt if he haunts the house? Why does he have to go?"

Mike answered reasonably, "it makes it hard for anyone to stay in the house."

"It's my guess that what keeps him here is something painful," Leo said.

They had all stopped at the top of the stairs where the senseless doodle had morphed into the beautifully rendered scarab.

"Why didn't mom stay in the house?" Cooper looked at his father with a look that Addie didn't feel she could confidently decipher. There was a little bit of accusation and there was the look of a younger child

186

allowing himself to be seen emerging from the eyes of a teenager. And there was just the simple question: Why? Why one person and not another?

Mike didn't dodge it. "You and me and Zoë and mom loved each other. She was sad, heartbroken to be leaving us, but we had a lot of time to prepare. We had time to get used to the idea that we were losing her. And she had time to prepare herself to go. It didn't make it less sad, it just made it," and here Mike paused, looking for the right word.

"It made it done." Cooper said

"That's right, it made it done. We accepted something that at first seemed impossible to all of us. We accepted it through loving each other."

Mike looked at Addie as if she might have a professional opinion. But Addie was crying and she gave him a little smile and wiped her eyes and nose with the sleeve of her sweatshirt. She and Sean had shared the love but they hadn't had any time to prepare. For five years she had viewed his death as completely unacceptable. As if her resistance would make him less dead. She had been the ghost, walking unconsciously through her days, haunting the life they used to have. She leaned against the stair rail. *Fuck it, I'm just going to cry.* Buck put his paws up on her thigh and licked her hand.

Cooper persisted, not aware of Addie's tears, intent on wanting to understand, "so mom didn't need to stay. When she died, she was finished with her life. And maybe this guy isn't done."

"Exactly," said Leo, "I think I see now what's so synchronous about the four of us being here, what brings us together." Everyone was quiet, waiting.

"We all lost someone, the one who seemed to be the one we couldn't live without. And I think we all shared what you were talking about, Mike, the clear sense that we loved this person and were loved deeply in return."

 Leo looked at all of them in turn and was met with agreement in each face.

"Between the four of us, we have a lot of experience with what it means to let go. Each of our stories comes with its unique twist. Cooper, you lost your mother when you were only ten. And Mike, you lost your wife and became a single parent of two children. Adeline, you thought you were in the middle of a normal day and Sean was just plucked out of your life like that." Leo snapped his fingers, which echoed in the emptiness of Pen House. "And I lost the woman that I grew up and grew old with." He paused and then, almost to himself, he added, "We kind of cover the gamut, from childhood to old age."

Addie felt the thrill of knowing that Leo's observation was exactly right. It seemed as if the four of them standing at the top of this staircase were having a discussion that had been booked in some cosmic calendar since the day she was born. For just a few moments it seemed like they were breathing in unison.

Leo brought them back. "What that means for this poor soul, we don't know yet. Shall we continue with our inspection?"

"Let's go back this way," Cooper said, indicating the hall to the right of the stairs. Leo and Cooper took the lead. Mike came up from behind to walk next to Addie. He put his arm around her and pulled her momentarily close to him and for a brief second she leaned her head against him.

They stood and stared at the red outline on the mirror. If anything, it looked eerier in the daylight, as if he had left this trace when he passed through the closed door. Buck sniffed along the bottom edge of the door but seemed otherwise unconcerned.

"I half expected all this stuff to be gone this morning," Addie commented.

"Why?" Cooper asked. Addie really liked this kid. In her mind she had taken to calling him 'good ol' Cooper' every time he asked one of his straightforward questions.

"Hmmm. I guess what I said wasn't literally true. What I meant was that the whole thing, the cold, the drawing on walls and mirrors, slamming doors, moving beetles, is pretty unbelievable."

"Where is the beetle, is it still on the post?" Leo asked. None of them had remembered to look. Mike walked back through the hall and down the stairs, far enough to see that the newel post was empty. "Not here," he called up.

He re-joined them and they walked into the bedroom. The bedroom was filled with indirect light, but sunny and warm-feeling nevertheless.

188

The room's walls were covered with ivory colored wallpaper that was patterned with dainty deep pink roses dappled between paler pink stripes. They looked around in a cursory way. Addie and Leo walked in and back out of the closet. Cooper looked out the windows that faced west. Mike came over and stood beside him.

"How're you doing, Coop?"

"I'm good. This place is pretty amazing." Cooper pointed out the view of the blue bay.

"Yeah, it is. It's got a little ghost problem is all." They both chuckled.

"Yeah, no big deal."

The foursome went out the north door of the bedroom and into the hall. Was it a little chillier here? Addie asked and all agreed the temperature had dropped slightly. They opened the door to the next bedroom and stepped in. The air was noticeably staler than anywhere else Addie had been in the house except, perhaps, the basement. As with the first bedroom, these walls were also wallpapered, albeit in a very different style. The light brown background with gold fleurs-de-lis running in neat, vertical rows exuded a stuffy, self important masculinity. Despite the west and north windows, the room felt dark.

"This room must be nicer in the afternoon when the sun hits it," Addie said.

"This room is gross."

"Why do you say that, Cooper?" Leo came over to where Cooper was standing by the windows.

Ignoring Leo's question, Cooper said, "looks like someone tried to start a fire."

Mike and Addie joined them at the window and all of them looked at the burn marks all along the sill.

"I've never noticed those before and I've shown this house a fair number of times."

"I think they would be easy to miss in here and I agree, this room is gloomy. I feel kind of sick in here." Leo paused to consider, "I guess they could be recent, which is pretty alarming. Do you know whose room this was originally, Mike?"

Mike shook his head slowly. "I don't know for sure but it must be the old man's. Seems like a man's room, doesn't it? This is the room the Jiao's want to recreate like a room in a hunting lodge. They must have picked up the 'manly' vibe as well."

Leo ran his finger over the bumpy surface of the charred wood. "I remember playing around with a magnifying glass, holding it so the rays of the sun went through it and eventually started to burn what I aimed it at. That's what this looks like to me."

"It does look like that," Mike said, bending over and sniffing the wood. "It certainly doesn't smell recent, I can't smell anything in fact."

Cooper bent over to smell it. "Me neither."

"Well that's a relief." Addie said, "The thought of him trying to burn the house down is pretty unpleasant."

"Look over here, there's a burn mark on the floor." Cooper had squatted down by the north windows and was staring at the tongue and groove flooring. "It looks like the letter C."

They all crowded around. Cooper continued, "Or maybe he was trying to make a circle and he had to stop before he was done."

"Initials are just the kind of thing a boy wants to do when burning wood with the aid of a magnifying glass. I speak from first hand experience." Leo turned from them and spoke out into the room, "What's your name?" He said it softly and they all waited as if an answer would float out of the air. But there was only silence. Beyond the room's quiet, they could hear birds singing, busy with the business of spring.

"Shall we keep going?" Leo asked. Everyone turned toward the door, glad to be leaving behind the sad weight that permeated the room.

In the back hall Mike pointed upwards, "that's the access to the attic. Shall we have a look around?" It was quite cold now.

"He's right here with us, isn't he?" Addie said, putting the hood of her sweatshirt up in an attempt to warm her ears.

"Here or very close," Leo answered. He took the black knit cap that Addie had loaned him out of his coat pocket and pulled it down over his ears.

"Why does he make the air around him so cold?"

"I have no idea," Mike shrugged, "you guys know why?"

Addie shook her head. Leo said, "When you're alive you radiate warmth. This cold feels like he's pulling the warmth right out of a room. The opposite of being alive."

"Maybe he's trying to get warm," Mike said, "and it ends up making other people cold, like when someone you're sleeping with hogs all the blankets." Addie and Leo both laughed. Mike smiled sheepishly, "no, seriously."

Addie apologized though there was still a little laughter left in her voice. "It actually makes great sense. He feels cold and he's trying to warm up."

Leo said, "he doesn't have a body, at least not a flesh and blood one, so if his perception is that he's cold, it would actually be a misperception. But it's kind of a moot point. If he's feeling cold then that's his reality."

"We feel the cold," Addie said, "so there is some real phenomenon going on here."

"Good point, Adeline. Maybe it is the nature of this kind of energy that it radiates cold."

"I still like my analogy that he's hogging the blankets."

"I like it too. It makes sense that his predicament is such that he keeps trying to gather warmth, as if the cold is out here somewhere," Leo waved his arms around vaguely, "without realizing he is the source of the cold."

"It's freezing just standing here, let's go up these stairs. If you give me a leg up, Dad, I'll pull them down."

Mike cupped his hands so Cooper could stand in them. Addie noticed that Buck was hanging back, sitting in the middle of the floor, staring at her. She walked back to where he was, noticing that he sat just beyond where the cold began. Addie waved her hand back and forth across the invisible line of temperature change. Buck was giving her that look that said: *I'd like us to do something different then what we're doing now.* She knelt down and scooped him up. His bobbed poodle tail thwacked her in the side.

"You can stay here if you want to." She set him back down and returned to the three men at the base of the lowered attic stairs. Their breath was thickly visible in the air.

"Where Buck is it's still reasonably warm." They all looked back at Buck, who had gotten tired of sitting and was now lying with his head on his front paws. His eyes were wide-awake, watchful. Addie realized he was whining. It was a low persistent grumbling, both complaint and warning.

"Buck doesn't approve of our going up here," Mike said as he started up the steps.

Mike went first because he knew where the lights were. Cooper and Leo went next and Addie took the rear. When Mike pushed the attic hatch open the cold streamed down and over them like a snowmelt waterfall. Buck's growling intensified and Addie shushed him in a kind voice. She got to the top and stood with the other three, looking around. She was surprised by how spacious it was.

"I don't know what I was imagining, but this place is huge." The rafters were a good four feet above the tallest of them and, except along the east and west walls where the roof sloped down, it felt cavernous to Addie. And empty. And cold.

"It's the full size of the footprint of the house." Mike had switched on the lights but there was also quite a bit of sunlight coming in through the windows. Addie was struck with a sense of unreality and recognized immediately that what was disconcerting was seeing the generous yellow pools of sun yet feeling no heat.

"It's like a meat locker up here, nothing like last time," Mike said, rubbing his hands together and blowing into them.

"There's an amazing view, look," Cooper pointed out the windows behind where the attic hatch penetrated the floor. They looked out over the trees and to the water. On the bay the whitecaps were doing a mad chaotic dance. To the east they could see the town, no more than a grouping of indistinct buildings.

Cooper and Mike had turned away from the window and started to drift toward the one place, in the southwest corner of the room, where there was a small collection of ratty furniture. Addie looked over at Leo.

"You OK Leo?"

"Yes. I think I'm fine except coming up the stairs winded me a little."

"Are you warm enough?"

"I'm fine. I promise I'll go back downstairs if I don't feel well." Once again, Addie wasn't sure she believed him.

"Let's just stand for a minute until you get your breath back," Addie suggested.

"No, it's too cold, let's get moving."

The floor was made up of thick planks that reminded Addie of the type of wood she'd seen used as flooring in old warehouses. The walls were a mix of exposed lathe and plaster and areas that were sheetrocked. Between the rafters that crisscrossed over their heads was insulation sagging with age and water damage. There were three large plastic garbage cans placed to catch leaks in the roof. Addie peered into the closest one and saw that it had just a small amount of water in the bottom. A dead housefly lay motionless on the water's surface. It was caught in a thin film of ice. Leo peered into the garbage can and they exchanged a look of wonder. After all, outside a mid-fifties spring day was in progress. The floor around the garbage can was water stained but it looked old and dry and the wood seemed essentially undamaged. They joined Mike and Cooper.

"Hey, look what's behind this furniture," Cooper said, pointing to three battered cardboard boxes. One had a faded French Market Coffee logo on it. The other two were plain cardboard. On one of them someone had printed with a shaky hand the words: *wrapping paper SAVE*. All of the boxes were held closed with brittle packing tape that had once been clear and was now a sickly yellow.

The beetle lay on its back on top of the box with the French Market Coffee logo. Addie reached down and turned it over onto its belly.

"I feel like he and I are engaged in a ritual. He leaves it on its back and I flip it back over."

It was after she said the words that they actually sounded true to her. They kept finding it in a death pose and then turning it over to mimic life. She had to admit that hers was the position that was mocking the reality.

"Let's get cracking and look through these," Leo said, taking the beetle off the box and setting it, right side up, on the seat of an old office chair tipping sadly due to a missing caster. "I dub thee Carl Gustav," he said, bringing his finger down like a sword and giving the beetle's back a feathery tap.

Addie opened up the box next to the one Leo was opening. Mike and Cooper started on the third and last box. It appeared to be filled with crinkled up newspaper. Nevertheless, Cooper and Mike carefully took each piece out one at a time, smoothed them flat and laid them in a neat stack.

"These aren't that old. Nineteen Ninety," Cooper said. He had stopped to look at a sheet of the Sunday funnies. Mike prodded him, "Let's not read the paper, Coop, it's too frigging cold up here."

"This box is filled with magazines," Leo held up a Ladies Home Journal dated from the mid-eighties. He too was going through them one at a time and making a stack on the wood floor. "So far they're all women's magazines and a few Reader's Digests. The oldest one I've found so far is nineteen eighty-one. Old but not super old, and definitely not very interesting."

Addie had been quietly going through her box which, true to its labeling, appeared to consist entirely of gift-wrapping. There were foils and tissues, spring flowers, birds, Santa Claus, snowflakes, stripes, polka dots. "I wonder who saved the wrapping from every gift they ever got?" She unfolded a gold foil sheet covered with stamped roses. "Some of these are beautiful." She carefully refolded it.

"I would say a woman," Mike said. "I can't imagine a guy doing that. Personally, when I open a present I rip the paper to shreds getting in there."

"I'll take that under advisement next time I get you a gift and not sink too much effort into the paper." Addie looked over at him with a smile and he winked at her.

"This box is history," Cooper said, lifting out the last piece of newspaper, a sports page from some long gone Wednesday in July of nineteen eighty three, "and it was a bust."

He stood up and went over to the window while Mike piled the papers back in the box. "From the dates on the this stuff, it seems like it was the old lady's. It's all dated before she moved out." His words drifted out into the cold room, his breath making a cloud. No one responded. Addie was absorbed in looking at each sheet of wrapping paper and Leo was still methodically lifting the magazines out one by one, glancing at the date on each of them. Mike stood up and joined Cooper at the window.

"You getting bored, Cooper?"

"No. I was just thinking how it doesn't make sense how cold it is. The heat's on downstairs and heat rises, right?" His father nodded. "Even the sun doesn't seem warm."

They both stared out the window at where the cars were parked. "They look weird, like alien vehicles from another life. It's hard to imagine kids being at school right now or anything normal and everyday." Mike put a protective arm around Cooper's shoulder.

Cooper continued, "we aren't alone in here, I know that. But it is so weird. I mean, right now, is he standing here listening to us talk?"

"I don't know."

Addie, eavesdropping, speculated that Mike wished he had something more definitive, a little more authoritative to tell his son. But Mike's wonderment and confusion was no less than Cooper's.

"Hey, look!" Leo's voice brought them all to one focused point of attention. He held up a leather folder, dark brown and fastened with string that wrapped in a figure eight around two battered but sturdy cardboard buttons. They all crowded around Leo excitedly. Leo got up from his knees slowly and painfully, handing the folder to Addie. "It was at the very bottom of the box. If someone was trying to hide it, they did a good job. That's the most boring collection of magazines I've ever seen."

"Let's take it downstairs and look at it where it's warm." Addie's fingers felt stiff with cold. Everyone readily agreed. She handed the folder back to Leo and started putting the wrapping paper back in the box.

"Adeline! Leave all that, let's get out of this freezing room and go look at this." Leo was smiling but he also waved his free hand at her impatiently. A gust of cold air rushed by them. *Our ghost is excited too.*

Buck stood in the exact spot where Addie had left him. He barked at the cold that had followed them like a little cloud. But he was also jubilant to see Addie and sprung up and down on his hind feet like a dancing circus dog. Addie scooped him up, told him what a good boy he was and planted a few kisses on his snout. He returned the love tenfold with a stinky bouquet of licks on her cold, red cheek.

They settled in the living room where the afternoon sun made it the warmest room in the house. Soon their invisible companion, if he stayed with them, would drive the temperature down.

There wasn't a lot in the folder but what was there was rich. There was a child's book, "A Boy's Guide To Insects." The cover was nearly detached and there was yellowing tape where inexperienced hands had done an amateur repair. There was no inscription. The book was in its second printing in nineteen oh six. On the inside of the front cover a child had sketched pictures of beetles. They were in pencil and there were nearly twenty of them marching higgledy-piggledy across the soft beige paper. They were from the hand of a young child, no more than seven or eight, and though they were childish, it was obvious that the hand was that of a promising artist.

The back inside cover had a sketch altogether different from the crowd of beetles in the front. It was a face, again childishly rendered. It was neither girl nor boy. There were no ears or hair, just an oval face with two large eyes stared intently at an imagined viewer. The mouth was open as if in the middle of a scream. They all stared at it, the cold now whirling around them. The foursome, unconsciously seeking both warmth and comfort, moved in to make a tighter circle.

Finally Addie spoke, "it's unbelievable how a few simple lines could communicate such anguish. It's as if this child feels flat like the paper, as if he's missing the dimension needed for his scream to be heard."

Carefully and wordlessly they looked through the book, aware of the chill cloud around them looking over their shoulders. Addie knew, as did the others, the artist was there with them.

She reached into the folder and pulled out what remained, a small stack of watercolors wrapped in tissue and tied loosely with a thin pink satin ribbon. Addie laid them down, five in all, in a row on the floor. These were not the work of the child. They were both meticulous and fluid. They had that sought after combination of technical mastery and freedom. There was nothing fussy or overworked. They were at once economical and complete.

"It's him," Cooper pointed unnecessarily to the picture that had already drawn them all. It portrayed a thin young man with his back to the viewer. He was looking out of the window, the glass revealing his face in a watery reflection. It was hard to tell if the eyes were sad or if the artist was merely capturing the intensity of his gaze as he tried to get it right. Addie thought both.

"It's extraordinary," Leo spoke for them all. "It's in the bedroom right above us, look, there's the wallpaper that's still up there."

"Right where we saw him last night," Mike said.

"Who is M.E.?" Cooper asked. In the lower right corner in black pen, small and precise, were the initials, M.E.

They looked at the other watercolors, three landscapes and one of the house, but none of the others were signed. Each, however, was titled with a carefree cursive using the same black pen: *Summer at Pen House; Looking North; The Hummingbird Tree*; and simply: *Pen House.* To the left of the words "Pen House" someone had written *Peony House* through which was drawn a decisive black line. To the left of that, in a messy scrawl, someone had written *House at the End*. For reasons unknown this second title had eluded the editor's pen. The edge of the paper was singed as if it had been saved from fire just before being engulfed. As if the arsonist's mind had changed at the very last minute.

"Peony House? Do you believe that, Leo?" Addie, whose voice seemed to have been snatched out of the air, wasn't sure she had even spoken out loud.

Mike, absorbed in his own discovery, laughed, startling the others who turned to stare at him. "M.E. Me!"

Leo was nodding, "yes, of course! I can't believe we didn't see it right away. The artist is just having fun with us."

Addie stared intently at the one that had originally been called *Peony House*. There was no barberry and instead of lawn there was an English style flower garden crowded with deep red roses, yellowy-orange gladiolas, purple iris, and lapis blue lupines. A vine maple and a tall dogwood sapling, each covered in delicate leaves seemed to move in a long-ago breeze. Drawing her eye most powerfully were two large flowering shrubs flanking the steps up to the front door. Addie thought the flowers looked like big poofy party dresses, ruffled and delicate, snowy white with a yellow center brightest at the very heart and then fading into the white. The deeply lobed leaves were crowded on their reddish stems. The perfect backdrop, Addie thought, for the show-stopping blooms, the weight of which had been exquisitely rendered by the artist.

Leo pointed to the white flowers, "those are tree peonies Adeline. I'm getting the distinct feeling that we are coming around full circle from the point you and I met."

Mike and Cooper looked to the other two for explanation.

Addie felt disoriented remembering her first misreading of the ad, remembering her first meeting Leo, remembering Virginia's dream about peonies. It seemed so long ago that discovering what appeared to be a continuing thread threw her. The cold circled her and she twitched against it.

Leo, who seemed to have maintained a measure of sang-froid, told them about Addie's flurry of close encounters with the flower.

Harkening back to their conversation of the day before, Mike said, "synchronicity, right?" Addie nodded. It seemed like she should be able to elaborate but she had nothing in the nature of genuine elucidation to contribute.

"Look how small the tree is." Mike pointed first to the picture titled *The Hummingbird Tree*, and then out the window at the grand tulip poplar just now coming out in new spring leaves. In the picture it was perhaps twelve feet tall and lacking the heft and authority it now possessed.

"But the house looks just the same," Cooper commented, "except in the painting it looks more," he paused, unsure of the right word, "alive."

"Yes," Addie said excitedly, wanting to move away, at least for the moment, from the conundrum of peonies, "it was a new house when these were done. Look at this one," she pointed to the one titled *Looking North*, "the trees in back are just saplings, maybe not even the ones that are there now."

The picture captured a corner of the rear of Pen House and then moved quickly to the back garden and its neat rows of young fruit trees and on to the bay. Addie thought the water looked as though it had been painted that very morning and it gave her a fleeting sense of comfort.

"Look here at the window," Mike indicated the picture titled *Pen House*. In the upstairs window was painted an almost imperceptible figure of a yellow-haired woman. Her dress, the most delicate blue and yellow, looked like a pattern on an old china saucer. She was just visible behind gauzy white curtains. She had her hand up, waving to the artist. It was utterly charming, all the more so because they had almost missed it.

It was Addie who first commented that the room had warmed again. The afternoon sun was covering the floor in honey-colored rectangles that mimicked the shape of the windows through which the light passed. The rays of sun were crowded with dust motes moving in an aimless dance. Buck, who had been stuck like glue to Addie, now felt comfortable enough to have moved away from her lap to a sunny spot on the floor and was lying on his side, asleep. No sooner had she mentioned the return of the warmth, they heard the slow creak of footsteps climbing the stairs. To her ears they sounded heavy, as if the climber could barely lift one foot in front of the other. They sat still, listening intensely, barely breathing. The footsteps continued down the hallway overhead at the same funereal pace. They heard the bedroom door open and close with a quiet click. And then, with an anguish so deep it felt like fingers digging into their bone marrow, the ghost let out one long animal howl.

38

Addie, Mike and Cooper saw Leo off, the three of them waving until his car disappeared around the bend of the driveway. It was late afternoon and Leo had suddenly needed to hustle to be in time for the ferry back to town. Addie and he had promised to connect after his appointment with the doctor the next afternoon. The three of them stood quietly until they heard the sound of Leo's wheels crunching onto the gravel of the chip-sealed road. Addie was at loose ends. She didn't want to stay the night in Pen House, alone. Wouldn't stay alone. Mike and Cooper couldn't stay. Cooper had school in the morning and Mike had insisted he not miss any more days. Mike had appointments, a life that needed tending to.

Cooper wandered away from them and started throwing a stick for Buck who was enjoying it tremendously, barking at Cooper to throw it again and again. Mike moved closer and put an arm around her.

"What now?" he said simply. She looked up at him. When exactly had they crossed over from property manager and tenant to this feeling of easy friendship tinged with more than a little excitement? She shrugged inwardly and leaned into him, willing herself to stop analyzing. If they had ever had such a formal relationship it had been shaken early and permanently by the events of the last few days. "I have no idea. I guess I need to pack up a bag for me and Buck and go get a room at that place in town." They were quiet for a moment then he said, "we're not finished here are we?"

"Nope." They stopped talking and stood happily watching Cooper and Buck whose shadows were now long and slanted in the golden light.

"You could stay at my house. We have plenty of room. I know Cooper wouldn't mind, he thinks your great." He was stroking her hair and when his fingers touched her neck she shivered.

"I think he's great, too. He's a wonderful kid. I feel like we've been through a war together. A quiet little war in Pen House." Mike nodded but returned to his original question, "So, you want to come stay with us?" Addie felt certain she was going to say yes but what came out was, "I don't think so. I don't think I'd better. Buck and I are going to go stay in town again." She was both disappointed and relieved by her own answer. Mike, still lazily running his hand through her hair simply said, "Ok."

Cooper and Buck had stopped playing fetch and were now walking toward them. Buck's tongue was hanging out of his mouth in a pant and she could see his sides heaving slightly. Mike gave the back of her neck a light squeeze, dropped his hand to his side and whispered, "I guess we better not kiss in front of the kids." Addie realized just how intensely she was looking forward to that kiss.

39

She met Mike for a late breakfast the next morning, by which time he had already seen Cooper off to school and been in his office for over an hour trying to catch up with his phone calls and email. Addie, on the other hand, still felt the sleep in her eyes. When she'd climbed into bed the night before she'd been reasonably certain the bed was too firm and that she was doomed to a night of tossing and turning. By ten, however, she was asleep and didn't wake up for eleven hours. Buck, too, had passed out without stirring and would have gone on sleeping had she not gotten up. She was mildly amazed that she'd slept through the street noise and the housekeeping staff, laughing and talking as they pushed their carts from room to room. After taking Buck out, she took her time getting ready. She luxuriated in a long hot shower, which she finally cut short when she realized she was thinking about Mike and his hand in her hair and on her neck. She suffered through the bad motel coffee, and managed to make a small and not very promising start on the Friday New York Times crossword. She even ironed a shirt.

She looked out the window at the day, sunny now but not at all a sure thing that it would stay that way. The clouds to the west looked like they could easily gather up into trouble. She put her rain shell over her arm and told Buck to stay. He looked at her forlornly and then, seeing she really meant it, hopped on the bed and curled up on the pillow where her head had recently been.

She saw Mike walking quickly down the street just as she was getting to the café door. An excited feeling rushed through her, swirled around in her stomach, and made her hands and feet tingle and blood rush to her cheeks. *Jesus wept*, she thought, both mortified and delighted. She saw him first, his face serious though not unhappy. He saw her and broke into a grin.

"Hey! How'd you sleep?"

"Unbelievably," She answered. They hugged a little awkwardly, both their arms going up and bumping. She could feel her face redden.

"Oops," he said, then pulled her close and they kissed. There. Just like that. Addie marveled at how simple it was. But it felt like the simplicity of the ribbon cutting that heralds the launch of a ship. She knew in that moment that she had genuinely been assuming, since Sean's death, that she would never kiss a man again. Never want to. But here she was in

Mike's arms feeling her lips where his had just been and already looking forward to the next time.

They lingered over coffee, stretching out their time together before ordering. They retold each other the story of Pen House up to where things now stood. They talked about Cooper, where he went to school, where he was thinking about going to college. He told her about his daughter, her plans to become a vet and work with farm animals. Addie told Mike more about what being a therapist had been like. She told him how she'd felt increasingly sure she never wanted to go back to it. He asked why. She told him that for the longest time she felt unqualified, fraudulent even. Now she recognized a new development; at long last a dawning sense of her own wisdom was leading her elsewhere. By the time the food came, Addie was famished.

"So, what's your plan for the day?" he asked.

"I'm going to go to the library here in town and see if I can find anything about the house, about the Davies'. I know I can't spend the night alone there. Not yet. And I can't let go of the notion that somehow I'm going to help the house heal. I just don't know what that means."

"Sounds like therapy to me," he teased gently.

"You know, I've thought about that and Leo and I have talked about it. I know you were kidding but I think there's some truth to it. Something happened to this guy, this amazing painter, as I now think of him. Anyway, something has kept him stuck for a long time and I feel this great unhappiness around him, in the house. Jesus, that howl he let out yesterday was heartbreaking."

"Cooper had a nightmare about it last night. He actually woke me up in the night to tell me about it. He hasn't done that since before his mom died. When he was really little he used to climb in bed with us pretty regularly because he was scared from a dream. I thought after his mom died he'd be with me every night but oddly that seemed to be the end of the nightmares."

Addie looked into Mike's face, checking to see how this piece of intimacy was making him feel. He smiled, his expression clear and frank. *He's so much farther down the road than I am. It isn't such a revelation for him that life goes on. Kids must force that on you. That, and time.*

"What did he dream?"

"You know that pencil sketch in the back of the bug book?"

"The silent scream, you mean?"

He laughed and shuddered at the same time. She knew the feeling.

"He dreamt he was home, actually it was in the last house we lived in. Anyway, he was looking at it, at the book, and that scream came out of the picture. I asked him what he meant and he said he couldn't really explain it any better, it just came to life off the page. He ran to find his mom even though he says he knew she was dead. And then he ran around the house looking for me, thinking I was in the garage working on the lawn mower." Mike paused, smiling at his prosaic dream role. "Then he remembered we had moved and it seemed like this impossible problem. He woke up trying to figure out how to get to the new house."

Addie felt the familiar urge to analyze and for the second time in less than twenty-four hours she resisted it. Instead she allowed herself to sit quietly and feel the emotion of the dream.

"What's wrong?" Mike reached over with his napkin and caught a tear rolling down her cheek.

"Nothing at all, actually," she said, smiling, wiping her face. "I'm so used to hearing people's dreams and going right to work with them to figure them out. I just resisted that urge and next thing I knew, I was crying."

Mike was quiet but expectant. Addie looked around inside her thoughts much like looking for misplaced keys. "I don't know what the dream is to Cooper," she said slowly, discovering her feelings along the way, "only the dreamer knows that. But the dream touched me. I feel that, emotionally, I relate to looking for *the new house*. And I've looked for Sean everywhere, even though I know he's dead." She stopped herself.

"Are you touched by me being in the garage working on the lawn mower?" *Damn. I blurt out a gooey emotional confession, and his response is to flirt with me shamelessly.* She decided to play it straight.

"Yes, Mr. Smart Ass, as a matter of fact, I am. Cooper knows you're there somewhere, fixing what's broken. He knows he can count on you." This last she said in a slightly exaggerated tone as if explaining something to a child. She had just gotten ready to trade some friendly barbs with him when he turned the table on her again.

"I really like you, Addie." He stood up, came over to her side of the booth and scooted in next to her. "Let's kiss again soon," he whispered.

Before parting he gave her directions to the library and they agreed to meet later for a drink and dinner.

Addie went back to the motel, got Buck and took him for a walk. It was short and she felt guilty leaving him behind again to go to the library. Buck milked it, giving her his most baleful expression from where he sat atop two snow-white motel pillows.

40

The library was surprisingly big for the size of the town. It was also quite new. Addie spent time looking at the computer, doing various searches. She thought wryly that if she'd been looking for information about the history of logging in Cedar County she would have had it made. Finally she went to the clerk at the check out desk who directed her to the head librarian. She and the children's librarian were standing in front of a bulletin board in the children's section. They were in the process of taking down a display of books about Ireland. There was a messy stack of large metallic green shamrocks on the floor.

"I'm looking for information about Pen House. It was designed by Edward Thomas and owned by the Davies family until the nineteen eighties?"

"Have you looked in the local history section yet?"

"I have but I didn't find anything except passing mention of the family. Nothing about the house or architect."

"We have a vertical file that's jammed with articles about the town. Have you looked there?"

"No, I haven't. It sounds intriguing if you'd just point me in the right direction."

The file was indeed full and the filing was only loosely correct. There was a folder marked history, which Addie carefully went through and found nothing. She checked the folders behind and in front of it and found enough items wildly out of order that it warranted a thorough search beginning with A. She dragged a chair over, pulled out "Apple Harvest" and got to work.

It was a slog. There had been a lot of parades. Editorials about the spotted owl debate were numerous and, on a quick glance, seemed to favor the logging companies about two to one. There was a graduate of the local high school who had become a Rhodes scholar. There had been a bar fight that had ended in a shooting death. The number of articles revolving around the doings in local churches made her head hurt. Finally she found something promising in a folder marked "Library/Remodel". It was a short article from the Sutton Bay Courier dated October first, nineteen ninety-one.

Laura Davies Leaves Gift To Library

The estate of Miss Laura Davies, lifelong resident of Sutton Bay and daughter of William Davies, has bequeathed ten thousand dollars to the Sutton Bay Public Library to be used toward the upcoming remodel and expansion of the library.

Miss Davies passed away in September of 1990. Marian Padilla, chairman of "Citizens for a New Library", told the Courier, "we are beyond delighted by Miss Davies' generosity. She was always a great friend of the library."

In addition, Miss Davies also left the library what she termed in her will a "brief and idiosyncratic history of Sutton Bay. Head Librarian, Ruth Jamesson, said she hasn't had the opportunity to read it yet and that it will need to be professionally bound before the public can view it in its eventual home in the library's reference section.

The remainder and bulk of her estate went to The Bentham School of Fine Art in Seattle.

Addie took the article to the head librarian who was back at her desk.

"Would it be possible to see this history written by Laura Davies?" She could barely contain her excitement.

The librarian looked at the article and shook her head, "I have no idea where this is. I've never seen it. Ruth Jamesson retired several years ago and I came to work here after the remodel." Addie glanced at the nameplate on the librarian's book and paper-strewn desk. It read: Janine Forstead. "Let me ask one of the clerks, they've both been here for ages." She walked away, article in hand.

Addie watched her briefly speak to someone at the front desk and then disappear into a back room. She was gone for about five minutes every minute of which Addie resisted the urge to dig out her phone and call Leo and Mike.

Ms. Forstead came back with an encouraging smile on her face. "Ms. Nealy remembers it. It's in the basement. Apparently it was put away for safekeeping before the demolition and it's been sitting there for what I'm embarrassed to admit is quite a long time. When things need repair it sometimes takes awhile to get around to it."

"Did Ms. Nealy say she's read it?"

"No. Well actually I didn't ask her. If you have time, I'll have Ms. Nealy go down and get it out for you." Addie assured her she did.

The wait seemed endless. To kill time, Addie went over to the computer and searched, *where does the name peony come from*? She impatiently threaded her way through the gardening sites, baby name sites, and ads for commercial nurseries. The story was small but interesting.

It seemed Asclepius, the Greek god of medicine and healing, had the so-named Paeon as his student. Paeon worked as a physician to the gods. He possessed a root of great power that could cure many ailments. When Asclepius realized that his student was in possession of something more potent than he had he flew into a rage and threatened to kill Paeon. At this point Zeus himself intervened, saving Paeon's life by transforming him into a peony flower. Jealousy, rage, revenge, intervention, transformation. Addie knew a metaphor-loaded story when she saw one. But she barely had time to begin considering it's possible meaning for Pen House when she saw Ms. Nealy, who didn't appear to be a day under eighty, coming her way, holding a book out toward Addie's eagerly outstretched hands.

The book, which was inside a black cloth-covered binder, was typed on old style eight and a half by eleven onionskin typing paper. Each of the pages, of which there were one hundred and twenty seven, including the title page and the table of contents, had been meticulously punched with a three-hole punch. Each of those holes had been protected from tearing by a white lick and stick reinforcement. Centered on the front cover was a white sticky label with a red border on which the book's title was typed: *The People and Places of Sutton Bay and Cedar County. By Laura Davies.* After providing her with a thin pair of white gloves and asking her to turn the pages with the utmost care, Ms. Nealy left Addie alone to read.

She looked first at the table of contents. Nothing jumped out at her so she started to read. After about twenty intensely disappointing pages she stopped reading and started skimming. The most impressive part of the book was turning out to be the perfection of Laura's typing and the seeming total absence of either spelling or grammar errors. She had no doubt that the book, once available to locals, would be helpful in sorting out chronologies as well as disabusing people of some long held beliefs. Who knew, for instance, that Joseph Branson actually settled in Cedar County nearly five years *before* Isaac Smith , according him the *rightful* claim of founding father? And so on.

So Addie skimmed the pages looking for key words; *Davies, Thomas, Pen House*, and even, improbable as she knew it to be, *ghost*. She did come upon a brief outline of the architect, Edward Thomas. It included his birth and death dates and a description of his achievements. In this context Pen House was included merely as an item on that list. There was no mention that Edward Thomas was her uncle, her mother's brother, and certainly no mention that there had been some kind of tension between her father and Mr. Thomas. It was as if Laura had gone to great pains to erase any hint of the personal. The only bit Addie found about Laura's father, William Davies, was equally flat and disappointing: He was an early resident of Cedar County and one of the founders of the Sutton Bay Savings and Loan, where he was the manager until he retired in nineteen twenty-one.

Although her eyes were beginning to feel heavy and she was wishing they had coffee shops in libraries, Addie trudged on, determined to view every page. When she turned over page eighty-seven and the words at the top of page eighty-eight began, 'To whom it may concern;' She felt momentarily lost. She looked down for the page number and there was none. She flipped ahead until she found page eighty-eight and saw that it picked up right where eighty-seven had left off, talking about a lawsuit brought by the Tate family against the Wilson/Patterson Lumber Company, something about an easement. She returned to the phantom pages and read, then re-read the extraordinary passage.

Feeling like a criminal, she looked around to assure herself no one was watching then carefully removed the pages of interest and copied them at the machine in the hall by the bathrooms. She then just as carefully returned the originals to where she had found them between pages eighty-seven and eighty-eight.

Now barely able to concentrate, she finished scanning the book. There was nothing else. But this was more than enough. The pages now folded in her bag seemed less like fifteen-cent copies and more like a sack of diamonds or a rare treasure map.

She called Leo first but it went immediately to the leave-a-message recording. She looked at the time and realized he must be at his appointment. "Call me as soon as you get this," was the extent of her message.

She then called Mike who picked up on the second ring, "hey, how's it going?" She filled him in, feeling almost giddy and even a little disoriented with excitement. They reaffirmed their meeting for dinner and hung up. Addie went and sprung Buck from the motel room and took him on another walk, this one long enough to make them both happily fatigued.

Leo finally called back just before seven as she was about to go out the door to meet Mike. By the time he called, Addie had become concerned that his not calling presaged bad news from his doctor. Leo's voice sounded completely normal, "No, nothing's wrong I just don't check this damn thing for messages. It never occurs to me. The only reason I got your message was because it tooted at me like a boson's whistle."

"How did it go at the doctor?"

"My blood pressure is a little high. She wrote me a prescription for that. I'm supposed to schedule a colonoscopy, blah, blah, blah. Everything was ok, no major alarms. But truthfully, I think the house temporarily wore me out...sorry to cause a scare. Not to change the subject, but," he laughed and Addie knew that was exactly what he wanted to do, "what's going on with you? You sounded excited or upset in your message, I couldn't tell."

Hearing that everything had essentially gone fine at his appointment, Addie felt a surge of relief. She realized then how worried she had been. Perhaps the house had been nurturing worst-case scenarios in her? Had she been seeing in Leo's seeming frailty a mirror image of her own anxieties? Perhaps the house had simply sapped him of his normal energy. In any case, the excitement over the new found document came back and rolled over her, swamping her introspection. It was the same rush of excitement she had been feeling in waves all afternoon. She told him about the letter. Leo was quiet for a moment and then simply said, "Wow."

"Yeah, you said it. Hey, I need to leave to meet Mike for dinner. Are you coming back tomorrow?"

"Are you kidding? I was just thinking about getting in the car right now."

Addie laughed. "I know what you mean."

"I can get the noon ferry and meet you at the house around two."

"Let's meet in town, in Sutton Bay. I know already that Mike has commitments until five or so. And I think it's important that Cooper be invited to come hear it as well. I want us to go there together." The letter, on Laura's request to the reader, whoever he or she might someday be, needed to be read aloud, in Pen House, to its intended recipient. Addie wanted them all to be there with her when she followed this directive.

Addie met Mike at an Italian restaurant in the center of town. He arrived first and had already gotten them a table and ordered a bottle of wine. He had selected a table at the back, far away from the restaurant's bustle. The overhead lights barely reached where he sat and as she approached him his face was shifting and unreadable in the light of the votive candle that flickered in its glass holder. He stood up to greet her, kissed her lightly on the nose, which made her laugh.

"Pretty dark back here," she said, knowing immediately that her jocular tone was a reflexive attempt to downplay her sudden shyness.

"I believe you mean romantic," he said, pretending offense. She let that go without remark, both charged and a little spooked by the comment.

He poured them each a glass of wine. "Let's make a toast. No, let's make two."

"Okay, shoot."

He surprised her by saying, "you go first."

She thought and then spoke, "to Pen House and its sad ghosts. May they finally find the peace they never had, in life or death." They clinked glasses lightly and drank. The sound of the other diner's inarticulate chatter was distant and there was a sense that they were profoundly alone, the sound of those other voices not unlike crickets on a still summer's night.

"Now you." She was almost whispering.

"To Addie. For her heart." They clinked again, drank again.

"Okay, may I see the letter?"

Later, when they were trying to say goodnight, Mike asked again if she wanted to stay with him. Again she declined. He walked her to her car and as they embraced he said, "I'm not going anywhere. There's no hurry."

She leaned up into him and initiated a kiss as long and deep as any kiss she could remember. They lingered at her car door, each of them having trouble admitting the evening was ending. Finally she said, "I need to take Buck out." Mike laughed, kissed her on the nose and said goodnight.

41

Addie and Buck led the way down the driveway to Pen House. Leo followed in his car and Mike and Cooper were behind him. The day had been blustery like the day before. There were blossoms littering the ground and the firs swayed like eccentric conductors leading a wild and dark symphony orchestra. The bay was whipped up and frothy and a seemingly endless stream of crows flew into the gusting wind on the way to their rookery. One or two occasionally let themselves be carried upward and away from the inexorable black swarm. There was still daylight but the falling sun was behind thick clouds and the light that remained seemed more like evening, less like late afternoon.

The house looked dark and sad. Addie couldn't remember if they had left any lights on. There were none on now. It didn't seem to matter. The letter had wiped out the urgency she had felt to note every odd incidence. In its place was a different urgency: A need to fulfill the wishes of the letter's author. The retreating daylight was such that they couldn't see into the windows but could only see distorted images of themselves in the old glass. Buck ran over to the birdbath and peed on it.

"Can you all give me a hand?" Leo pointed to his backseat, which was crowded with bags of groceries.

"What are we making?" Addie realized she was looking forward to getting inside, turning on lights, cranking up the heat and getting dinner going.

Leo ticked off the menu on his fingertips. "My quickie version of Chicken Biryani, naan, store bought I'm afraid, salad and wine. And I made a loaf of cranberry tea bread for later."

Addie hugged him, "I feel nervous about reading the letter out loud. I don't know what to expect."

"Let's just proceed as kindly and calmly as we possibly can."

Loaded up with groceries and a pile of extra blankets that Mike and Cooper had brought, they approached the front door. They heard music coming from inside.

"Cinderella Suite?" Leo asked. Addie nodded. It wasn't particularly loud. The door wasn't even latched and Addie simply bumped it open with her hip. She turned back to her companions, "he's been waiting for us to come home."

The entryway was bitingly cold. The beetle lay on its back atop its customary newel post perch. The light in the house was fluid, shifting with the fast-moving clouds, an occasional sunbeam breaking through the gradations of gloom.

Cooper dumped the blankets on the living room floor and followed the other three into the kitchen. On the way Addie pointed to the twenty or so CDs that had been taken out of their jewel cases and strewn carelessly on the top of the sideboard. Had he really been listening to Ry Cooder? West Side Story? Prince? Beethoven? The Prokofiev was now uncomfortably loud in the room. Addie, unwilling to listen to it at all, turned it off. They continued into the kitchen, firmly closing the door that separated it from the dining room behind them. Buck was quiet, his tail was down and he stuck close by Addie.

They switched lights on as they went. Addie turned the thermostat up to seventy-five. The cold followed them into the kitchen.

"It's weird to be back," Cooper said, echoing a thought Addie was reasonably certain they all felt. "In a way it feels like a million years ago and in a way like we never left."

"The house definitely has a funny way of dealing with time," Leo said.

"I hope it warms up soon," Addie said, hopping from one foot to the other as she unpacked the food. Suddenly a new CD started. They all stood still, Addie at the counter, Cooper leaning against the old wood-burning stove, Mike next to him uncorking a bottle of wine, Leo at the sink. Like a backwards game of musical chairs, the sound of the music had been a command for them all to freeze. His choice surprised and amused Addie; the soundtrack to Monsoon Wedding. She had paid fifty cents for it at a yard sale and fallen in love with it. Later she rented the movie on the strength of it. She'd loved that too. She found it weird and amazing that he had selected something that seemed targeted to compliment the dinner Leo was making. She inwardly shook her head. Somehow he was both lost in the past and very much here now and one of their group.

Everyone seemed to have quickly shaken it off and Leo, who along with Mike and Cooper seemed not to have registered the simpatico nature of the change in the music, said, "Cooper, would you grab the coat I left on the passenger seat of my car? It's unlocked." Cooper nodded and Mike said he'd go along with him. Addie wouldn't want to let her kid out of sight here either. The cold stayed behind with Addie and Leo.

"So, Adeline, is something up with you and Mike?" Leo's voice was casual but when Addie looked over to where he stood, cutting chicken into hefty cubes, she could see the hint of a smile on his face. She felt her face redden. Well, at least it provided a little bit of warmth.

"I like him but it freaks me out too." Ok, not her most eloquent moment. She was about to give him a more erudite explanation but he was quicker, "I imagine it is freaky. Mike is the first man you've been interested in since Sean, yes?"

Addie felt the cold come up close to her. It was as if he was standing shoulder to shoulder with her, not wanting to miss a word. She reached her hand out to the side where he seemed to stand and waved it lightly. "Are you listening?"

"Of course I'm listening, the suspense is killing me." Leo now had his back to her and was grinding spices with a little mortar and pestle he had brought along with him. The smell of the spices wafted over to Addie's nose. The sweet fragrance, which so powerfully evoked heat and light, was completely at odds with the cold room and the petulant sky fading quickly to black outside the window.

"I was talking to Charles," she said almost whispering. "He's standing right next to me, I'm pretty sure." She paused, bringing back to mind what Leo's question had been, "yes, Mike is the first. And I never thought there would be anyone again. I didn't want it. It just seemed exhausting and pointless to even think about it. No one could replace Sean. I didn't want them to. In a way the scariest thing is the thought that if I follow my attraction to Mike I'll lose Sean forever." The cold seemed to be stroking her arm, the back of her neck. She felt the hairs in both places standing up and yet she didn't feel afraid exactly. It wasn't a threatening move, it was more like he was trying to hear her, as if this was the bit he really needed to understand. So she continued, not so much now for Leo, but for Charles. "And it doesn't make sense because Sean is lost to me, he died. Five years ago. In a motorcycle accident." Leo had turned and was watching her intently. He recognized that she was speaking both to him and beyond him.

"But Adeline, don't you also see that Sean is never lost to you? Relationships don't cancel each other out. Your budding relationship with Mike is a different relationship. It doesn't compete with anything you and Sean shared." Addie nodded. That was starting to become more in focus for her though her thoughts still often told her she was somehow cheating on Sean.

Mike and Cooper came back in to the kitchen. Leo thanked them as he put on the camel hair coat. "Ahh. Much better. Now all I need are two pairs of wool socks and a space blanket."

"This is definitely the cold room," Mike said. "The rest of the house is toasty compared to in here."

"Charles is in here with us and I think he'll probably remain with us," Leo said, nodding toward Addie.

"Can I help?" Cooper asked. Leo instructed him in putting some oil in the large cast iron skillet and turning the heat up about halfway. "When you're done, why don't you set the table?"

Mike walked over to where Addie had reached down wine glasses and was pouring them each a drink.

"Five glasses?"

"One for Charles," she answered. "Maybe he can't drink it but he can be included in spirit."

"So to speak." Mike smiled.

Five glasses poured, Addie carried them over to the table.

"I'd like to propose a toast."

Cooper, Mike and Leo came to stand around the table, each taking up a glass of the rich cherry-colored pinot noir. The fifth glass sat on the table next to a tall candle Addie had lighted. The mossy color of the wax glowed. The sound and smell of sautéing onion, garlic, and spices seemed to push back against the cold. Buck whined at Addie's leg and she scooped him up with her free hand.

"I guess it's not so much a toast as a prayer," Addie started thoughtfully.

"To our most unusual companion here in Pen House, who has been waylaid from finding his joy. My prayer is that we can help him find the road he most longs to travel."

They tapped their wine glasses and the pure ringing of the crystal seemed unnaturally long in it's sustain. Addie added, "these were a wedding gift to Sean and me." She lifted her glass again, "to Sean. I hope you've found your joy."

"To mom," Cooper added.

"To Alicia," Mike said. Had Mike ever told her his wife's name? She didn't think so. *Alicia. What a lovely name.*

They all looked to Leo, who nodded, lifted his glass and whispered, "to Teddy."

"And last but not least, to Laura." They touched glasses one more time and then watched, spellbound, as the glass on the table, moving in slow motion, came to rest on its side and spilled its wine like thin blood onto the flagstone floor.

42

Dinner was done. The CD's final track, a spacious and dreamlike amalgam of a couple of the film's most thematic songs, came to an end as the dishes were being piled in the sink and the counters and stovetop wiped down.

The foursome moved into the living room by way of the back hall. Addie carried the candle and a wad of napkins with her, Leo a bottle of scotch, Cooper four jam jar glasses and Mike carried a plate of sliced cranberry tea bread. They arranged themselves in a tight circle, creating seating out of Mike and Cooper's bedding. The cold whirled around them. It felt as if it was running in circles around the knot of human warmth they had created. The energy was frantic. Addie consciously tried to not get caught up in fear, to slow her heart, which wanted to pound.

The wind had picked up and the gusting had been replaced with a constant low roar. A branch of the tulip poplar occasionally bent over far enough to make a scratching noise as it rubbed the window. Buck tried to get comfortable on a blanket, circling round and round, but couldn't and showed his anxiety by growling almost continuously.

"Do you have the letter?" Cooper asked. He was the only one of the four who hadn't yet read it.

"I do." Addie reached in and pulled the neatly folded sheets out of the front pocket of her sweatshirt. "Should I light the candle?"

"The overhead lights are plenty bright," Cooper said.

He sounded apprehensive and Mike stepped in to soothe him, "I don't think Addie was suggesting we turn them off. But listen to that wind. It's possible we could lose power and it would be nice to have the candle in that case."

"I also think the candle gives off at least a perception of warmth that the overheads don't provide. Is this the only one?" Leo looked over at Addie who was shaking her head and rising at the same time. "I have plenty. I'll go grab them." When Mike started to get up to accompany her she added, "No, that's ok, I'm fine to run into the next room. Anyway, I want Buck to go back and stay on the bed. His growling is adding to the tension and I think he'll be happier anyway."

The cold ran alongside her to the dining room. She retrieved a box of votives and some extra safety matches from inside the sideboard and told Buck to stay where he was, sitting on her pillow. The cold ran down her arms and out to her fingertips. It seemed to be clinging to her. Why? *Because you have the letter. Because your pain is the freshest.* She forced herself to breathe deeply, slowly, and assure herself she was fine. On the way back to the living room she paused at the newel post. It seemed like the beetle should be with them in the other room. She held out one hand so she could push the beetle into it with the other but paused. She hated touching bugs, dead or alive. In the split second she paused there was a little cold gust that blew the beetle off the newel post. Without thought she caught it with her cupped hands before it could fall to the floor. As mightily creeped out as she was, she had to smile. *You tricked me into holding it!*

Addie placed the votives around the room and lit them. She returned to sit in the circle of friends, unsure if the flickering of the extra candles was adding any warmth or reassurance. It seemed to her to only make the room look more distorted. Still, she reasoned, they'd be glad of the extra light if they lost power.

Mike had poured himself, Leo and Addie a small tot of whiskey. The fourth glass also had a little in it but not for Cooper. Mike said one glass of wine was enough. Cooper didn't argue. Addie reckoned that, under the circumstances, it felt comforting that his dad was taking charge. Mike had placed the fourth glass in the middle of their circle and Addie had placed the beetle next to it. She had put it there with great solemnity but they all laughed spontaneously at the sight of the dead bug next to the glass of liquor. Their laughter was cut short by the cold spinning around them again. It was as if their laughter wound him up into frenzy. Everyone sat quiet and unmoving until the whirling slowed and finally stopped. Now the cold was still and stung their cheeks. *All right*, Addie thought, *let's get started*.

"I can feel you in the room Charles. It seems to me I can feel you listening. And maybe it's my imagination or wishful thinking, but I sense that you are longing to hear what I have to say to you." She looked at each face in turn for confirmation that she had put the right foot forward. Each of them nodded and Leo said, "go on Adeline. Just follow your instincts."

She could feel Mike's body next to hers. Absurdly it seemed like she could feel the beating of his heart through where their cross-legged knees touched. Her mouth felt dry and she took a very small sip of whisky, swished the smoky hot liquid around her mouth and let it slide down her throat leaving a trail of heat.

"So I'm going to just go forward with what I have to say and trust that you will hear me out and know that I have the deepest regard for your feelings and situation." She still felt awkward, a little embarrassed, a little juvenile, as if they were playing with a ouija board and someone was going to suggest spin the bottle at any moment.

"Yesterday I found a letter tucked in a book and it was from your sister, Laura, to you." She felt that cold breath on her neck and Cooper, who was to her left, felt it too. "Jesus!" he blurted.

Addie kept her voice calm, "I know, Cooper, it feels scary to me too. I just have to keep reminding myself that I, that we are fine. This is just something we don't understand."

"I'm ok," he said, "that just surprised me."

They fell into silence again while Addie gathered up her thoughts. Outside, the wind had lessened some. She was about to go on when Leo, who was facing the window, nodded to them to look in that direction. The ghost's reflection was in the window, revealing him to be standing behind them, between Addie and Cooper. His hands were clasped behind his back and she could see his face in profile, impossibly sad. He wasn't looking down at them or off into the distance. His gaze seemed to fall into some middle place. His reflection, of which they could see only from the waist up, showed him to be clothed formally in a suit jacket, vest and high collared white shirt cinched with a fairly wide tie. His dark hair, parted down the middle, was wavy and thick. They were mesmerized by his reflection, and feeling their eyes on him, he turned to the window and looked back at them. Addie had to shut her eyes and turn back into their circle.

She continued, "in the letter Laura instructs that it be read aloud to you and that's what I'm going to do." She opened her eyes but kept them down and on the letter in her lap.

To Whom It May Concern: When this letter is found I will have gone to whatever, if anything, the afterlife has in store for me. I am asking you, a total stranger, to do me a very great favor and that is to take this letter to Pen House (anyone in town will be able to direct you) and read it aloud. I pray the house is still standing and that if it is occupied the new owners will allow you to do this or, at the very least, take on this task themselves. Anyone currently living there may be more open to this suggestion than you might imagine. In the event the house is no longer standing, please simply read the letter aloud in the area where it stood. Beneath the grand tulip poplar, should it still be standing, would be a good place to bury the letter once it's been read. In the end, we are all seeking some kind of peace and I thank you for helping us to find ours.

> With Deepest Gratitude,
>
> Laura Marie Davies, May 4, 1990

Addie stopped. There was no sound. Almost imperceptibly Leo directed them to look at the window. There he was again. Standing in the same place but now he had covered his face with his hands and was swaying ever so gently from foot to foot. When Addie closed her eyes she could feel the tiny ripples of cold created by his movement. His fingers were long and elegant and the bright white of his shirt cuffs made for a stark contrast with the grayish green of his skin. Addie and her companions huddled as tightly as possible for warmth and courage.

"Go on dear," Leo prompted.

Dearest Charles,

In all honesty I don't know how you could ever forgive the wrongs done to you. But I must put my best foot forward and try to at least explain why things unfolded as they did. Most likely I will never know if this letter reached you or, if it did, whether it helped. For myself, I don't hope for heaven or, for that matter, fear hell. But I admit to hoping we are reunited after my death, which, thankfully, can't be far off now. In any case, all that is in my power at this point is to tell you how deeply I regret my failure to be your champion, my dear sweet brother. I know you believed in me, looked up to me. After all, my words of love were the only ones you ever heard. But I was not your champion. I was selfish and afraid of jeopardizing what little love there was in Pen House.

As you know, I was nearly eleven when you were born. That was when we still called the house "Peony House", which was inspired by Mama's beautiful garden and which I described to you many times. I was so excited as the day of your arrival grew near. I felt sure I would love you as much as I loved Mama, which to me was all the love in the world. All of this you know because I told you many times how delighted I was when you were born and how I doted on you.

What I never told you was that Papa and Mama were fighting terribly throughout her pregnancy. More accurately, Papa was badgering her constantly. He had become convinced that he was not the father of the baby but that her brother, our uncle Edward, was the real father. Imagine making such a shameful accusation! Uncle Edward and

219

Mama were close, after all they were siblings, but Papa's claim was nonsense. Papa was jealous whenever Mama and Uncle "E", as I called him, spent time together. Papa's ranting, for that is what it was, was ridiculous. If anyone could have seen you and Papa stand next to one another they would never, ever have mistaken you for anything other than father and son. I used to hide in my bedroom closet when he would start in on her. I could hear him shouting and she would protest her innocence until all that was left for her to do was cry. You were there when all this unhappiness came into our lives, there in Mama's womb with no place to run and hide. This was the terrible beginning of Papa's unwinding and of my childish complicity.

Mama lived only hours after you were born. The midwife, and I, under her direction, worked to save her but we were no help. All this time, Papa was mostly in his room. I could hear him stamping around next to us, yelling, cursing. I could see too that the midwife was afraid of him. I don't know what I thought. Nothing I suppose. I was a child and he was just Papa. I felt as if I were in a dream.

And you! What a beautiful baby you were! You seemed to know right from the start that making a fuss would not be the right thing to do. The midwife showed me how to warm the glass bottle of milk and put the little nipple to your lips. And from then forward, I was the only mother you knew. Poor Charles!

When Uncle E came to see Mama and the new baby, Papa broke the news to him that his sister had died. He did it more gently than I could have imagined. Sometimes Papa seemed to awaken out of his angry nightmare. Still, holding you in the room next door, you suckling quietly at your bottle, the midwife now gone and Mama washed and laid out on the bed in which you were birthed, I could hear Uncle E fall to pieces. Unsurprisingly, he blamed it squarely on Papa. He told him his cruelty and hectoring had made her weak at a time she most needed strengthening. And I don't doubt the accuracy of his words. Pretty soon they were both yelling and I heard Papa say, "the little bastard died right along with her." I couldn't believe my ears and even looked down at you to double check the tender rise and fall of your small chest and see the bloom of life on your cheeks. I had never known Papa to simply tell a lie. But this was a lie and a monstrous one that pulled us like straw into the deadly turning of a tornado.

Uncle E was quiet then. I don't know that he mourned when hearing he had lost his infant nephew. He never knew you. But he seemed to regain his composure. I assume it was because he had the decency to realize that Papa had lost everything. I heard him say in a normal tone of voice, "I'd like to see her now." Papa told him gruffly to wait. He came in and shooed us out of the room. As I was making my way out the opposite door he looked at me with more anger and confusion in his eyes than I had ever witnessed. I realized when I got a little older that that terrible lie picked him up and hurtled him to a distant place from which he couldn't return. He said, "keep that bastard quiet or by God, he *will* be dead." I got away as quickly as possible.

So this is how the fiction started. Papa said you were dead and we lived that lie day after day, year after year. Mama's coffin was delivered. Papa took one of my baby dolls, my favorite, which I had named Gladiola, and wrapped it round and round in a sheet. He let it be known there would be no service and that he would lay his own wife to rest in the coffin. He put the little bundle that he said was you in the coffin alongside Mama. No one saw but me. No one visited. No one asked questions. Papa was a grieving widower and the president of the bank, both of which commanded tremendous respect and deference. I often wondered about the midwife. She had delivered a healthy baby boy and then signed off on a certificate saying the child had been delivered dead. Had she ever said anything to anyone? Did Papa pay her for her lies and silence? I assume so though this is something I never knew. I never saw or heard of her again after she left our house. In any case Mama and my dolly, Gladiola, were picked up by the undertakers in their horse-drawn hearse and taken to the county cemetery and buried. Uncle E wanted to buy an elaborate granite headstone for her but Papa refused. So the most simple of markers is all that remains.

Papa never even gave you a name. He would tell people "my boy" died. And so your death certificate, which I saw only after Papa died, simply said, "baby boy Davies." You know of course what was written on Mama's headstone because I took you once to see it:

Eliza Thomas Davies

1871 – 1901

Baby Boy Davies

God's Lambs Now Called Home

It was me who named you Charles. I always told you that it was Mama who named you and that she said to tell you she loved you. But in truth she never spoke after you were born but was lost in a high fever until she passed. But I know she did love you. She said so to me when she was pregnant with you and of this you can be sure: she was a good, kind mother. So I hope you know that this is the least of my lies and that I felt confident that Mama would have approved of it.

Papa said you must stay up in the attic and forbade me to ever let anyone see you. He said if anyone were to find "the boy", you would be taken from us and never seen again. Sometimes, for good measure, he said I might be taken as well. In hindsight the monstrosity of his words have become obvious as the cruel but empty threats they were. But as a child I believed him completely.

He did not come up into the attic and so I felt free to make you a room as comfortable and cheerful as possible. I moved up there what nursery things of yours I could manage. The greatest miracle is that I got you through babyhood safely. I had nothing but Mama's old childcare books she'd consulted when I was a baby. You were born in June and that attic was unbearably hot on many summer days. We would sit by the open north windows getting any relief to be had from the bay breezes. Fortunately Papa was always gone during the weekdays and I had the run of the house. We spent lots of time in the garden, you on one of your blankets and me pretending to play house with a real baby. I missed Mama terribly and I put all of that sorrow into loving you. It was as if she was present with us in the love and care I gave you.

As for Papa, somehow he was able to utterly separate his home and public life. He went to work and everyone saw him as the pitiable man who had lost his lovely wife and newborn son. Somehow he fulfilled his duties as an upright citizen and bank manager. I don't know how because at home he was a tyrant and often made no sense.

He would always ask about you. He called you "the boy" or worse, "the bastard boy", though you were never that. He would make me tell him all about the day and would even praise me for my efforts. I am mightily ashamed of it but I must admit that I came to feel like a sort of wife to Papa. I took care of you, I tried to keep the house reasonably clean and I cooked. I look back now and know I did only a child's job with all of these tasks.

The idea that I would return to school just disappeared. I don't remember that it was ever spoken of. Papa brought home lots of books but gave no instruction other than that they were mine to read. I regained the lost time in my education when I began teaching you. Eventually, what I taught you caught me up to where I might have been.

Oh Charles, Shame on me! I was so proud to be the little mama and sometimes Papa would put me on his knee and stroke my hair and tell me what a good girl I was. Invariably he would push me away angrily, but I looked forward to his gentle voice and hand even when I knew how it would end.

We had many close calls. Times you fell and hurt yourself and I tried my best to stop a cut from bleeding or bring down a lump on your head. When I got the mumps, Papa was forced to call in the doctor. I know Papa went up to the attic and warned you, just a little lad of three, that you were not to make a noise or I would never come to see you again. And even then I felt a little pride because I knew you loved me so much that you wouldn't make a peep. You came down with mumps then too but Papa wouldn't call the doctor for that. I nursed you as best I could, doing what I had seen the doctor do for me.

You started to draw as soon as you could hold a crayon or pencil and I knew early on that you were not only a good artist, but in fact a gifted one. I made sure you always had plenty of paper and supplies. At first I told Papa of your talent, tried to show him pictures, but he wouldn't look or listen. In the end I had to tell him I needed the supplies for my own picture making. I don't think he ever really believed me but it was the only way he would allow himself to provide the materials you needed. You see how sick we were? I could feel our sickness in my heart and my bones. Why didn't I run away and tell someone? Beg them to help us, save us? I only know that I felt as if I too was now as invisible to society as you. I imagined that people thought I had died with Mama. If anyone asked Papa about Laura, I never heard about it.

But now I think I am falling into self-pity and excuses. In truth I stayed quiet because I was afraid. Afraid that you and I would be separated, yes, but much more shamefully, I was terrified of losing Papa's love. Here I am, finally having been forced to leave Pen House due to this damn hip, and on the verge of being a drooling fool, and only now can I find the words. I can never say I am sorry enough times to make up for what you suffered.

I had a great plan for you. Once you were old enough you would go to art school and become a famous artist. I was sure you would be given a scholarship once they saw your work. You used to say I would come along with you to school, maybe become a teacher. It sounded grand but in truth I could not imagine ever leaving Papa alone. You told me you wanted to travel to Egypt and record all you saw in your sketchbooks. And I imagined that you would be able to, once you got away from here. We spent many happy hours lost in fantasies of the world beyond Pen House.

Remember how you loved the beetles we would find in the yard, under the back steps? You said you were the beetle who would be born again, transformed. In the last year or two I could feel you beginning to chafe under my care. And you even spoke angrily about Papa, though never to his face. You were beginning to mature and I think, given time, you might have confronted him. I wasted so much time defending Papa, defending our little institution. If I wasn't his little pretend wife and your pretend mother, who was I? No one at all. And so I continued to defend the indefensible.

The flu came in 1918, just as the war was ending. By then I went into town regularly and did the shopping. After all I was twenty-four years old. The people in town were so kind to me. Perhaps to them I was some kind of heroine, giving up her own life to take care of her dear Papa. If only they had seen the reality! In any case, I began to hear about a flu that was going around, the worst flu anyone could recall. Do you remember when we used to read about the war? I'd bring the paper home and we'd read together? I remember thinking that the one silver lining to the dark cloud our life comprised was that you would never have to go to that dreadful war. And then, in 1919, the flu came to our house. First I got it and I was no sicker than with any other flu I'd had before. Then Papa came down with it and it was an entirely different matter. I thought he might die. I was with him night and day. The doctor couldn't come, he was too busy and said there was nothing to be done but try my best to nurse him back to health. After about two weeks he rapidly improved. But there was no time to feel relieved because by then you were sick.

I assumed you would come through it as I had. And at first that seemed the case. You had the aches and pains, and a terrible sore throat. The symptoms seemed to clear a little and then roared back in just the space of a day. Your fever shot up and I couldn't get it down. I pleaded with Papa to get the doctor. I told him we could say you were a cousin visiting from out of town. But he refused. He said there was nothing a doctor could do. A proper parent would have begged for a doctor to come no matter how hopeless.

But I can't blame it all on Papa. I was a grown woman and I could have gone. But I didn't. Once again I obeyed him. Once again the fear of losing his love dictated my actions. And in my defense, you begged me not to leave your side.

Charles, dearest Charles, you died the night of April 10, 1919, at nine PM. Your fever was raging and finally you lapsed into unconsciousness and passed within minutes. I don't know how long I held your hand in mine but when I finally let go it was losing its warmth and elasticity. All along I could only babble, "you're fine, don't leave me. Don't leave me alone with Papa."

You didn't leave, Charles. Every time I felt the weight of your unrealized life on my shoulders, which was every minute of every day, I should have let you go but instead I clung more ferociously. I heard you walking the floor of the attic before I released your cold dead fingers from mine.

Papa lived another nineteen long years. He retired not long after you died and sunk quickly into full-fledged madness. He heard you walking, opening and shutting doors, banging on the piano. I spoke openly to you in his presence, perhaps to torment him. But I never heard your sweet voice after the evening you died. I don't know that he ever saw your window reflection trick but I'm sure he saw in his mind's eye visions a thousand times more fantastic and terrifying. His madness was brought on by his cruelty, I am sure. And his madness, his paranoia, his head full of voices and visions, reflected how he had lived his life.

After you passed I lost my ridiculous pride. I took care of Papa for the rest of his life but it was no longer because I was desirous of his love and good opinion. I had come to hate Papa. What kept me there was my refusal to leave you alone with him in Pen House. And I could not bear the thought of losing you. I felt that if I didn't affirm your presence every day, you would slip away from me forever. I could have done what millions and millions have done before and since, I could have let go, wished you well. But I held on. In the confusion of my mind it even seemed somehow predestined. After all, you were always the ghost of Pen House from the moment you took your first precious breath.

I came to see how, at first, you and I were both Papa's prisoners. But then I became your jailer. I didn't mean to, just like I never meant harm in anything I did. But there you are, harm I did. I think now of what it would have been like if you had gone to war with the other boys your age. And I imagine you dying in a mud-filled trench in France, thousands of miles away. As horrible as that seemed at the time, it is an infinitely sweeter vision than the reality that haunts me. To think you might have soared to heaven sixty years ago!

I am old now. I haven't been home for over a month and don't expect to see it again. Sometimes I feel bad thinking of you alone at the house. But I know for you time is standing still. I saw you countless times in the window wearing your same coat and trousers, the same unruly hair. I shrink and bend and wither and you are in the same dream you slipped into on April 10, 1919.

I am writing this Charles to implore you to wake up out of your dream and pass on as you should have all those years ago. I am writing this to tell you that as foolish and wrong-headed as I was, I can only beg you to understand that I was a child when you were given into my care. And even when I came into my woman's body, I was still a child in my mind. But now that I am old enough to be forgetting what happened five minutes ago, there is a part of me that is finally becoming wise. I cannot change the past but I hope this letter will influence the future. At first I fought to get out of this place and back to you. Now I know I dare not return to Pen House lest I slip back into my old habit of holding on to you. I trust to God, though I don't know if I believe He exists, that this letter will fall into the hands of someone with the compassion to go to Pen House and read this to you. Though I have nothing to base it on, somehow I believe it will be so.

And let me end by calling the house by its real name, what you and I always secretly called it, the name Mama always wanted it to have: Peony House. It was Papa's cruel humor that made him shorten it to Pen House. He said it was a more fitting name since "pen" is the Welsh word for both head and end and we were, after all, situated at the end of the road and on a headland of sorts overlooking the bay. But I knew it was just more of his poison that made him deny her and the beauty she represented, even in death.

Papa and I buried you under the Hummingbird Tree. I never told him that was our name for it. He didn't deserve to know such a sweet secret. I forced him to make that the place we laid you to rest and for once he was quiet and bent to my will. Go and see now, Charles. Go and see that you are buried there and what I've told you is the truth. I have always loved you with all my heart. Laura.

Addie had been reading through tears for the last several lines of the letter. Mike had put his arm around her shoulder and Leo handed her a crumpled but clean tissue he had fished out of the pocket of his coat. She looked over at Cooper who had his face in his hands and was crying quietly. She turned to him and took him into her arms where he willingly laid his head on her chest and continued crying. The room was warm, uncomfortably so under the layers of clothing they all wore.

"He's not with us. The cold is gone." Buck had joined them, his tail wagging madly.

"It started to warm up just before you finished." Mike said.

"Where is he?" Cooper asked, wiping his eyes. They were all standing now, stretching the kinks out of their legs from having been folded so long.

"Are you OK, Leo?" Addie went to him.

"I'm OK. I feel like a wrung out dishrag but I'm OK. And to answer your question, Cooper, my guess is he's gone to the Hummingbird Tree."

"Where is it?"

"It's right there." Leo pointed out the west window into the blackness. "It's the tulip poplar in Charles' painting."

Mike, breaking his silence, said, "I think we should go out there." Buck, hearing the word *out*, ran for the front door with a jubilant, happy-to-be-alive series of yips.

The night had cleared, the earlier wind and clouds proving to be an empty threat. The stars looked hard and bright and the air was fresh, full of the ripe promise of renewal that is spring. The moon was out and gently illuminated the way.

They wandered slowly around the front garden, avoiding a straight walk to the tree. Buck took a long pee on the birdbath. Mike was holding Addie's hand. She felt relaxed, unhurried and gloriously released, as if she had been let out of prison. Her feelings for Mike, Cooper, and Leo, as well as for herself, felt huge, unbounded. For the moment, she had entirely lost the sense of sadness and fear she had been carrying for all the years since Sean had died. Instead her thoughts were about how lucky she was. She had married a fine man who had been her best friend and he had died. She had suffered but she wasn't holding on anymore. Contrary to her fears that her grief was all that could keep his memory alive, Sean now lit up the inside of her heart with more presence and reality than when she had so desperately clung to him. She didn't know what was going to happen with this guy holding her hand. But she liked him. A lot. And she wanted to find out what was around the next corner with him.

The foursome made their way to the side of the house. Cooper said, "look!" His voice was whispered but urgent. At first Addie saw nothing but then slowly Charles came into focus. He was kneeling, hands plunged into the wet soil at the foot of the tulip poplar, head down as if in deep meditation. With an unspoken respect, Addie, Mike, Cooper and Leo stayed back. Buck sat by Addie's foot.

Addie hoped with all her heart that whatever was next for him would be filled with joy and love and peace. He looked up as if he had heard her thoughts. He had the same expression that Sean had had in the dream. A look that said, "I can't stay, I have to go." Addie smiled a small smile and nodded to him. *Yes, go.*

Each of them described what happened next a little differently. Mike said Charles seemed to smile directly at him before he faded. He said he was reminded of a candle being slowly deprived of oxygen, of the way it dims and flickers before going out.

To Leo he seemed to be solid one moment and then flash out of existence like the sudden breaking of a light bulb's filament.

Cooper saw the ghost became elongated, stretched thin until he was just a fog-like wisp that was consumed by the dark night.

The Charles that Addie witnessed glowed with a pale and exquisitely delicate golden light. He had a look of sublime ecstasy on his face, and his arms were outstretched as if welcoming his beloved. Addie watched him fade, leaving Peony House forever.

Buck ran to the base of the tulip poplar, seemingly drawn by a powerful smell. He pawed at the wet and mossy ground only to find that the rich, exotic odor had faded entirely.

Made in the USA
Columbia, SC
08 January 2019